FAITH, HOPE, AND DR. VANGELIS

Happy reading,

Steve Gordy

FAITH, HOPE, AND
DR. VANGELIS

All the best from
Aiken, SC

STEVE GORDY

Palmetto Publishing Group
Charleston, SC

Faith, Hope, and Dr. Vangelis
Copyright © 2019 by Stephen L. Gordy
All rights reserved

This book is a work of fiction. Any references to historical events, or real people are used fictitiously. Other names, characters, places, and events are products of the author's imagination, and any resemblance to actual events or places or persons, living or dead, is entirely coincidental.

First Edition

Printed in the United States

ISBN-13: 978-1-64111-151-5
ISBN-10: 1-64111-151-8

DEDICATION

To Ruth, my soul and inspiration

ACKNOWLEDGEMENTS

THIS BOOK EMERGED from a time of trial in my life. In late 2013 and early 2014, I experienced the deaths of my business partner, the young son of an admired colleague, my mother, and two much-loved cousins. In the aftermath of these losses, I dwelt at length on the question, "How do those who face the reality of death every day cope with the brutal fact of death?" The book started out as a very long short story, or possibly a novella. As I got into the writing, I found that the characters took control of my efforts. They allowed me to say, "That's enough" when I reached a logical stopping point.

I ran up many obligations during the writing of this book. First thanks go to my fellow writers of the Assassins Guild in Aiken, specifically, Sasscer Hill, Mary Beth Gibson, and Bettie Williams. I've had the good fortune of having my work critiqued by three ladies who are better writers than I. Likewise, my thanks go to Ronald Nelson and Evelyn Beck, my beta readers.

A shout-out to Aurelia Sands Wilson of Deer Hawk Publications for her confidence that this work was publishable.

Also, a thank-you to Meredith Hawcroft for her editing craftsmanship on the manuscript, and to Prof. Vicki Collins and to Jeff Wallace, who both recommended her.

If you like this story, the credit goes to Lukas, Diana, Katie, Andy, Timmy, and all the others who took control of my life. If you don't like it, I'm accountable. Happy reading!

PART I

WARNINGS

Your old men will dream dreams, your young men will see visions.
- Joel 2:28

1

LUKAS VANGELIS HAD been a man of dreams and visions for many years, yet the visitation he experienced on that spring night in 2004 shook him. He'd seen his mother, dead almost eighty years now, seemingly as alive as he was. "My son, hear what I must tell you" were her only words. They bore the moral authority that only a mother's love can imprint on a person's soul. She had left him with a brief injunction to watch and wait.

Unable to go back to sleep after this jarring apparition, his bleary eyes focused on the reflection in the mirror. It showed a man on the tall side of average height with salt-and-pepper hair and tired dark brown eyes. His Aegean features bore a three-inch scar on the left cheek, a memento of an encounter with a hot andiron as a child. An observer would have pegged him as a professional man in his early fifties. That would be half right. Lukas was a physician, now in charge of a hospice, but he was also much older than he appeared.

These things had happened before. They manifested themselves in two ways: dreams without voices and voices without images. A dream-disturbance typically posed a problem to be solved, a situation which would lead to a definite, but unknown, conclusion. Luke likened it to coming to a locked door and trying out a number of different keys until he found the right one.

A voice-disturbance was hearing a few words, repeated again and again until he recognized the speaker's voice. The voice always started at a low volume and pitch, so indistinct he had to strain to make it out. The message repeated, an endless loop, until he heard it clearly and could name the speaker and acknowledge the words with a simple "yes." The wounds in his soul ran deep. He seldom had bad nights, but when they came along, the wounds bled anew. Such was the case on this night, except that it was more upsetting. Lukas's memories of his mother, Eleni Vangelis, had rested in the amber of almost six decades of separation. When they reawakened, in the 1980s, they always took the form of what he called a "voice-disturbance," a message from her in an unmistakable voice, down to Eleni's Anatolian Greek accent. He never saw her, but the experiences were as real as a phone conversation with his niece, the only close living relative this side of Athens. He'd gone by the name Luke for a long time; Eleni was the only one who still called him "Lukas."

He left the bathroom and went to the kitchen where he poured and tossed down a shot of ouzo. Proceeding in darkness to the living room, he settled into his favorite chair and closed his eyes.

———

THE VIDEO THAT played behind his closed eyelids was a panorama of a beach. Sand dunes stretched left and right, as far as he could see. The air was still, the sea calm. An orange sun had just cleared the horizon when she appeared from behind one of the sand dunes, clad in black from head to foot.

She stretched out her hands to him. "Come, my son, and be at peace."

He wanted to believe, wanted it as much as a small child on Christmas Eve wants the endless night to pass. His years of medical practice forced a question from his mouth. "Mama, is that really you?"

"Yes, my son. You see me as you remember me. Someday soon, you will see me as I am."

A soft moan rose from his throat. "Is this the promise when you left us?"

"My promise and the promise of those who sent me." She turned and gestured toward the ocean. A host of shadowy figures appeared, their features not quite distinguishable in the early morning light.

"When?"

"At the right moment, when your understanding is complete."

Lukas felt his mouth tighten into a downward bow. "Why? Is my understanding now not complete?"

"You lack two things. First, you need to know how I found my powers. You already know that I passed them to you, but you still must learn. Don't open your eyes. If you do, the chance will be lost."

He obeyed. The scenes that unfolded in the theater of his mind were as if he were in the midst of a movie whose script lay open before him. He was in the movie, yet not of it, removed from every ability except to watch and listen.

SMYRNA, TURKEY, MAY 1919

Greek officers led their troops into the ancient city of Smyrna, marching beneath an ornamental gate draped with blue-and-white flags. Banners displaying Orthodox crosses hung from light poles. The commanders' tunics bore medals won in the Balkan Wars that had deprived Turkey of most of its European territories. The ranks of soldiers, marching with arms shouldered, battle-ready, underscored that this was a conquerors' procession.

The inhabitants reacted predictably. Turks in fezzes looked on in dismay at the khaki-clad infantry, the *Evzones* in skirts and tasseled caps. An elderly man leaning on a cane turned his head and spat.

Most of the Greek citizens beamed, applauding at the precise stride of the elite units. Some tossed flowers. A few daring young women dashed into the street to plant kisses on soldiers' cheeks.

Eleni Vangelis stood with her parents and watched from the quay. Her face was a kaleidoscope of emotions.

Lukas, the mute witness, stood in the midst of this jubilation, invisible to everyone except his mother. Next to Eleni stood the grandparents he had never known, Demetrios and Irina Mavreles.

Demetrios looked at his daughter. "Why are you so unhappy?" he asked.

Eleni bit her lip. "Andreas says that any time war comes, nothing good can result."

Irina shrugged and gave a soft cackle. "Only three weeks married and already your husband is all-knowing? Does he have any idea how long we've had Turkish boots on our necks?"

"He knows, Mama, but he thinks that, sooner or later, the Turkish army will attack. Then blood will flow on both sides."

"The Turks are finished," Demetrios said. "They're too busy trying to keep the damned British and French from gobbling up all their territory."

Eleni said nothing. She had heard that the Turks had a rising leader, Mustafa Kemal, who had different ideas about how the Ottoman remnants should be run. *Eventually, he'll look in our direction.* Even in defeat, the Turks could be formidable. *The oldest, most broken-down alley cat will fight if cornered.*

The gunshots riveted the crowd's attention. Heads turned in the direction of the reports. Most of the onlookers seemed to think this was only a few Turkish diehards whose opposition would be rubbed out in short order.

Once again, Eleni's thoughts were darker. *Please let this be only a skirmish. God grant it's nothing worse.* At the same time, intuition told her this prayer was in vain.

Lukas heard Eleni's thought and realized that he was seeing things as she saw them, privy to her innermost thoughts and emotions.

"So now the war comes and seeks us out."

Eleni, Demetrios, and Irina all turned at this new voice. Yochanan ben Shalom had joined them. This was one of her late father-in-law's closest business associates, a wine seller. For years, he'd passed himself off as a Romanian, going by the name of Josef Brancusi. After a pilgrimage to Jerusalem, just before Europe went up in flames, he'd dropped all pretense and adopted a Hebrew name. It was a well-kept secret that the Vangelis family had done business for decades with a Jew.

"Do you object to being free from Turkish rule?" Demetrios' lip seemed to curl downward into a sneer.

"Not at all. Still, our British friends promised the Jews a homeland in Palestine. Lately, they've been so busy gobbling up land they've forgotten their promise."

"Why is this a bad thing?"

"It's simple. Soon, the British will be so busy with settling Arab affairs that they'll have no time to keep the Turks off our backs."

The older man gave a contemptuous laugh. "The Greek army will give them a good slap in the face. They'll remember that."

"Yes. The wrong way."

Eleni tapped Yochanan on the arm. "Would you mind walking me home? Papa and Mama may want to stay here a while. I need to begin dinner for Andreas."

They excused themselves and headed up the quay. A short walk brought them to a building bearing a sign that advertised, in six-inch letters:

VANGELIS EXPORTS
Purveyors of fine produce

This was the seat of Andreas' business realm, the location from which his family had for four generations shipped the famous Smyrna figs, as well as olives, raisins, and dates, across Europe, and, lately, across the Atlantic as well.

They were a few feet from the door when another flurry of shots erupted, this time much closer. Yochanan flattened himself against the nearest wall.

Eleni didn't move. She slowly raised her face toward the sky. After a moment of silence, she began walking again, this time down the street that ran along the eastern wall of the building.

"Eleni, don't! You don't know who fired those shots. Come on, let's go inside."

She said nothing, continuing on her way. When Yochanan unfroze, he started after her but halted after only a few steps. He turned on his heel and ran into the building.

Yochanan and Andreas emerged a minute later. They dashed down the street in the direction Eleni had taken, running as fast as possible, dodging broken paving stones and heaps of horse manure. As they ran, more shots rang out.

Panting like dray horses, the men came to a sudden halt at a cul-de-sac on the opposite side of the street. Eleni was kneeling in a courtyard that led to a Turkish business, Ersin Ozkardesh's tobacco shop.

Ersin, a family friend for years, lay on his back, his dead eyes seemingly staring at the bullet holes in the door of his shop. Another man lay face down. Blood streamed from a head wound which his fez only partially concealed.

Eleni bent over and cradled a young man, whispering words of comfort. He was dying. Gouts of his blood stained the stones, and his breath came in tortured gasps. He turned his face to the young woman and said, "Why . . . never . . . hurt . . . anyone."

She stroked his cheek. "Forgive them. They've gone crazy."

As he gave a weak nod, his eyes took on the glassy sheen of death. Eleni's tears, held back until now, began streaming down her cheeks. She crossed herself.

She turned toward the men and spoke, but not to them. "Your road is near its end. Soon he will be ready to bear your burden."

———

"OPEN YOUR EYES, my son."

The movie in Lukas's mind stopped. "Now I know why I always had the desire to be a healer. But what is the second thing I need to know?"

"The one who is to follow you will soon appear. You must find him."

"How can I?"

"You will know at the right moment."

Luke leaned back in his chair. As he took several deep breaths, the beach vista came into view, this time with Eleni directly facing him. He saw her head bow.

In a voice close to breaking, she said, "There are still trials ahead, my son. The road will challenge you."

He wanted desperately to reach out and touch his mother, but a sixth sense told him he dared not take the risk. He asked, "What trials?"

"I know that they will come from those whom you love. That is all I know."

"Diana?"

Eleni didn't answer. She pointed to the shadowy figures that had reappeared behind her. Another figure came down the beach, a being wreathed in light so brilliant he had to turn away. When he looked again, both the bright being and the shadows had vanished.

She smiled. "My love goes with you."

Eleni turned and stretched out her arms, a cruciform shape facing the sun. Without another word, she disappeared.

2

LUKE SPENT THE rest of a sleepless night pondering his mother's words about obstacles that might be posed by those he loved. Both of his parents, his wife, his brother, and his sister-in-law were dead. The only person he could consider a possible threat was his niece, Diana Vangelis Karras.

He left home and took the Metro to a stop near the offices of Eleni Hospice, the firm he'd established in 1985 as a memorial to his mother. Amid the sounds and smells of a jam-packed Metro car, he brooded over the silent fear that Diana might be a Trojan horse. He debouched from the exit at the Capitol South station. It was cherry blossom season in Washington, and the fragrance of the cherry trees around the Tidal Basin rode a westerly morning breeze, giving a momentary lift to his spirits as he walked the rest of the way to Seward Square.

"Good morning, Dr. V," said the receptionist.

"Good morning, Wanda. Is Diana in yet?"

"Yes, sir. She's been at work in her office for almost an hour now."

Luke looked at his watch: 9:17. "Wait a minute! I've been off all morning on what time it was. Why didn't anyone call me?"

"Diana told me not to. She said you probably overslept, but it's not a problem."

Luke shook his head ruefully and went to his office.

On the way, he passed a conference room where Diana was briefing two of the hospice's nurses about their patient visits scheduled for the weekend. "Good morning, everyone. What's on tap for today?"

Diana's eyes flashed the color of black opals, which Luke knew was a sign of a wisecrack in the offing. "How nice of you to join us today, Doctor." She delivered this with a wink, motioning him to a chair across from her.

He shook his head. "Sorry, I'd better get right to work. It's been a while since I overslept like that."

"We're all human, aren't we?"

"Yes. Just keep reminding me."

Luke checked the scheduling board, making mental notes about case files that needed review. He went to work and was focused on these folders when Diana walked into his office. Setting aside the stack of files, he asked, "Had any *visits* lately?" His accent on "visits" conveyed the special meaning of this term.

"Not since January. Are you expecting one?"

He tapped his lips with his right forefinger. "Not sure. It's just odd that three months have gone by, and nothing has changed."

"That's true. Before we go any further, would you like a cup of coffee?"

"That would be divine. Thank you."

She left the office, returning a minute later with two mugs from which vapors rose like incense. "This new special blend you've started buying is terrific," she said.

He didn't answer at first, thinking, *She's been my rock, the one on whom I could absolutely depend. Did Mama warn me not to trust her? How can I know?* After a pause of almost a minute, he said, "You never met Mama. I think it's time."

Her mouth wrinkled. "You've got a reason for saying that. So?"

"So, I think she's trying to signal both of us. She spoke to me last night and it disrupted my sleep. That's why I overslept."

"You're saying I should expect to hear from her. How will I know it's really Grandmama?"

Luke took a sip of coffee and stared at the portrait of his mother that adorned one wall of his office. "Just a hunch. Why don't you come over tomorrow morning and let's talk? I would suggest after work, but I need to catch up on my sleep."

"Right. Tomorrow morning. Nine?"

"That's fine."

———

WHEN DIANA STEPPED into the foyer of Luke's townhouse in Georgetown, the honey-rich aroma of baklava greeted her.

Luke appeared, apron-clad, wiping his hands with a dishtowel. "I didn't sleep any better last night than the night before, so I got up and did some baking."

"Damn it, Luke, I just had two crowns put in. I don't need any more tooth decay." Her mocking smile was reassuring to him.

"It's a special occasion. I think something's about to happen. Let's go to the living room."

Two glasses of Retsina stood on the coffee table. He handed one to Diana and raised his own: "To Mama and the truth."

She said nothing. Luke sat down in his favorite chair, and she took a place on the sofa. Several minutes of conversation followed while they sipped wine. When a timer dinged in the kitchen, he excused himself for a moment. He came back with two pie plates, each of which held a small slice of the delicious pastry he'd fixed. They ate and drank in silence, both trying to clear their minds of any distractions. Luke finished his wine and leaned back, signaling that Diana needed to do the same. They closed their eyes. The silence that descended over the room was profound enough to drown out the noise of traffic from nearby Wisconsin Avenue.

After an indefinite interlude, Luke and Diana opened their eyes and looked at each other. Neither spoke until Luke broke the silence. "Tell me what you saw."

"I was in a strange city, somewhere on the other side of the earth."

"You were in Smyrna, or Izmir as they call it nowadays. Athanasios and I were born there."

She gave him an account of the events they'd both experienced in the sun-drenched room. When she finished, he smiled at her. "You've just described in perfect detail what I saw."

"There's something that puzzles me. I saw all this clearly, but I didn't see Grandmama. I wonder why?"

Luke, noting that the silence which accompanied the vision still held sway, said, "Let's try it again, okay?"

"We've never had to do that before."

"This may be a time when we *should* try it."

"All right." Luke cheated, keeping his eyes open until he sensed the inner tranquility that flowed from her. Only then did he close his eyes.

The entire scene replayed – yet again – but this one time with a difference. When he heard his mother's voice, he violated the rules they followed when in a vision; he looked at Diana. He saw her lips moving, forming words in Greek with Eleni's intonations. He closed his eyes again.

Diana emerged from the vision and said, "I still didn't see her. Someone said, 'There are still trials ahead of you. The road will challenge you.' But I couldn't see who said it."

The sound of a car horn from the street broke the stillness of the living room. *Okay, the vision's gone for now. What's next?* He swallowed and said, "I think Mama spoke through you."

"What?"

"I believe you saw the scene through Mama's eyes."

Diana's face scrunched up as if battling some deep inner emotion. "Oh, I *so* wanted to see Grandmama. Why couldn't I?"

"I don't know."

She put a hand up to her forehead. "There has to be some reason why we both saw this, even if it was different. Do you remember anything else that happened that day?"

He shook his head. "Keep the chronology in mind. I remember Papa telling me about the Greeks landing in Smyrna, but that was a couple of years before I was born. I think that was the day Mama got the gift as she comforted the dying man. It was a gift of grace."

Diana's dark features brightened. "My grandmother. What a lovely person she must've been."

He nodded.

"How long have you been having visions of Grandmama?"

"They started after the day we both saw Connie and Athanasios. Even if you never saw her before, your gift comes from her. It's easy to understand how it can pass through a bloodline."

Diana's eyes glowed. "We need to meet whenever either of us has a vision. Maybe we'll gain some understanding of where we are now."

"Yes. And now, if you don't mind, I need a nap. Wine in the morning always makes me drowsy."

She rose, kissed him on the forehead, and went out the door.

Luke felt a wave of relief wash over him. *At least, if there are conflicts, they won't come from Diana.* With this comforting thought, he went to bed.

———

LUKE NAPPED ONLY on rare occasions, but this time, he slept soundly. The peace of a deep slumber wrapped its arms around him.

He woke up and noted that it was nighttime. His mind was alert, but his body still cried out for relief. He went to the kitchen where he consumed more baklava and wine.

He hadn't mentioned Eleni's last words in the vision. Diana obviously hadn't heard them, which told him those were for him alone.

That night, a new dream appeared. It was a fall day in Boston. He and Athanasios walked arm in arm to the Greek Orthodox church of St. Makarios the Great. As they passed a newsstand, headlines proclaimed that Herbert Hoover, newly elected as President, was proclaiming an era of continued peace and prosperity.

All right, 1928. Papa was so busy with the fruit business he'd stopped going to church.

They reached the church and went to the basement. Father Ilarion greeted them at the door of a small classroom with a blackboard on one wall. A fellow student, coated with chalk dust, rushed past them. *Father Ilarion was always fond of making us clean the board as a means of discipline.* The board held a cryptic inscription: ISAIAH 11:6-9. Then darkness wiped out the dream, leaving only the Biblical citation as if written in characters of fire.

Luke, a confirmed agnostic, couldn't recall the verses. He got up and went to his study. From a fireproof storage box bolted to the floor in the kneehole of his desk, he tenderly removed a linen-wrapped parcel. The Greek words HOLY BIBLE were printed in gilded letters on the cover. Turning the fragile pages with care, he sought out the prophetic verses, which he read and re-read. After a dozen readings, he replaced his mother's Bible in the lockbox and returned to bed. He dropped off into peaceful slumber while meditating on the verses he'd read. His last conscious thought was to wonder if they had something to do with his successor.

3

Luke knew he was walking into a minefield, concealed amidst the glitz of a hotel ballroom. The message he'd gotten in his latest voice-disturbance was cryptic: "You must find them. They will lead you to her, and she will lead you to the one who is to follow."

The next night, a vision followed, one that showed the hotel ballroom before him. Now, he scanned the room and turned to Diana. "How can I locate guys I haven't seen in fifty years?"

Diana said, "Trust your dreams. They're like a radiation detector. You don't really know how strong a message is or what it means until you're right on top of it."

"Yes, but lately they're less and less clear. I'm still trying to figure out the one from a couple of months ago."

The banner over the dais at the far end read, "Our Nation's Capital Welcomes D-Day Veterans."

Luke wrinkled his brow. "I'm walking into a room full of infantrymen. Back in the day, I was a bearer of bad news. I'm pretty sure who I need to find. Will they remember me?"

He fished the printed pages out of the inside pocket of his tuxedo jacket and ran down the list until he found "101st Airborne Division,"

17

followed by roughly threescore names. His eyes roamed until he spotted a clutch of men gathered beneath a wall banner displaying the white-and-gold-on-black Screaming Eagles emblem.

As Luke scanned each face, there was a flash of recognition: A tall white-haired man in a dinner jacket, chatting with a stocky man in a gray suit. Target in sight.

He walked up to them and said, "Do either of you dogfaces need a drink?" He stuck out a hand. Both men gave him quizzical looks but shook his hand.

The shorter man stiffened as if an electric arc had jumped from Lukas's fingers. "Sorry, trooper, I can't recall your name? Were you airborne?"

"Nope. 367th Field Hospital, Third Army."

The man stared at Luke's name badge for a few seconds. His eyes lit up. "Son-of-a-bitch. Bastogne, wasn't it?" Brian turned to Diana and said, "Pardon my profanity, ma'am. Us old soldiers never change our ways."

She gave him a wink and a smile. "No apology needed. My late husband served in Vietnam."

Luke spoke up. "Right, it was Bastogne. You've got a good memory, Brian Thompson." Brian's name tag had the stripes and rockers of a sergeant major. "I see you made a career of the army."

"Forty years' worth."

The other man's eyes crinkled. "I'm George Burton." He looked at Luke. "I don't remember you from Bastogne, but someplace else. I just can't remember where or when."

"Sounds like a good title for a popular song," Luke said. "Seoul, as I recall, '51 or '52. You'd gotten into a jeep accident." Burton's tag bore the two stars of a major general.

A waiter passed, bearing a tray of champagne glasses. Luke flagged him down and took four glasses. "To all our comrades in arms, living and dead."

As they drank their toast, two other women appeared. One was a handsome middle-aged woman with sky-blue eyes and strawberry blonde hair. "Daddy, I've got the four of us seats a couple of tables away."

Brian said, "Bonnie, this is Lukas Vangelis. He saved my life in World War II. Lukas, this is my oldest daughter, Bonnie Warren. She's my escort to these shindigs."

Luke said, "Just call me Luke. Lukas sounds too formal."

George said, "This is my granddaughter, Caroline Segura. She's my date for tonight."

Luke noted that Caroline's looks screamed, "California beach baby." She wore an Air Force dress uniform. "Sharp threads, miss."

"Actually, it's Mrs. I'm an old married lady."

They exchanged handshakes and George said, "Care to join us?"

"Thanks. It would be a pleasure."

George said, "Your name's familiar for some other reason. Did you ever teach in medical school?"

"No, but my brother Athanasios, Nate for short, did."

"Where?"

"Johns Hopkins."

George's face brightened. "Okay, now I know why your name rang a bell. My son was a medical student at Johns Hopkins, and I recall him talking about one of his teachers, a 'Dr. Vangelis.' Is your brother still teaching?"

Diana shook her head. "No, my father died in an auto accident in 1981."

"That's too bad."

"That's life."

Luke said, "Your son's a doctor? Where does he practice?"

"He runs an oncology clinic in Tampa. He's been pretty successful. Referrals from doctors all over the eastern seaboard."

"I admire him. That's a specialty where you have to get used to pushing a rock up the same hill, again and again."

"Clark says something like that, but he's dedicated. He says he couldn't do anything better with his life."

Diana turned to Brian and said, "You look like a man who's held up remarkably well through a lot of tough years."

He nodded. "I've turned into a sunbird. Moved to Jacksonville in '75, where I can hunt and fish until they put me six feet under."

A bell rang in Luke's head. *Florida. If the message is really about this guy, Florida will come into the picture somewhere.*

Diana said, "I've never had much urge to move to the Sunbelt. Maybe I ought to reconsider."

A waiter came up and asked for drink orders. When he left, Bonnie asked, "Luke, do you still practice?"

He smiled. "Doctors, like old soldiers, don't die. They just fade away. I'm the medical director for a small hospice in Washington. Diana is my head nurse and deputy."

"Goodness. That must be depressing," Bonnie said.

"Not really," Luke said. "When you face death every day, it helps to put things in balance. Your dad knows what I mean."

The other men nodded. Brian said, "War and disease are a lot alike. Nobody in his right mind goes looking for 'em, but they happen anyway."

The ringing of a knife against a glass, magnified by the speaker system, caught everyone's attention. "Ladies and gentlemen, please stand for presentation of the colors." The entire crowd came to its feet.

The ballroom doors opened, and a color guard marched in, followed by a military band playing the theme from *The Longest Day*. As if by a single word of command, hundreds of hands snapped to foreheads, saluting as the colors passed. The music stopped, and a hoarse roar erupted from hundreds of throats as the color guard placed the flags in stands flanking the dais. There was a clatter around the tables as the attendees took their seats. Waiters scurried around the room.

Luke took several slow, deep breaths. His encounter with the two men he'd come to find had gone well so far. *Why was I so worried? There's something more here. I just can't see it.*

He turned to his dinner companions. "Brian, tell me a little more about your family. Do you have any other children?"

"Five others, plus twenty-three grandkids and two great-grands. Us Irish Catholics like large families. How 'bout you?"

He bowed his head. "My wife and I weren't able to have kids. God knows, we tried."

The conversation flagged, but the arrival of liquid refreshments sparked a renewal of talk. Luke turned to Bonnie and asked, "How many children do you have, Mrs. Warren?"

"Three girls: Kathleen, Christina, and Margaret. Kathleen, or Katie, is the oldest, but she has no children yet. My other girls have given us grandkids."

At her words, Luke shivered, as though the temperature in the ballroom had suddenly dropped by thirty degrees. *What the hell? Am I coming down with pneumonia?* "Well, we all have good moments and bad, don't we? My mother died when I was young, but I hope she'd be happy with what her sons have done with their lives."

George asked, "What about you, Diana?"

"I lost my husband and two kids in an accident. My family came from Greece in 1922. We have only a few close relatives in the U.S. How about you?"

"I have two daughters and two sons. My oldest was killed in Vietnam."

Caroline said, "I really don't remember my dad. I was only eight months old when he died. But my aunts and uncle and Grandpa here have told me a lot about him."

Luke's lips tightened. "Losing a parent is difficult, but nothing compares to losing a child."

Bonnie gave him a gentle smile. "I completely agree."

The talk turned to pleasantries and, later, to war memories. The rest of the evening went by without incident.

Luke couldn't shake a vague feeling of discomfort. As he and Diana left the gathering, Brian said, "Keep your eyes and ears open, trooper. The woods are full of snipers."

It wasn't until much later that Lukas grasped the full import of these words.

4

LUKE DREAMED THAT night, as he often did after meeting new people. These dreams weren't like his recent encounter with his mother; instead, they helped him "place" people, helped him get a sense of how they might affect his life or how he might affect theirs.

His dream after the reunion sounded a discordant note. He found himself in the parlor of his father's Bostonian house in 1948.

When Luke walked into the room, his father was asleep in a rocking chair with a shawl around his shoulders and a blanket covering his legs. A fire blazed in the fireplace. The tang of well-seasoned wood was palpable, aroma and warmth banishing the December chill. Luke felt beads of sweat forming on his brow.

He shook his father's shoulder. Andreas Vangelis slowly opened his eyes. After a few seconds, Andreas's blank expression changed to a half-smile. "So, my son the doctor decides to honor his father. Is this a special occasion?"

"It's Christmas Eve, Papa. I'm out of medical school until after the New Year."

Luke heard the front door open, followed by the voice of his brother Athanasios. "Papa, are you all right? Is someone in there with you?" Athanasios's tone was one of suspicion.

Andreas said nothing. Athanasios appeared in the door to the parlor, followed by an olive-skinned beauty. With a jolt, Luke recognized Nikkoletta "Nikki" Pappas, Athanasios's fiancée. He got a second shock when he saw the look on his brother's face: anger, almost hatred.

Athanasios said, "What are you doing here? Did we invite you?"

"I knew Papa was very sick, Nate. That's why I came." He used the familiar form of his brother's name.

Athanasios, unmollified, took two steps toward Luke. "You're too late. He's already dead."

Luke half-turned. Andreas was slumped in his rocker, his left arm dangling limply at his side. His eyes were shut, but his mouth hung open.

Luke stepped quickly to his father's side. When he pushed up the eyelids, he observed that the eyeballs had rolled back, leaving only the whites visible. A quick check of the carotid artery failed to locate a pulse. Luke thrust a hand beneath the shawl and his father's nightshirt. The skin was clammy.

He rose and spun to face his brother. "Papa was alive before you walked in."

"Seeing you here like this probably caused him to die of shock."

The brothers faced each other with only a foot or two between them. Luke felt the fingers of both hands curling into fists.

Nikki stepped between them. "A fine pair you are! Will it honor your father to fight here in his presence?"

Luke relaxed and stepped back.

Nate asked, "Are you here after your share of the inheritance?"

Luke felt his face flush, and his anger began to mount again.

Nikki tried again to calm the furies that gripped both men. "Lukas, I think you need to be going. Let us handle this."

His mouth taut, Luke said, "Okay, I'll go. But I don't give a damn for the inheritance. You can have it all." He picked up the suitcase he'd brought with him and strode toward the door.

Nikki caught him in the foyer. "Lukas, please try not to be angry. Don't mistake what I'm saying. Athanasios is the way he is because of World War II. While you were off in the Army, people looked down on him. Some called him a draft dodger, which was unfair. It cut him to the quick. He's worn himself down, trying to take care of Andreas. That's what made him so touchy."

"Why didn't he call me to tell me how sick Papa was?"

"He knew it was your father's time to go. You would've just tried to cure him."

"Curing is my business."

"That's where you're wrong. You need to be a *healer*."

His eyes narrowed. "Is there a difference?"

"Yes. Only the dead are truly healed. We understand that because we're dead ourselves. You're not. You'll understand in time. It won't be long now. I can tell how tired you are."

In the next instant, the entire scene vanished, and Luke found himself sitting up in his own bed. He muttered, "What the hell was that? I didn't know Nikki then. I only met her when she and Athanasios got married." Another thought crept into his mind: *How could I remember this? I wasn't there when Papa died.*

He looked at his bedside clock. It showed the time as a few minutes before five. Reckoning it useless to try to go back to sleep, he got up and went to the living room. As he settled into his easy chair, Nikki's words came back to him: "Only the dead are truly healed." In a mind befogged with weariness, these words sounded over and over, their warning unmistakable.

5

THE MORNING USHERED in a typical summer Sunday in Washington – plenty of sunshine accompanied by the all-pervading mugginess that had once led Great Britain to designate its American embassy as a tropical hardship post.

Luke poured himself a mug of coffee and opened the *Washington Post*. The first section was dominated by coverage of the death of Ronald Reagan, which caught the capital unawares despite general knowledge of his precarious health.

He was halfway through the national news when the doorbell rang. It was a surprise to see Diana on the front stoop; Wednesday afternoons and Sundays were her only regular times off from the hospice, and she often fled the city at such times.

"Morning," he said. "Coffee's ready."

"Thanks. When I heard the news on the radio, I thought about the day Reagan was shot. You would've been on duty at the GW Emergency Room, except . . ."

His mouth twisted. "Yeah. Bad day for both of us."

"Why did you insist on going to that dinner last night? You've never joined any veterans' groups."

"Mama told me I should."

26

Her eyebrows lifted. Despite her years of experience in maintaining professional tranquility, her mouth dropped open. "She told you just what to do. Has that ever happened before?"

"No."

"I missed the message. Are you sure?"

"Absolutely. It *was* her."

Diana turned her head, as if expecting her grandmother to appear in Lukas's den. Her eyes tightened, radiating melancholy. She put a hand up like she was fending off some unwelcome news. "I wish you'd told me."

"I didn't because I wasn't sure."

"Of what?"

"There was always the chance that my mind might be playing tricks on me." Luke quickly tried to change the subject. "Well, it's a nice day so far. Let's go out to the garden."

The lilacs Luke had planted at each corner of the stockade fence around his patio showed the early effects of the summer heat. Diana filled up the watering can and gave each of them a cool drink. *She's even a nurse when she's off the job. I wish Connie and I had been able to have a daughter like her.*

They sat in rattan armchairs Diana had given Lukas as a Christmas gift several years earlier. She asked, "What did you mean, 'my mind might be playing tricks on me'?"

"Most of the time, our messages have come from Sonny, right? This wasn't like the messages we've gotten from him in the past. You know, when one of us has heard from him, within a day or two, the other has had some experience that confirmed what he said."

At the mention of Sonny, her lips trembled. The down-and-out Vietnam veteran and reformed thug had been pivotal in reorienting their lives. Since his death, he'd become a channel of strange prophetic messages. She gave a slight nod. "It didn't happen this time."

"It was a delayed reaction." He put his left hand up, as if the sunlight had gotten too intense. "I got it, oh, I'd guess it was three weeks ago. I didn't hear anything from Sonny, which made me recognize that what Mama said was different."

"Okay, I'll bite. What was it?"

"Her words were, as close as I can recall, 'The end of the road lies ahead.'"

"Did you know you were supposed to look for those folks we shared a table with?"

"Not at first. I had to look at the names of all the attendees to solve the puzzle. Or rather, to take a step or two toward solving it." He scratched his head, a pensive moment that made him look very old. "Nothing comes easily. As far as I could tell, Burton and Thompson are linked to what I'm supposed to do. I'm just not sure how."

"Maybe they're related in some way."

He sat up in his chair and slapped his forehead. "What the hell?"

"Something odd?"

"I'd forgotten. You remember Bonnie, Thompson's daughter, the one who lives in Florida?"

"Sure. Why?"

"When I shook hands with her, I noticed a slight tremor. It was as if she touched something that scared her. I blew it off then, but I think that's a part of the picture too."

He sat back, his hooded dark eyes settling on the butterflies that circled around a potted lantana by the back gate. A breeze swirled around the little enclosure, cooling the sweat on his brow. "I think Bonnie will come into the picture, but I don't know where or when. Maybe tomorrow, maybe sometime in the future."

Diana rocked back and forth, an unconscious gesture Luke sometimes noticed when she was trying to follow the wanderings of his mind. She pursed her lips. "Okay. Grandmama has started sending messages with some special significance. Why her and no one else?"

He bowed his head for a long minute. "Do you really want to know the most important thing she said?"

"Of course. Spit it out."

"What Mama said the first time I heard from her was, 'Teach her how to forgive.' I'm sorry. I know it isn't easy to hear that. It isn't easy to say it either."

He saw her bite her lip and duck her head for a few seconds. "I'm sorry. I couldn't lie to you. I knew it would hurt."

Diana gave a mute nod. When she had composed herself, she said, "You never told me, but that's what you were pushing me toward, all those years ago."

"Yes. She wanted you to forgive the man who killed your children."

"Well, this experience, whatever it turns out to be, could be just as painful as that one was."

Luke smiled; it was a wry smile. "You're right. Although Mama didn't say it in so many words, there's some forgiving I still have to do. I just don't know who else is involved."

———

DIANA LEFT LUKE'S condo and walked aimlessly around Georgetown for a while – she didn't know how long – before getting in her car. She took New York Avenue and followed it out of town through suburbs that sprouted like dandelions around the Beltway, where the road became U.S. Route 50. She continued through Annapolis, across the soaring bridge that spanned the Chesapeake Bay. On the Eastern Shore, she continued a short distance on U.S. 301, turning on a dirt road that led to a small patch of woodland perched along the shore. A graveled lane led to a wrought iron gate. Diana parked and unlocked the padlock that secured the gate. She went inside and continued to a clearing that looked out on the waves of Chesapeake Bay, stirred by a summer breeze that bore the fragrance of wildflowers.

Two granite boulders rose inside the clearing. Diana paused for a moment in front of one which bore the following inscription:

ATHANASIOS DEMETRIOS	NIKKOLETTA PAPPAS
VANGELIS	VANGELIS
1921-1981	1923-1968
FATHER	MOTHER

The other stone was inscribed:

HECTOR LEONIDAS	ANDREW PHILIP	ATHENA ELENI
KARRAS	KARRAS	KARRAS
1945-1982	1974-1982	1977-1982

She continued a few steps further, to the second, bowing her head before the surface.

The sun is too hot here. It seemed as though the day's brightness was breaking through every barrier she could raise. Even the tears that started flowing, the convulsive sobs she couldn't stifle, couldn't cool the heat that was choking her. She crumpled to the ground.

When she opened her eyes, the sun, just past the meridian when she arrived, was now well down toward the horizon. *God, how long was I out cold?* She had started to get up when her vision fell on the first name on the inscription. Her lips curled into a sneer.

Diana fought down the impulse to spit. *Not now, not here, not where my angels rest.*

Arising, she returned to the gate, locked it, got in her car, and drove home.

6

TWO MONTHS LATER

Luke and Diana hadn't had any more discussions about the mysterious experiences of the spring. Two decades of hospice work had taught them that the path to understanding such things couldn't be rushed. All of their energy was occupied with the day-to-day demands of helping the dying to live out their lives with as little distress and as much dignity as possible.

It was a typical August day in Washington, a prolonged sojourn in a sauna. At dusk, Diana, feeling like a wet washcloth run through a microwave oven, stepped off a city bus across from the National Cathedral and entered her apartment building. *I'm too tired to cook. Just a glass of wine and a piece of cheese for me.*

She prepared her evening repast and carried it to her living room. After doffing her crepe-soled shoes, she sat down and tried to relax, taking the wine in sips, chewing each bite of cheese with the deliberateness of a ruminant.

She turned on the radio to a classical music station. An orchestra was playing the "Lullaby" from Khachaturian's *Gayane* ballet, its serene strains a balm for weary spirits. The deep purple fell on her before she finished eating. A long interval of unmoving restfulness followed. It ended when she woke up with a start. She was in the same chair, inside a room with deep gray walls but with no windows or doors. Her dead husband sat a few feet away in a straight-backed chair.

Twenty-plus years of separation hadn't quelled her anger. She glared at Hector. "What are you doing here? And where are the kids? Can you see them?"

"What's that you're asking?"

"Where are Andrew and Athena?"

"Hell, I don't know. I can't see them. I think it's because of where I am. I'm stuck someplace alone, where I can see other people, but I can't talk to them or even get them to notice me. I guess that's my punishment."

"Why are you bothering me? What do you want that I could possibly give you?"

"I need your understanding. You were always there to listen, except for that last time. I never had the chance to tell you what went down that night. You were on duty at the hospital. Think about what the weather was like. It was thunder and lightning like I hadn't seen since I left Nam. Maybe that's what did it. Maybe the weather caused me to flashback."

Diana felt the heat rising inside her. "Are you seriously trying to make excuses for what you did?"

"No, but you don't know the full truth."

"What difference would that make?"

Hector's swarthy features seemed to grow darker in the subdued light. "I don't know. Will you at least try? Don't judge me until you hear the full story."

"All right, I'll listen."

"Anyhow, back to Nam in '69. I was on a listening post one night during the monsoon season and the weather was giving us a serious ass-kicking. Now when you're on LP duty, you got to constantly scan the perimeter, looking for Cong or NVA infiltrators. That's what I was doing. My buddy, we called him Frenchie 'cause he was a Louisiana Cajun, he was kind of a goof-off. He wasn't paying attention to his sectors. Before you knew it, they were on us. Frenchie caught it with the first rounds they fired. That's when I got wounded. Anyhow, I had enough sense to play dead. I pulled him on top of me and the infiltrators figured they'd gotten the both of us."

As he paused for breath, Diana quietly said, "Yes. I remember Sonny telling me about that night. Was he anywhere near you?"

Hector shook his head. "No, he was on the other side of the camp. Anyhow, right in the middle of the attack, I lost it. I shifted, and Frenchie's body rolled on top of me. His eyes were wide open, and there were two ugly holes in his forehead. I'll never forget that look. It's like he was saying, 'Hey, buddy, come on and join me.' That moment stayed with me for years after that."

Diana said, "You're not the only person who has nightmares."

"Would you please shut up and hear me out?"

"Yes. Go on."

"The nightmares always brought back that vision of Frenchie, the wounds, the look. After a while, it hit me: He'd never stop until I joined him."

"It happened again that night in '82. Right in the middle of that storm, I was trying to keep Andy and Athena calm, and there he was, standing right in front of me, saying, 'Hey, buddy, come on and join me. Bring your kids along.' When I looked up, I was back in the jungle, in that dark foxhole with that dead face staring at me."

Diana's lips quivered. She said nothing but put her hand in front of her mouth.

"I knew the VC were about to overrun us, and I knew what they'd do to the kids. It was better for me to smother them before I shot myself. Now they're at peace, at least I hope they are, and I'm stuck here in this cold, lonely hell."

She started to reach out to touch his hand. Before she could, the scene vanished. The lamp beside her chair was shining in her eyes. She looked at the clock on her radio, which was blinking "12:00." The rumble of thunder reminded her that the day's weather forecast had included the possibility of late evening thunderstorms. *Power must've gone out for a few minutes.* She got up, reset the clock, and went to bed. The rest of the night passed in peace, undisturbed by recollections of her talk with a child-killer.

7

The noise in The Swamp rose to jackhammer levels as the Florida Gators completed their Homecoming game with a romp over the South Carolina Gamecocks. In the Fernandina Beach Gator Club seats, Andy and Katie Lyle whooped it up with their friends, until the final buzzer, when everyone stood to sing the Alma Mater.

As they made their way through the crowd leaving the stadium, Andy heard a raucous voice. "Hey, Randy Andy, what's shaking?"

Katie chortled as her husband scanned the throng. She spotted a knot of fans near a concession stand with a sign that read, "Builders Club Class of '94," and said, "Aren't those some of your classmates?"

Andy followed her pointed finger. He grinned when he saw Bennie Tarpley, his roommate for his first year at Gainesville. Husband and wife plowed through the human swarm toward the sign, Katie wrinkling her nose at the smell of sweat and spilled beer that pervaded the crowded walkway.

"Bennie, you halfbreed sumbitch, what the hell's going on?"

"Nothing, you crazy bush hog. Hi, Katie."

"Hiya, Ben. It's been over three years since you were in our wedding. It hardly seems like that long."

36

"Sure doesn't."

Andy asked, "Well, Bennie, are you still the shadiest builder in Palm Beach County? You still paying off the building inspectors to overlook all the shortcuts you throw into your work? And who is this lady?"

A bleached blonde standing next to Bennie extended her hand. "Ali Forester. I'm Bennie's office manager. Pleased to meetcha."

Andy and Bennie exchanged winks. Bennie asked, "You guys got any plans for after the game?"

Andy shook his head. "You got something in mind?"

Bennie said, "Well, we're staying in a motel near Bivens Arm Lake. I know they had vacancies this morning. Let's go get some barbecue and beer, then head out there."

"That all right with you, babe?" Andy said to Katie.

"Are you sure you wouldn't mind us hanging around? I mean, we can always head home after supper. We weren't really planning on staying overnight."

Bennie said, "No problem. You can pick up some toiletries after we eat. West Palm Beach is just too damned far to drive after watching our guys stomp the shit out of some bunch of sad sacks."

Katie said, "Hey, we don't do this very often." She rubbed her nose. Her hazel eyes seemed to flash with hidden mischief. The late after-noon sun cast a dazzling sheen on her blonde hair, an inheritance from "Oma," her Austrian grandmother. Her rich tan bespoke her Florida upbringing. When she and Andy were dating, he introduced her as "my golden girl." Sometimes, he still did.

They chatted until the crowd dispersed and traffic died down. After dining at a barbecue place on Highway 441, they gathered at the mo-tel, drinking beer and swapping stories. The night air in north Florida was fall-ish; it would get cold in January, but there were still traces of summer in the air. The party went on until after midnight.

Around two o'clock, Katie whispered in the dark, "Hey, sailor, are you up for a little fun?"

Andy said, "Sure, it's the perfect way to celebrate a victory." He reached for her and pulled her close. The sounds of nocturnal passion interrupted the nighttime stillness.

Both couples departed for home the next morning, Andy and Katie still basking in the afterglow of their celebration.

———

KATIE'S PERIODS HAD been irregular since she went off the pill in the summer. It didn't bother her until a new month dawned, and she realized *I'm late*. She didn't want to say anything to Andy until she'd seen her gynecologist.

Andy came home from work ten days before Christmas to a spectacle. Crepe paper festoons hung from the chandelier and the walls of the dining room, giving the little space a carnival atmosphere.

"What's going on? Is there some special occasion I don't know about?" Andy snapped out these questions before catching sight of Katie. When she appeared, she was wearing a T-shirt that read, "Under Construction," with an arrow pointing down toward her belly.

His expression went from inquisitive to stunned in the blink of an eye. "Huh?"

She beamed. "Don't look so surprised. You were in on this from the beginning."

He stammered in his search for words. "You-you-you're..."

"Pregnant. I would say you're going to be a father, but that's already happened. In eight months or so, you're going to be a daddy."

His eyes danced as he took her in his arms. "Are you positive?"

"Dr. Walters says so."

"God, this is amazing. All of a sudden, I'm scared shitless."

She kissed him. "Didn't we both want this? That's why I stopped taking the pill."

"Yeah, but I guess it's kind of unbelievable until it really happens."

An endless moment passed, as the young parents-to-be held each other, looking deeply into each other's eyes. Katie thought, *We'll always remember this, forever, until the end of our lives.*

"I love you, girl. You're going to be a great mother."

She laughed. "Was there ever a baby who was more wanted than ours? I can't wait to tell Mom and Dad."

Dinner was festive; Katie had put champagne into an ice bucket. As they drank toasts to their impending new arrival, Katie said, "Farewell to alcohol for the duration. I'll miss my beer, but from here on out, I'm not taking any chances."

The day's cares vanished in the euphoria they shared.

———

SINCE CHRISTINA MUELLER Thompson's death, her eldest daughter assumed the primary responsibility for the Christmas festivities, starting with midnight Mass at St. Matthias Catholic Church. Andy, a dyed-in-the-wool Baptist, accompanied his wife's family, although the liturgy made little sense to him. After the service, the out-of-town relatives went to the house of Katie's parents, Bonnie and Art Warren, setting up cots and throwing down sleeping bags so that everyone could share being together for the following day.

At breakfast, Katie served mimosas. It was another family tradition for her maternal grandfather Brian, the patriarch, to offer the toast. Katie whispered to him just before everyone sat down, and, when he stood for the toast, he said, "Here's to my next great-grandchild, and may he have a life as full of blessings as I've had. Katie, my love, you've given me a gift to brighten my last years."

The dining room turned into a mosh pit as aunts, uncles, and cousins crowded around the parents-to-be, offering hugs, kisses, and congratulations. The tangible fragrance of familial love mingled with the cheerful aroma of bacon, eggs, and coffee.

8

After the announcement of Katie's pregnancy, her grandfather's visits became a weekly affair. Brian's face had a special glow when Katie was around. She found this a little bit puzzling; her sister Christina had already given the old man a great-grandson and a great-granddaughter. Her wondering continued until a rainy Saturday in February when Tom and Ginny Lyle, Andy's father and stepmother, were also paying a call.

Katie brought her grandfather a Harp lager. "Opa, I don't mean to be rude, but why are you making such a fuss over our baby? I know you love Chrissie's kids, but this seems different."

The Irish laughter in Brian's eyes died. He bit his lip and bowed his head for a few seconds. When he looked up, he said, "Katie-poo, there's something I've never told you. Your mother knows, but I didn't see any reason to disturb you."

"Is it something bad, Opa? You look upset."

He nodded. "I had a younger sister named Kathleen. She died of the flu when I was five. The first time I saw you, you were her again, come back to life."

41

She leaned down and kissed him on the forehead. "That's sweet. Now, I know why Mommy and Daddy picked the name they chose for me."

"Things just fell apart when she went. My Da always loved his whiskey, but he'd kept it under control until little Katie died. After that, he'd sometimes go to work drunk. He was drunk the day of the switchyard accident that killed him. That was why we got a pittance from the railroad for the accident."

Katie fought down the urge to cry. "All those years, you've carried that with you. I guess I know why I was your favorite, but why didn't you tell me about this? It might've helped you deal with it."

The old soldier's mouth trembled.

There was silence in the den. The rain drummed harder than ever on the roof, as if some benevolent force were trying to wash away the memory of the words Brian had spoken. Ginny put down the glass of bourbon and soda she'd been sipping. "Mr. Thompson, was this the right moment to tell Katie that story?"

Tom spoke up. "Ginny, I don't think we need to say anything. You hardly knew my father. As he was dying, he told me the worst year of his life was the year I was in Vietnam. Plus, you know how you'd feel if Don or Carl died. It's harder than losing a parent."

At the mention of Ginny's sons by her first marriage, Andy nodded. "Opa, I don't care what anyone says. You did the right thing."

Ginny wasn't willing to back down. "I mean, we're all supposed to be happy about this, right? It's just, uh, we shouldn't talk about bad things at a time like this."

Brian turned toward her. "I'm old now, and it doesn't bother me as much as you think. I've seen lots of bad things in my life. It won't be long until I see little Katie again, her and Ma and Oma." He mentioned his late wife with something that sounded like a lilt in his voice. "To be honest, wasn't there a time when you didn't want to hear people talk about your husband? But I'll bet there came a time when speaking his name aloud helped you to heal, didn't it?"

The mention of Ginny's late spouse caused her to fall silent, but only briefly. "I guess you're right, it's just that--"

Tom shook his head. "Let's just let this go, okay?"

Ginny had a pouty look on her face, but she said nothing.

———

THE FOLLOWING WEEKEND, the weather improved enough for Andy to grill steaks on the deck. He'd bought a twelve-pack of Harp, and he and Brian tended the grill while watching a Bulls-Celtics game on a portable TV. As a reminder that winter was still around, the bright sunshine was tempered by occasional chilly breezes from the Atlantic.

Brian was in a fine humor as the game progressed, with the Bulls running up a hefty lead. "I guess I ought to be a loyal Irishman and pull for the Celtics, but I'm too much a Windy City boy at heart."

Katie emerged from the kitchen with a plate of chips and nuts. "Didn't you try to take Oma to a basketball game once? I think I remember you telling me she wondered what it was all about."

Brian grinned. "Yep, Christina was always Austrian at heart. She couldn't understand why Americans didn't love soccer. Not long before she died, the World Cup was held in the U.S., and she tied up the television for days on end, watching every game she could get."

Katie sat in an Adirondack chair, facing her grandfather. She sipped a Diet Coke and watched the men banter back and forth. After the game, she reached into a bag under the chair and extracted a DVD. "Here, Opa. It took me some searching to find this, but it was worth it."

Brian seldom smiled, sensitive about his false teeth, but he broke into a great rainbow of a grin when he saw it was *Lili*, a long-time favorite. "Katie-poo, that's just the thing to make me feel young again."

Andy shot him an inquiring glance. "What's that, Opa?"

Brian held up the box, which showed a winsome Leslie Caron carrying a leather-bound suitcase. "I took Bonnie to see this movie in 1953, not long after I came back from Korea. She made me search every store within twenty miles of Ft. Sam Houston until I found the record. It wore out in less than a year, the way Bonnie played it all the time."

"Record?"

Katie started whistling, which brought a startled look to Andy's face. She finished up and told him, "That's what Mom always remembered from the movie, a song called 'Hi Lili Hi Lo.' She said Opa would sing it to her when she was feeling down. It always bucked up her spirits."

After supper, they watched the movie. By the end, even Andy was whistling along with Brian and Katie.

———

KATIE HAD ALWAYS been a dreamer, although her dreams had become less frequent with the onset of pregnancy. The one that came calling this night was a familiar one, from the end of the movie. Lili was walking down a road, fleeing a hopeless love, accompanied by the four puppets who were the interlocutors in her romance with Paul, the puppeteer.

The dream always included a special memory: her Oma singing "Hi Lili Hi Lo" in German. This led to the requisite happy ending when Lili left her companions and returned to the carnival and Paul's waiting arms.

It was the same dream until the moment Paul appeared in the road in front of Lili and her friends. But this dream ended with the appearance, not of Mel Ferrer's dark good looks, but of a small child. Katie couldn't see the child's face, but it was obviously a boy. Like Paul, the child was silent.

In the dream, Katie blinked. When she looked again, Lili wasn't Leslie Caron. Lili was herself. An involuntary "Oh!" escaped her.

Andy stirred and turned toward her. In a groggy voice, he asked, "What's wrong?"

"Just a strange dream. I woke up before it got bad."

He pulled her close. "Your knight in shining armor, Sir Andrew, is on the job."

She chuckled. "Thank you, Sir Andrew."

Andy dropped off at once. Katie remained awake just long enough to whisper a prayer. "Please don't let anything be wrong with my baby. Watch out for my baby, Oma."

———

A MONTH LATER

Katie stirred, nudged awake. At first, she couldn't recognize it. Then it happened again, and she knew: Her baby was moving. She muttered, "Oh, God. Oh, God."

Andy's eyes were still shut, but he mumbled, "You're talking in your sleep, darling. Just settle down. Everything's all right."

She kissed him and moved his left hand down to her belly. "Feel that?"

"Huh?"

"The baby just moved. There, did you feel that?"

He sat up. "I couldn't feel it. Are you sure?"

"Of course, I'm sure."

He pulled her close. For a moment, they held each other, an embrace punctuated only by the sounds of soft breathing. Then Andy said, "It's real now. It's different. I'm really going to be a father."

She kissed him again. "You're already a father, big shot. But like I told you, you get the chance to be a daddy."

They held each other for a long time. Eventually, slumber overtook them, and they drifted away, the same couple that had gone to bed now in a relationship transformed by a special knowledge.

9

Eric Grueneberg put down the letter of admonishment from the Metroplex Medical Society. His successful oncology practice had lately turned sour. The cause of his discontent was a radiological technician named Winterthur, whom Eric had fired for mixing his job duties with an aggressive brand of fundamentalist proselytizing of seriously ill patients. The family of one man whom Winterthur had advised to "get right with Jesus" had complained to Eric. No sooner was Winterthur out the door than he had launched a guerrilla campaign to undermine Eric's reputation.

When Eric showed his wife Marina the letter, she said, "Maybe it's time to look somewhere else. Oncologists with your reputation are scarce."

"You may be right. The politics in the Medical Society have gotten so nasty lately that I may not have a reputation much longer. I have it on good authority that one of my colleagues told Winterthur I was a 'self-hating Jew' whose real specialty was making people miserable."

"I knew there was more to it than you let on. We've got a great life here, but don't take on unearned misery. I told you what it did to Pop."

Marina's father, a Baltimore cardiologist, had died of a heart attack at fifty-three, an affliction blamed on too much job stress.

With this prod from his wife, Eric began an online search for greener professional pastures.

————

"AAAAAYYYY RICO! WHAT'S shaking?"

These words made Eric smile in spite of himself. Clark Burton, a medical school classmate and fellow oncologist, called him "Rico" and greeted him in a manner reminiscent of Fonzie on *Happy Days*. "Nothing worth mentioning, soldier boy," he said, alluding to Burton's Army-brat background.

"The grapevine says you're looking to move out of Texas."

"Uh huh. Marina and I have always loved it here, but the atmosphere has gotten nasty lately." He proceeded to give Clark a condensed account of the clash between him, Winterthur, and the Medical Society.

"Well, Rico, we know the woods are full of vindictive assholes, but I just heard about something that may interest you."

"I'm listening."

"There's an oncology practice in Jacksonville that's looking for a managing partner."

"Where's Jacksonville? How far is that from you?"

"About two hundred miles. Hell, we'd practically be neighbors."

Eric zeroed in with a series of additional questions. After listening to Clark's sales pitch, he said, "Okay, I'm interested."

Eric and Marina flew to Jacksonville three weeks later. Eric grinned when he saw Clark waiting for them near the ticket counter. Eric was dressed for a business meeting. Clark wore plus fours topped by a yellow shirt and green bowtie, as if ready for a high-society golf game. He was tall, moon-faced, and almost completely bald. The two old friends bear-hugged, and Clark kissed Marina.

Eric gave Clark an appraising look. "Why the costume, soldier boy?"

Clark punched him in a playful manner, a light tap on the shoulder. "Just a little encouragement to relax now that you're in the Sunshine State. Maybe we can get in a round of golf while you're here."

Eric cocked an eyebrow. "I didn't bring my clubs. This was supposed to be a business trip."

"Studies show that doctors who mix business with pleasure live longer."

This drew a laugh from Marina. "Don't try talking sense to him. You're battling too much hereditary Jewish immigrant workaholism."

Eric shot her a look of mild vexation. "Who says I don't know how to relax?"

"You're Heinrich Grueneberg's son. I only met your father twice, but I could read him like a Harlequin Romance. He and Pop were two of a kind."

Clark's eyes had a mirthful twinkle. "Exactly. If my dad had put more emphasis on his golf game back in the day, he might've wound up with three or four stars on his shoulder, instead of just two."

Marina turned to Eric. "Do you think you can change? I don't know if we can expect either of us to be different persons."

"Well, I can try." He looked at Clark. "Why are you being so helpful?"

He saw an expression that betrayed uncertainty on his friend's face. After an uncomfortable silence, Clark said, "I need someone I can trust nearby."

"What does that mean?"

"I'm getting into immunology and not just focusing on chemotherapy. We can work together. It's been a long time, hasn't it?"

"Okay, I'm interested. Go on."

"We have more tools than ever for a coordinated attack on cancer. You're one of the best radiation oncologists in the country, but you've been too far away. A lot of my patients couldn't go to Dallas, even though you could be just what they needed."

The luggage arrived at that moment. Clark shepherded them to a Ford Explorer in the parking lot. They drove into the city, whose appearance left Eric unimpressed. *It looks kind of run-down compared to Dallas. I hope the practice is in a better neighborhood.* He voiced his doubts to Clark who replied with, "Just wait a few minutes."

The conversation livened up when I-95 took them past downtown. Eric said, "You think we can put together a functioning partnership?"

"Yes, that's it, just what I had in mind. That's how we'll get the upper hand on cancer. I'd trust you with my life. Remember what that prof. at Johns Hopkins said, what was his name…?"

"Vangelis. Athanasios Vangelis."

"Yeah, Vangelis. He said that to convince patients to trust us with their lives, we needed to do the same with each other."

"Uh-huh. Now I remember. I think that was over a beer one night. He was talking about how he and his brother always had trouble trusting one another."

The mention of this long-ago conversation brought a pause to their current discussion. After they crossed the St. Johns River, the landscape began to look more like Eric's images of Florida: boats, palm trees, and houses built in ersatz tropical architecture. Three miles south of downtown, Clark pulled into an office park; low-rise stucco-and-glass buildings were set amidst live oaks adorned with Spanish moss. As they crossed the parking lot, the scent of mimosa blossoms rode a light breeze.

Their visit to the property went well. The oncology practice had a well-stocked patient list with four physicians, one of whom was retiring. They offered Eric the chance to buy into the practice and become its managing partner. After two hours of office discussions followed by a business lunch at a restaurant overlooking the river, the participants agreed on a price for Eric's buy-in. With a verbal agreement concluded, Clark, Eric, and Marina checked in at a nearby motel.

The next morning, after breakfast, Eric asked, "Any residential areas you'd recommend?"

Clark smiled. "Already interested in houses?"

"Marina's fallen in love with the area. She never made much of a fuss about living in Florida before, even when we took the kids to Disney World, but I'm afraid she's hooked now."

Marina said, "I'm seriously interested in places with good golf and tennis opportunities."

Clark said, "I've got friends who live in Ponte Vedra Beach. You want to head over there?"

As they drove down Highway A1A, they passed a billboard advertising a new residential development. "Coming Summer 2005. Mimosa Estates. Contact LYLE & SONS BUILDERS." An artist's conception showed a proposed neighborhood clubhouse. There was also a photo of three men in hardhats with the caption, "Tom Lyle, Andy Lyle, and Tom Lyle Jr. invite you to stop in and have a look at our selection of over thirty floor plans."

Clark said, "That's a firm with a good reputation, or so my friends tell me. You might want to look at their homes if you're coming to the Sunshine State."

Marina replied, "All right. Lyle & Sons. We'll check into them."

———

AS THE DISCUSSION about relocation progressed, Lyle & Sons was gearing up for a normal business day.

Andy Lyle's normal responsibilities included managing Lyle & Sons' office operations. Since he got to the office before Mindy, Tom's administrative assistant, he screened the mail at her workstation for obvious discards.

This morning, he spotted an envelope whose return address bore the name "Wilmer Lupton." He checked the address and found it was in a rundown apartment complex near the Amtrak station. Andy gritted his teeth and murmured, "Lowlife asshole. We don't need any of his whining." He tossed the unopened envelope into a wastebasket.

Subsequent letters from the same individual, arriving at monthly intervals thereafter, met the same fate.

10

SPRING 2005

Luke was accustomed to dreams in which a mysterious female voice spoke Delphic words. Circumstances eventually made the meaning of these verbal visitations clear. It usually took only two or three months for him to discern the prescribed course of action. This time was different. There were no words at all, only mysterious manifestations that always seemed to give him a headache.

Almost a year ago, he'd encountered two men whom he'd known decades earlier. He did not receive any revelations from this encounter, which frustrated him. Diana had felt the need to warn him that it threatened to undermine his relationships with the hospice's clientele.

What do Brian Thompson and George Burton have to do with my business? He'd expected their conversation at the D-Day celebration to result in a follow-up call, a request for his services for a family member or friend. There'd been no further contact in the ten months since the meeting.

I don't need to waste any time in fruitless wonderings. The Washington climate isn't beastly just now, and I need to get out more. These thoughts over his morning coffee led him to review his calendar. *Nothing requires my presence in the office today. If Diana needs me, she'll call.* He dressed in a green hoodie bearing the words "I'm Greek – I Don't Speculate, I Philosophize." It was

53

a gift from a patient a few years ago, a fellow immigrant. Donning khaki slacks and running shoes, he set out for a long walk.

He left his dwelling in a relaxed mood, strolling along Q Street NW toward Rock Creek Parkway. He knew the rhythm of the seasons; the rising sun was just now clearing the dome of the U.S. Capitol. Hidden from him today by a thicket of buildings, it was a sight he loved, a reminder of how coming to America had altered his life's trajectory. Patrons sitting outside a coffee shop laughed at the sight of a silver-haired man ambling along, whistling the melody of Neil Diamond's "America." *Well, I'm no professional, but I give it my best shot. It's part of my payback to this country. This is my world now. Papa never felt completely at home in Boston. But what would I be if we were still in Smyrna?*

A freshening breeze from the river brought the scents of spring: flowering dogwood, azalea, and, most refreshing of all, cherry blossoms. As he crossed Rock Creek, he leaned over a railing and waved at the scantily-clad female runners running along a path below. He'd lived a celibate life for many years, but the sight of good-looking young women could still stir him. *Amazing how they can get out with no more on than they're wearing. It's still a little cold for me.* His pullover shielded him from the occasional gust. *My blood's thinned out. I need to find a place out of the cold.*

He headed down Massachusetts Avenue. Approaching DuPont Circle, the city's noise and bustle forced him to abandon his musings, concentrating on dodging traffic and other pedestrians. From the circle, he proceeded down Connecticut Avenue, pausing at Rhode Island Avenue, looking toward the cathedral to his left. Memories of a cold fall day, a little boy saluting his father's coffin, reminded him of a similar day in his own past. He continued, doing a half-left at K Street, passing down 15th Street to the Mall.

Luke threaded his way through the crowds already gathering at the National World War II Memorial. He drew his hoodie close around his face, so his thoughts wouldn't be disrupted by any bystanders. He passed the Korean War Memorial, which brought other bittersweet memories. *Funny how, out of the millions who served in World War II and Korea, I encountered Brian and George in both wars. There's a reason for that, but I'll be damned if I can figure out what it is.*

On these walks, he always paused at the Lincoln Memorial. The clean Greek lines of this American temple drew his aesthetic approval, but it was the words inscribed inside that always moved him: "In this temple, as in the hearts of the people for whom he saved the Union, the memory of Abraham Lincoln is enshrined forever." *Father Abraham, that's what his soldiers called him, even when he sent them into slaughter by the thousands. It was the Iliad all over, with men fighting and dying for reasons they sometimes only dimly comprehended. No wonder I've always felt a kinship with Lincoln. He lost his mother as a boy too.*

Luke returned via 23rd Street, through Foggy Bottom. At the George Washington University Hospital he thought, *I had some of the best days of my career here… and some of the worst.* As he pondered this, the pain came, sudden and sharp, as though someone had whacked him in the back of the head with a club. His stoic bearing failed him, and he hobbled to a nearby retaining wall, seating himself with an audible exhalation. A young woman wearing a white coat stopped and asked him, "Are you all right, sir? Do you need help?"

He looked up at her. Her features, dark hair and eyes, and her accent told him she was probably an Arab, or perhaps an Indian or Pakistani. *It's a different world now. I could never have become a doctor in Athens, and she could never have become a doctor wherever her family's from.* He took a deep breath. "No, it's just a migraine. I sometimes get one when I go for a walk. Thank you for stopping and asking."

"You're sure?"

He nodded, and she continued into the complex. As he leaned back, the inner voice intruded, this time a familiar one, the raspy tones of Merle "Sonny" Widener, conveying a hard truth that he found strangely comforting. "Your time is coming. He will take your place. You must keep faith with us."

Sonny. That means something's about to change. But what? And who is "he?" Luke closed his eyes, trying to will the pain into submission. After a few minutes, he got up and resumed his walk, a man of many steps heading toward a destination, redirected by a few words only he could hear.

———

He called the hospice and left a message for Diana. She came by that evening. Her first words when she saw him were, "Are you okay? You look worn-out."

He shrugged. "I went for a walk today, down to the Lincoln Memorial and back. It never tires me out, except perhaps in midsummer. But near the end, I got a call from Sonny, if you catch my drift."

She sat down and asked, "What did he say?"

"It was something like, he will take your place if you keep faith with us." His omission of the first words was deliberate.

She put her hand up to her forehead, as if to brush back an errant lock. "This time it's not Grandmama or Mama. This is the first contact from Sonny in, what, two years?"

"Actually, closer to three. I remember it was just before that Vietnam veteran, uh, what's his name-?"

"Tony Capelletti."

"Right, it was just before he died. What Sonny said was, 'It's time for you to let him go. We'll take care of him.' That, or words to that effect."

"Sonny mentioned someone he just called 'he.' I wonder who he was talking about?"

He gave her a long, placid gaze. Her eyes widened. "A successor?" she said.

"Possibly. But it's obvious that the message was just for me, not for both of us."

Her lips tightened. "I thought it would always be the two of us, that one of us wouldn't get a successor and leave the other behind." Her eyes radiated something else – a sense of alarm. Luke hadn't seen this in Diana for a long time.

"Not to worry. It will take a long time to prepare whoever it is. I don't think I'm about to be recalled right away."

"So, what should I do?"

"Just keep me posted on any messages you get."

"Don't I always? That's part of the agreement."

He got up and went to the kitchen. "I see a nurse who's had a long day and would probably appreciate a glass of wine."

When he handed her the glass, she asked, "Do you think I would've made a good doctor? Athanasios thought so, but I wouldn't take any advice from him." The tone in which she uttered her father's name was devoid of filial affection.

"It's not too late. In the end, you may have to be the doctor for both of us."

She shook her head. "I don't think the District of Columbia would approve of me practicing medicine without a license. Maybe some-place else or in another karma."

Luke had seated himself in a rocker. He leaned forward so sudden-ly that he spilled a few drops of wine on the hardwood floor. "Damn! I think that's the clue I've been looking for."

"The clue to what?"

"You remember those two D-Day veterans I met last year at the sixtieth-anniversary celebration?"

"Yes. What about them? Nothing's come of the meeting, as far as I can tell."

"The older guy, Brian, said something about Florida. When he said that, I felt a kind of tug, as though something was pushing me in that direction. Mind you, I've never had much of an urge to retire to the Sunbelt, but there *must* be some reason I got that feeling when he mentioned Florida."

"Well, as you said, it probably won't come to pass right away."

Diana finished her wine and departed, saying that she intended to take a bubble bath and go straight to bed.

Luke was sitting up in bed reading a magazine when the sudden pain struck again. It was severe enough that he involuntarily closed his eyes for a few seconds. His inner determination to not become a slave to painkillers battled his good senses and the knowledge that he badly needed a good night's sleep. In the end, the wine took over. It relaxed him, and he dropped off quickly.

———

HIS PUZZLEMENT OVER the message from Sonny, coupled with the latest episodes of pain, led him to call a medical imaging lab located next to the Johns Hopkins medical school. Two days later, he drove to Baltimore and submitted to an MRI. The results showed no evident physical basis for the pains. When several weeks passed with no recurrence, he concluded that he'd either endured a psychosomatic episode or some transitory phenomenon that had no greater significance. He returned to work as usual and resolved not to yield to any infirmity until he got closer to unraveling some of the mystery about his designated successor.

11

LUKE HAD PUZZLED for months over the spectral visitation from his mother. A few days after the MRI, he remembered that the first anniversary of this experience was upon him, but he still wondered about the message she'd given him. The past year had been a series of dogs that had barked once then fallen silent.

He knew enough psychology to understand that, in some way, his mother's reappearance arose from his unresolved grief of losing her as a child. On the anniversary of the vision, a new question lanced into his mind as he drank coffee on his enclosed patio: *What about Papa?*

Andreas Vangelis's death, the result of an undetected case of coronary artery disease, had been sudden, leaving no time for father and son to fully air their differences. *What could I have said to Papa? I've never been good at handling deep emotions. Anyway, Nate was there to look after him, and that meant more to Papa.* When the dreadful phone call from his brother came through, Luke put the memories of his father into a locked closet. Andreas had long since ceased to be a significant influence on his life.

His father's return from the shadows occurred that evening. As he often did, Luke dozed off while relaxing in his favorite chair. He heard his name, a voice unmistakable despite its long absence from his life: "Lukas."

"Who's there?"

"Your father. Don't open your eyes."

Silence followed. Luke broke it by saying, "Papa, is that really you? Why are you here?" He already knew the answer. His questions were a feeble attempt to play for time.

In a tone different from any Luke had ever heard his father use, Andreas said, "I'm here to help you find what you need."

"What do you mean?"

"I want to make things right between us."

"I don't understand."

"You will if you can listen to me."

"Very well. Please speak."

"I know you think I'm a rogue, or perhaps something worse. Still, I am your father, and I expect you to listen to me. If you listen, you might understand why I am the man I am.

"I was born in Constantinople in 1888, as you know. Can you imagine what a magical place it was in those days before the world fell apart? The evening light on the Golden Horn had a quality you will never see in any other place on earth. From our house in Pera, we could look across to Hagia Sophia. That's a sight like nothing in America.

"Constantinople was a seductress. It seduced my father, your grandfather. When he had to return to Smyrna to take over the exporting firm, he never got the Golden Horn out of his blood. When he abandoned us, I was twenty-two and still sowing my wild oats. Of course, he died a few months later. The fact that he emptied out the firm's till meant that I had to break my back to keep us solvent.

"I was meant for a better marriage, perhaps a daughter of one of the prominent families in Constantinople or Kusadasi," he continued. "I did truly love your mother, but there was always the fact that she was the daughter of Demetrios Mavreles, whose peasant crudeness and money-grubbing ways combined the worst features of the city and the countryside."

"Alright, Papa. I know you're bitter over the way your father treated his family. Is this an excuse?"

"No. It's part of the story. Because I worked so hard to rebuild our family fortune, I couldn't spend time with you and Athanasios when you were boys. Perhaps this is just regret for the life I didn't have."

"Could things have been different?"

"Things *would* have been different if your mother's other baby had lived. She had a daughter, you know, before you and Athanasios. The child died before reaching her first birthday. Something died in Eleni when that happened. Even before that drunkard in Boston took her life, she was dying inside."

Luke was at a loss for words, shaken by how this revelation hit him. *Damn it! You never cried in front of him before. Don't start now.* "You should've told me about my sister."

"What good would that have done? You were too young, and we didn't want to frighten you."

"Was that your decision or Mama's?"

"It was Eleni's choice. Your mother had a kind of wisdom that you very seldom see. When the Greek army landed in Smyrna in 1919, she knew it wouldn't end well. She and Yochanan ben Shalom convinced me to stash as much of the firm's wealth in our safe as possible. Even she didn't foresee that, when we had to flee, having to put all those gold coins into a suitcase left us vulnerable to brigands. When I was beaten and robbed, I wanted to die. I thought that losing the firm's wealth undid all the hard work I did to restore our fortunes. Your mother assured me it didn't matter, but I knew it did. You were only eighteen months old and couldn't understand that at the time. I hope you understand now."

Another long pause. Lukas wanted to open his eyes. *Maybe I'd see something in Papa's face that would help me understand this, but I can't take the chance he might fall silent. There are still things I need to know.* "Why did you dislike Mama's parents? Mama never told me anything bad about them."

"Don't be a fool, Lukas. Your mother respected her parents in spite of the kind of people they were. Demetrios and Irina were killed when the Turks seized Smyrna. My brother, Philip, and your mother's brother, Nikos, vanished in all the turmoil. We never learned what happened to them."

"What about your relatives in Athens?"

"The rest of the family wasn't much help, either. My Uncle Constantine had drunk the heady wine of Greek victory. Whatever loss of face he suffered when the Turks routed the Greek army, it was a minor annoyance compared to our family's plight. Thank God for Uncle Ioannos. He and your cousin George sent the money for us to come to America. Would we have been happier if we hadn't? Would your mother have lived a normal life span? Even now, I don't have the answers to those questions. At least by escaping Greece, we escaped the worst effects of World War II. Uncle Constantine's family suffered dreadfully. Two of his sons died in German slave labor camps."

"Well, even after we came to America, we didn't live some fairy-tale life. We lost Mama."

For a few seconds, Andreas said nothing. Luke could sense that his father was building up to something major. *Another shocking revelation?*

"Let's go back to something that I know is a great affliction to you, even though you don't speak openly of it. You believe I always favored Athanasios. I can't deny that. By the time we fled to Athens, you were firmly established as your mother's favorite, while Athanasios always stayed close to me. After we lost your mother in such a tragic way, I tried to change the way I treated both of you, but I couldn't change my thinking. When he was almost killed in that accident with the delivery wagon, perhaps I thought it was a signal to me that I needed to pay special attention to him."

"Papa, I understood that long ago. You don't have to apologize for loving Athanasios as much as you did."

"Perhaps. I needed to tell you personally. You were both of great help to me in the 1930s. Believe me when I tell you that I could never thank you enough for how hard you both worked to keep the fruit stand in business during those terrible years. There was a subtle difference, though, between you and him. You were obviously the better student, perhaps because of lingering effects from Athanasios' injuries. I must have known, deep inside, that sooner or later you'd leave to follow your star, but I knew Athanasios would always remain close to home. When he finally did leave, our business was successful, and I could let him go."

Despite the solemn nature of this talk, Luke couldn't help laughing. "Actually, Papa, I don't think leaving to follow my star had much to do with it. You remember there was this thing called World War II that came along."

"You were a different man when you returned."

"That's true. It helped me decide to become a doctor."

"And so we ran out of time. Because I died while you were in medical school, and we never had the chance to say our final good-bye, I suffered the tortures of a damned soul for many years. It became worse when Athanasios died, and I had to confront my own role in making him the man he became. When you and his daughter were able to forgive him, my own soul awakened from a spiritual coma."

What is Papa saying? Am I in a spiritual coma? "Now I understand things more clearly. I'll admit I was too quick to judge you."

"It's taken us a long time to reach this moment. I've taken my share of responsibility for the estrangement between us. Could you hear my pleas to you over all the years since I died? Or were you too preoccupied with being a healer to others that you couldn't spare a kind word for your own father? For the sake of a man who tried, however feebly, to do his best for you, I pray that you will someday say the words that will make it right between us." In the seconds that followed this request, there was an almost inaudible sound, like the popping of a soap bubble.

Luke sat in silence and darkness for a long time. When he opened his eyes, the room was empty, but a strange fragrance lingered. It took his weary mind several minutes to search the files of his memory. Then, in an instant, he knew.

It was the pungent smell of Andreas's special blend of pipe tobacco.

12

TIMOTHY JAMES LYLE was born on a midsummer evening. In the smothering heat, only the fireflies had the energy to move, while humans stayed indoors or immersed themselves in swimming pools.

There were exceptions, of course. Those whose duties required it or those with a mission went about their business.

Art Warren was a man on a mission. He left the hospital and drove to Brian Thompson's apartment. When he pulled into the parking lot, Brian was sitting on his veranda, smoking a Camel and sipping iced tea from a plastic bottle. The fireflies flickered in the darkness, like beacons to travelers in a strange land.

"Ready to roll, Dad Brian?"

"You bet, trooper. I've been chomping at the bit since Bonnie told me Katie had gone to the hospital. Why did it take her so long to call me back?"

"It was a tough delivery. Katie was very brave, bearing up under a lot of pain."

"That's my girl. I've always known she had enough faith and courage to take whatever anyone threw at her to get the mission done. How's she doing now?"

"She's had a chance to hold Timmy for a few minutes. Now she's resting. He weighed in at nine pounds, seven ounces."

"Healthy little tyke. Can you tell who he looks like?"

"He's got Andy's nose and chin. His hair color is a lot like yours when Bonnie and I were dating, except darker. I can't tell about the eyes, though. They don't look like anybody in particular."

"Odd thing, that. Usually, the eyes do as much to determine resemblances as anything."

Grandfather and great-grandfather chatted about the weather and sports for the rest of the drive to North Coast Hospital. When they parked, Brian said, "Seems like it's gotten hotter since we left home. This feels a lot like Korea in fifty-two."

"That's one place Bonnie and I struck off our 'must-see' list."

Timmy's crib was at the front of the nursery. Art and Brian wig-wagged until the nurse on duty came to the viewing window. In response to their hand-signals, she picked Timmy up and brought him to the window for a close viewing. The baby's gaze darted from side to side, taking in the panorama of the world in which he had just arrived.

When Art turned to Brian to ask what the old man thought of his newest great-grandchild, the words stuck in his throat. The look on Brian's face was one Art hadn't seen since Christina's death; his mouth was taut. "Is something the matter, Dad Brian?"

Brian looked up. "He has my sister's eyes, little Katie's. I'll never forget what her eyes looked like. Even when she was just a few days old, she could look at you and it was like she was peering all the way into your soul."

Art had to admit that Timmy's eyes *were* different. They were dark gray, a shade distinctly different from Andy's dark blue and Katie's hazel. As they turned away from the window and headed for Katie's room, Brian said, "He has the gift. I hope he lives to exercise it."

The comment puzzled Art, who said nothing in response.

TIMMY'S CHRISTENING WAS set for a Sunday eight weeks later. Katie's sister Chrissie and her husband Eddie were to be the godparents. When Katie suggested inviting Marilyn and Jack Pilcher, Andy's mother and stepfather, his frown flashed, "Don't go there." She decided to let the matter rest for a few days.

Marilyn forced the issue. The phone at the Lyle house rang the next afternoon, a few minutes after Katie had succeeded in getting Timmy to go to sleep. She'd turned the ringer off, but when she heard the answering machine kick on, she dashed to the phone.

"Katie, is that you? This is Marilyn Pilcher."

After a pause of a few seconds, while she searched for something to say, Katie replied, "How are you doing, Mom Marilyn?"

"I'm a little worried. Audrey McKenzie called and told me my grandson is being christened. That's the first we've heard of it."

"Uh, yeah, we've made some tentative plans in that direction."

"Audrey told me it's set for next Sunday. That doesn't sound tentative to me."

"Well, uh, it's going to be a very Catholic affair. We know you're Baptists and don't go in for such things."

"For my grandson? We'll go anywhere for something like this. I mean, I'd go all the way to Mecca if I had to."

You considered the Lyles a bunch of no-culture hicks, according to Tom. Now Andy's given you a grandson and you want to get back in his good graces. Okay, you win. Katie said, "Well, then, I guess we can expect you. It's at St. Matthias at 3:00 p.m. Do you need directions?"

She didn't intend to wait for Andy to come home to break the news to him. Dreading what he might say, she called his office. When she learned he was out, she called his cell phone. When she still didn't contact him, she took it as a sign to wait until he came home.

It was obvious he'd had a tiring day. That, she thought, was the main reason he didn't blow a gasket when he learned he'd have to face Marilyn. He just said, "I guess it'll be okay, as long as we keep Dad and Jack from getting into a pissing contest. You know what Dad thinks of lawyers."

The christening itself went well. Marilyn seemed fascinated by the rites, with the godparents holding candles, the anointings with oil and salt, the priest's question to the godparents, "Is it your will that this child should be baptized?" to which they responded, "it is."

Having yielded to his mother and stepfather's desire to attend the christening, Andy said nothing when they invited themselves to the parish hall for the christening party. Things went surprisingly well, with Marilyn and Jack blending in easily with the Warren and Thompson clans. When Brian and Tom went outside for a smoke, Art and Jack went along.

The men returned just as Marilyn handed the new parents an envelope. Andy opened it, removing a check, which he unfolded. With a whistle, he handed it to his wife.

"Mom Marilyn, are you serious? Ten thousand dollars."

Marilyn beamed. "Timmy's our first grandchild. We want to give all our grandkids a head start on college."

On that note, the Pilchers bade their farewells and headed back to the airport.

———

THE CLIMATE CHANGED ten days later.

"Mr. Lyle, there's a man here to see you." Mindy's voice came through the intercom.

"Ask him his name and find out what he needs."

A minute later, Mindy's voice quavered as she said, "Um, I think you need to come out here and talk to him yourself."

The man was from FedEx. "Are you Thomas Lyle?"

"The very same. What's your business?"

"I need your signature to accept delivery of this," the man said, handing over an envelope.

Tom signed the acknowledgment. The envelope came from Caldwell, Prosser & Pilcher, Attorneys at Law, and showed an Atlanta address. Taking it into his office, he muttered, "What the hell?"

His consternation escalated as he sat down and read the envelope's contents. Andy, who had been at a commercial project site, came in midway through Tom's perusal. Noticing his father's flushed face, he asked, "What's up? You look like you're about to burst."

Tom's response was the growl of an aroused bear. "The son-of-a-bitch. All the time he was here smiling, he was cooking this up. Go ahead, read the whole thing."

The delivery was notice of a lawsuit filed in Federal Court in Jacksonville. Wilmer Lupton, a former construction supervisor at Lyle & Sons Builders, alleged wrongful termination on the grounds of discrimination because of age and disability. His counsel was John J. Pilcher, Esq.

Andy's face tightened as he read. "Boy, that motherfucker has a pair of king-size ones, suing us. He's lucky his screw-ups didn't put us out of business."

The plaintiff had been fired twenty months earlier in the wake of a construction accident in which two workers were electrocuted when a crane boom came into contact with energized power lines. An internal investigation had revealed that he had given permission to move the crane without a spotter to make sure it could pass safely under the lines.

Andy had handled the termination interview, which turned into a disaster. Lupton had begged for another chance. When told there was no chance of reconsideration, two other employees had escorted him to his car. Lupton had grabbed a pistol from the trunk and forced his way back into the office. A possible shoot-out was averted when local police showed up and took him into custody.

"I'll bet he didn't tell his lawyers about the write-ups we had given him before then for cutting corners," Tom said. "I should've canned him ten years ago. That way, he couldn't have claimed age discrimination."

"Not to mention all the time he spent off the job with that 'bad back' of his. So, why didn't you fire him?"

"He and I served together in Vietnam. I know that sounds too simple, but it carries some weight with those of us who were there."

"What? How come you never told me that?"

"I never thought it would make much of a difference."

Andy gave a resigned sigh. "No, I guess not. How much of a risk is this?"

"Jack Pilcher may be a snake in the grass, but he's not stupid. He ought to know how all of this will come out when a jury hears the case."

Andy smirked. "He knows it'll never come to trial. If it does, Lupton's already got an alibi."

"I don't follow you."

"Remember, he'll bring up the fact that a doctor diagnosed him with severe depression because of his oldest boy's death in that boating accident. If that came out in trial, Jack would play the jury like an orchestra. He'd have 'em all sobbing before he finished. In the process, he'd make you look like Simon Legree. No, Jack wants a nice, fat out-of-court settlement, a suitable price for silence."

"He won't get it. Anyway, who the hell is Simon Legree?"

Andy decided not to enlighten his father. He also saw no reason to mention the furor to Katie.

———

WHILE TOM AND Andy discussed the Lupton lawsuit, the plaintiff's attorney and his wife were wrestling with emotional complications of their own.

Jack Pilcher sat facing the door of a Buckhead bistro, regularly cutting his eyes from the plate of veal marsala in front of him toward the entrance. This was a habit of his when dining out. Today, Marilyn found it distracting. "Jack, why do you keep looking at the front door like that? Are you afraid some gunman's going to walk in, looking for us?"

"Sorry. When I was in law school, there was this *trattoria* in New Haven that was famous because all the seats faced the door. It got to be a running joke. I guess I'm just reminiscing."

"I wish you'd stop. Right now, it's getting on my nerves."

Jack took a swallow from the glass of Sangiovese before him and looked at Marilyn. A recollection intruded: the taste of a stick of alum-coated gum a practical joker had slipped him in high school. Marilyn's mouth looked as though she'd just gotten the same taste in her mouth. "Alright," he said, "I'll try to stop. What else is bugging you?"

"We started this custom of meeting for lunch one workday every week, so we wouldn't drift apart. But you haven't said anything work-related. That's not like you, and it's bothering me."

He rubbed his chin, pondered this remark for a few seconds, then it hit him. *She's resentful about the lawsuit against Lyle and Sons.* Accustomed to thinking on his feet in a courtroom, he was momentarily at a loss for words. On the pretext of answering a call of nature, he rose and left the table.

He decided on an indirect approach. When he sat back down, he said, "How well did you know Wilmer Lupton, back in the day?"

She saw through this gambit in an instant. "Why do you ask? Do you think I'm mad because you're his lawyer?"

"That's what it sounds like to me." His mouth turned down. "Okay, you got me. Is there a reason why you're upset?"

"Not that so much. There's just something I never told you about him and Tom."

"Now's a fine time to drop this on me. I don't care what it is, you need to tell me."

Marilyn swallowed and hesitated. "It goes back to Christmas of '69, right before Tom asked me to marry him. I was at the Jacksonville airport with his parents, just waiting for his Eastern flight from Atlanta to come in." She looked down at her lacquered fingernails. "When they rolled the stairs up to the plane and people got off, I started jumping up and down and waving. He didn't see me *or* his mom and dad."

In a voice far gentler than he normally used when questioning someone, Jack said, "Are you telling me you resented him for that?"

She looked down again. "I guess so."

"What does this have to do with Wilmer Lupton?"

"The reason Tom wasn't looking at me was that Wilmer Lupton got off the plane with him. He and Tom were so tied up in their own conversation, he didn't even see me until after he bent down and kissed the ground."

"Okay, I get the picture." He reached across the table and squeezed her hand. "What was his excuse for not noticing you?"

"While we were on the way to Big Daddy's house, Tom told me that Lupton had saved him from being killed or seriously wounded. Something about Lupton stopping him from hooking up explosives to a detonator wrong."

Hmmm. Maybe this will come in handy in court. "Who else knows about this?"

"Well, Big Daddy heard the whole story, but he's dead now. So, as far as I know, there's only Tom, you, me, and Wilmer himself, of course."

"Whew. Given what you told me, I wonder why Tom fired him."

"Actually, I suspect it was mostly Andy's doing. He's got that hard edge where the business is concerned."

Jack's brow wrinkled. He'd heard Marilyn's grievances, chapter and verse, against Tom Lyle. But this was the first time he'd heard her disparage her eldest son. "Remind me not to get on your bad side, Mom."

"I didn't mean it quite the way it sounded. Andy may go a little overboard when he thinks he's defending someone he loves."

"That's not always a failing, is it?"

"No. I guess it's a part of what makes us human."

They finished their lunch and Marilyn left to attend a Bible study class at their church. As Jack drove back to his office, the phrase "what makes us human" kept playing over and over in his mind.

13

ANDY LYLE HAD loved the water since boyhood when he and his brother had helped their father build a St. Lawrence skiff, the source of many hours of pleasure on the waterways of northeast Florida. On this glorious September day, he'd decided to initiate his six-week-old son into the pleasures of boating. Now, as he headed south on the river, Katie took the baby to the boat's small cabin for a bottle and a nap. Andy kept the wheel, basking in his love of the river. Even the rotten-egg stench from a paper mill didn't bother him. The brilliance of reflected sunlight on the water, the roar of outboard engines, and the cawing of gulls were part of a world in which, it seemed, nothing could go wrong.

Marriage had changed him more than he'd ever thought possible. In college, his good looks and rustic charm made him the life of a hundred frat parties. He'd gained a reputation as a hell-raiser, but no girl came close to putting the hook of matrimony in his mouth.

He'd known Katie was different, almost from the first. They'd met at a Panhellenic Day, a once-a-year lollapalooza on the Jacksonville riverfront. A highlight of the day was a series of fraternity-sorority alumni face-offs on the volleyball court. When Delta Chi faced the Tri-Delts, he was matched against a tall blonde who, as it happened, was deadly in placing her spikes where the guys couldn't return them. In an effort to block one of her shots, he'd jumped at the same instant she did, causing a collision at the net. They landed in a tangle of arms and legs, serenaded by raucous laughter.

After the game, he bought her a beer and apologized for his miscalculation. Three days later, he'd asked her out. He was nervous and it came as a pleasant surprise when she accepted. When she explained that she was on the rebound from a failed relationship, he'd disregarded his first inclination, to press home an attack head-on. Instead, he'd moved slowly, steering clear of the party scene in favor of afternoons on the river and long beach walks in the moonlight.

The blat of an air horn interrupted his reverie, prompting evasive action to miss a cabin cruiser that had the right-of-way. As he completed his swerve, he heard a thump, followed by the squalling of an infant suddenly awakened. "Babe, are you okay?"

"I just stumbled. I'm all right. But I don't think Timmy's interested in going back to sleep."

Andy steered for the east bank, scanning the shoreline until he found a cove where he dropped anchor. He let out a long sigh of relief. *What if I'd hurt her or the baby?*

Katie came up on deck, still trying to quieten Timmy. "Would you take him for a minute?"

"No sweat." He nestled Timmy in the crook of his left arm as he rocked him. "Sorry I can't sing to you like Mommy does, but you'd never go to sleep if you heard me."

"Owwww. I guess I got a little too much sun."

He noticed that her golden glow had been overpowered by redness on her shoulders and upper back. "I'm sorry. I was the one who forgot the sunblock."

"Just make nice with the baby oil when we get home."

"You got it. Would you please get me a Coke?"

She did, and they relaxed. Timmy dropped off to sleep in a little while. Mother, father, and child enjoyed the serenity of being enveloped in a cloud of love and happiness.

Katie took Timmy back to the cabin, where they cuddled up on a bunk. When silence from below decks assured Andy they were asleep, he plugged a set of earbuds into his iPod and settled back, listening to John Mellencamp's "American Fool" album. *Small town boy from Indiana. My kind of guy.* He closed his eyes.

When the album finished up, the sun was far down toward the western horizon. Andy slipped into the cabin and gently touched Katie's shoulder. When she opened her eyes, he mouthed the words, "Time to go. I'm going to crank up." She nodded and pulled her son closer.

As they headed downriver, Andy thought back to the near-miss with the other boat. With a shudder, images of what might have happened played in his mind: the bigger boat slicing through the Bayliner, being tossed into the river, frantically trying to reach the sinking boat to rescue his wife and son but failing, the piteous cry of a baby who doesn't know what's happening to him.

Andy gave two or three involuntary gasps at the thoughts that crowded into his head. *If I could save one of them, which one would it be? At least Katie can swim. Katie and I could have other children. What if she got hurt and I had to save her? How could I let my son drown? Why do I feel that Timmy would be a greater loss to the world?*

No answers came. The questions pestered him all the way home.

———

ANDY OPPOSED THE idea of a mediation with Wilmer Lupton. When Tom got the letter from Jack, proposing a meeting for that purpose, he handed it to Andy and sat back to await the reaction.

When Andy said nothing at first, Tom spoke up. "Hmmm. I wonder what brought on this change of heart?"

"Could it be Jack recognizes he's got a real loser for a client?"

Tom leaned back in his chair. "I don't think so. I've known Jack Pilcher almost twenty years, ever since we co-chaired the building fund drive for Oceanview Baptist. He's one smooth SOB. He's not the kind who folds early in the game, even if he's got a weak hand."

"What should we do?"

"Sit down with him. It could save us a court date."

The mediation session came to pass two weeks later. Tom and Andy, both accustomed to chambray shirts and chino slacks, chafed in dark two-piece suits. Roland Walsingham, the agreed-upon mediator, waited with them in the anteroom to his offices.

Andy and Tom exchanged sideways glances when Jack Pilcher and Wilmer Lupton walked in. Jack, attired in a Brooks Brothers dark blue pinstripe suit, white shirt with ivory stripes, and dark purple tie with grey polka-dots, looked every inch the heavyweight litigator.

It was Wilmer's appearance that shocked Andy. He was dressed in a light grey suit and was clean-shaven, peering from behind a pair of bifocals that sat on his nose with a slight skew to one side. His skin was the color of old parchment, his eyes rheumy. The day of his firing, he'd been a sunburned, lean-muscled physical specimen. Now he looked gaunt, as if rehearsing for a meeting with an undertaker.

The group adjourned to a conference room, and the back-and-forth conversation that characterized such meetings got underway. There was legal jockeying but little progress at first.

After two hours, Roland called a recess. Jack leaned over and whispered something in his ear. As Tom, Andy, and Frank Foxworth, their lawyer, went to the waiting area, Roland pulled Jack off to one side, a frown on his face. The conference room door shut, leaving the two lawyers in a one-on-one.

"Wonder what that's all about?" Tom asked.

Frank drummed his nails on a glass table laden with glossy magazines. "Well, they haven't put an offer on the table yet. They'd better get it done or old Rollo's likely to kick them out. He hates it when people waste his time."

They drank coffee in silence for a few minutes, until Roland emerged from the conference room. He beckoned Frank, who went back inside with him. Speculations bounced back and forth between father and son for about ten minutes.

Frank came out. "Okay, now we're getting someplace."

Tom said, "Where are we going?"

"It's a strange thing. Pilcher is asking for a settlement, but he wants it in the form of an annuity for Lupton's wife."

"Huh?"

The lawyer's mouth tightened for a minute. "Lupton is dying. Cancer and cirrhosis of the liver. According to Pilcher, he's got a few months at best. He and his wife have run through their savings since he got fired. He doesn't want to leave her a pauper."

Andy said, "That's tough. There are two people who died because of his fuckups. I say no."

Tom asked, "Has Pilcher mentioned a specific sum?"

Frank handed him a slip of paper on which was written "$125K" with Jack Pilcher's initials. "You want to consider this carefully. On paper, he hasn't got a strong case, but juries are notoriously sympathetic to deathbed sob stories. He'll die before we go to trial, but Jack's got friends in the media. You could be in for some very damaging publicity, particularly if the proposed settlement gets out – which it will. Paying higher insurance premiums is cheaper than trying to rebuild your reputation."

Tom's face reddened and his eyes closed for a moment. "Any other conditions?"

"If you agree, Lupton wants to make a statement for the record."

Andy started to jump back in but stopped at his father's upraised hand. "Deal. Let's get it over with."

In the conference room, Roland explained how the settlement would be executed. A secretary came in and handed him a formal statement of concurrence, which the parties and their attorneys signed. Then everyone sat back as Wilmer got to his feet. "I just got to say, Mr. Lyle, I know I done wrong the day of the accident. I'd just heard from my doc a couple of days before that, 'bout the cirrhosis and all, and I wasn't doin' good. I'm sorry now, and I'll be sorry for however many days the good Lord gives me. That includes the way I carried on the day you fired me. I can't make it right, but you can."

In a half-whisper, Tom asked, "How can I do that?"

"You can forgive me. That's all I really need now."

Andy blurted out, "What about those two guys. Will that do them any good?"

Jack took off his glasses and started to clean them. Roland drew back, as though someone had dropped a serpent on the conference room table. Frank held a balled fist to his lips. In a near-growl, Tom said, "That's enough. Let the adults settle this." He turned to face Wilmer. "Yes, I forgive you. For all we've been through together, I don't have any other choice."

He rose and held out his hand. With a visibly shaky grip, Wilmer grasped it.

As the gathering broke up, Tom walked over to Jack. "If forgiveness is what he really wanted, why did you go through the rigamarole of a lawsuit?"

"You didn't respond to any of the letters Wilmer wrote."

Tom's eyes widened. "What letters?"

Andy looked down at the floor. "I, uh, I didn't want you to have to bother with them, so I intercepted them."

"What did you do with them?"

Andy shook his head. Tom said, "Let's get back to work."

———

NEITHER TOM NOR Andy talked about the Lupton case thereafter. Andy focused his efforts to erase from memory the embarrassment of the mediation conference.

A couple of days later, he had a checkup with his dentist in Fernandina Beach. When the checkup ended, it was too late to go back to work, so he drove home. Katie had left a note reading, "Timmy and I have gone to grocery store. Back by 5."

Feeling a little footloose, he drove to Ft. Clinch State Park. He decided on a stroll and headed down a path through a marsh, listening to the honk of migrating geese, the cawing of crows and gulls. The fetid smell from the marsh seemed laden with a hidden promise.

He was alone, about half a mile from his truck, when the voice spoke. "Andrew."

"What? Who's talking?"

"Continue with your walk. You can't see me, but we can still talk."

Andy slapped the side of his head, as though trying to reset his mental circuits. "This is crazy. I won't go any further until I know who you are. And why are you following me?" He looked around, but could see no one else near the path or on the water.

"Your grandfather, the one you call Big Daddy, sent me. He's worried about you."

"Big Daddy died a long time ago."

The voice didn't reply at first. In the stillness, it struck Andy that the speaker, whoever he was, had a strong accent, so he said, "Where are you from? And how do you know Big Daddy?"

"Your grandfather and I both dwell in the house of guardians, those whose mission is to watch over the living. My name in life was Yochanan ben Shalom. I lived in Palestine, what today you would call Israel."

"Why didn't Big Daddy contact me himself?"

"That knowledge is not for you. Let us just say he worries about you."

Andy could feel his temper percolating. He would have turned around and headed back to the parking lot, but his legs refused to respond to his command.

"Patience, Andrew. That is one thing you lack, but it is not what worries your grandfather. He worries at how unforgiving you are."

"That's bullshit. What makes you say that?"

"You brood about a wrong done in the past. What happened could be something good if you learn from it."

Lupton. That's what he's talking about. "Okay, I'm willing to learn. Teach me."

"Such impatience, Andrew. You remind me of a friend I had in life. His name was Andreas, or Andrew, if you wish. He never truly learned to forgive. We both lost all our possessions. He never forgave those who had stolen from him. I learned I *had* to do it, or I would have died from my anger."

"Is that all you're trying to tell me? Something that simple?"

"It isn't simple when you have to practice it. And you will have to. Be ready when the time comes."

"When what time comes?"

Silence filled the marsh. Andy's final question was carried away by the autumn wind.

14

THE FOLLOWING WEEKEND, Art and Bonnie were at Andy and Katie's house. While helping Katie sort through dirty laundry, Bonnie asked, "Honey, what's that on your back?"

"I don't know. What does it look like?"

"It sort of looks like a rash, just a little odd in color."

"Well, I did get a sunburn out on the river three weeks ago. It'll clear up, just give it some time."

"Promise me you'll keep an eye on it."

"I will, Mama."

In the press of demands that fill a new mother's time, Katie forgot her pledge. In early November, before cold weather set in, she used a cookout at her parents' house for Art's birthday as a reason to don her favorite halter top. It gave her the chance to show off how she was shedding the extra weight she'd gained during her pregnancy.

Another guest was Joe Francis, who had been the Warren family physician for twenty years. As she brought a tray of beverage refills to his table, he noticed something unusual. "Katie, you've got something on your back that seems odd. May I look at it?"

"Sure."

He got up and examined the discoloration Bonnie had previously noticed. "You'd better get that checked. Do you have a dermatologist?"

"I haven't needed one since I was a teenager."

Joe's florid face paled a little. "I'd recommend Bruce Morton. He's a top-notch guy. Would you like me to refer you?"

"Yeah, I guess maybe I've overdone it with the sun worship."

"You don't need that, what with your healthy complexion. Take care of that spot pronto."

"I'll do that."

Dr. Francis's referral got her a prompt consultation with a specialist whose appointment calendar was always jammed.

———

THE DERMATOLOGIST GAVE the patch a prolonged examination through a monocular viewer. His comment was a soft, "Hmmm. That's odd."

"Excuse me, what does that mean?"

"I can't tell for certain. It's mostly a reddish patch, but it looks like there are some dark brown granular structures. I can also make out a dark purple, pearl-shaped structure."

"And?"

"It could be skin cancer. I need to send you over to a lab for a needle biopsy."

"Is it that serious?"

"Yes. We need a biopsy to get a definite answer."

The lab report took only five days before another call came from Dr. Francis. He asked Katie to bring Andy and come to his office at six o'clock the next evening.

She sucked in her breath when they walked into the doctor's office. Bruce Morton sat next to Joe Francis. A few blond strands of hair attempted to conceal the wrinkles in Morton's forehead but failed.

Joe cleared his throat. "The first thing you need to understand, Katie, is that this is serious, but we have lots of room for hope."

"Is it skin cancer?"

Bruce nodded. "I'm afraid it's the worst kind: malignant melanoma."

Andy sagged in his chair. "What does that mean? Are you telling me Katie's going to die?"

"As Dr. Francis says, it *is* serious, but there are a number of treatment options. I would recommend surgery, possibly combined with radiation therapy for the tissues around the cancer."

Katie asked, "How long will that take?"

"I'll contact Dr. Ted Moore tomorrow. He's at Emory University Hospital in Atlanta and is probably the best surgical oncologist in the southeast. Once the surgery's done, the radiation treatments will probably be every day for a few weeks."

Andy asked, "In round numbers, what are the odds?"

"Ninety percent favorable, if we've caught this in time."

"How long will it take us to know for sure?"

"As much as five years to be relatively certain, but every month the cancer doesn't show up after treatment, the more confident we can be."

Katie said, "We've got a three-month-old son. Can these treatments be done locally?"

"Yes, but I strongly urge you to use Dr. Moore for the surgery. If radiation is indicated, you're in luck; one of the best radiation oncologists in the U.S. relocated to this area not long ago. If you like, I'll make the initial contact with him. His name is Eric Grueneberg. He's board-certified with over twenty years in practice."

She and Andy looked at each other for endless seconds. "Yes, I'd appreciate it if you'd give him a call."

Katie held back the tears until they were in the car.

———

KATIE LOOKED AT Andy as they crossed the river heading home. "You're mighty quiet."

"I'm in shock. Cancer is something that happens to other people."

"It's our life now. I'll fight this with everything I've got. I have faith we can beat it."

"You're a lot calmer than I would be."

"Yes. You're a man and feel like you've got to take charge of the battle. But that's why we've got good doctors. We have to trust in them and hope for the best. Will you promise me one thing?"

"You know I will. What is it?"

"Let me be the one who decides how to tell our families. I've got to come to grips with it myself. Do you think you can keep it inside until I do?"

"Anything for you, babe."

"One thing hasn't changed. I still love you as much as I ever have."

Andy couldn't take his eyes off the road, but he kissed the fingertips of his right hand and placed them on her lips.

15

Ted Moore's appearance, gazing through bottle-bottom spectacles, seemed reassuring to Katie. He said, "In layman's terms, we're going to remove the cancer and the tissues around it. This is not only to get the cancer, but to determine whether it's spread. We use 'metastasis' to describe the spread of cancer, which is what we want to avoid. Are you still with me?"

They nodded. Katie asked, "Then what?"

"We'll remove the lymph nodes in the area that might enable the cancer to spread. This will involve the area of your left armpit. You may have a lymphedema. That's a temporary swelling due to obstruction of the lymph vessels."

She turned to Andy whose taut lips betrayed an inner struggle. *Okay, I've got to take the lead here.* In a tone of forced calm, she asked, "Are there any other problems or dangers we need to know about?"

Ted removed his glasses and rubbed his eyes. Katie saw something there. Was it fear? Uncertainty? She couldn't tell. The doctor said, "It's troubling if we find evidence of 'angiogenesis.' That's where cancer cells connect to a blood vessel. We definitely don't want to see that. It makes metastasis much easier."

Andy said, "Dr. Morton talked about that. He said Katie could get radiation when we get home."

"Correct. I've already talked with Dr. Grueneberg to make the arrangements. We do radiation therapy to stop the spread of cancer through the surrounding tissues."

Andy squeezed Katie's hand. "Can I be with her during the surgery? I was in the delivery room when our son was born."

Ted shook his head. "I'd say probably not. It's not good practice for this kind of surgery. Don't worry. There's a waiting room nearby. We'll make sure you know anything important as soon as possible."

Bonnie had accompanied them. She asked, "How soon can we take Katie home? Christmas is only three weeks away, and it's always a big occasion in our family."

"She'll be home in plenty of time. I must warn you that Katie's radiation treatments and their effects may well interfere with her enjoyment of Christmas."

"We understand. We just want her home with us."

Katie reached out and touched her mother's shoulder. "I'll be there, Mama. I promise you nothing's going to stop me."

———

THE SURGERY WENT well. After a few days of recovery at Emory, Andy, Katie, and Bonnie drove home.

When they pulled up to the Warren house, Art, Tom, and Andy's sisters Lisa and Fran were waiting in the driveway. They unfolded a banner: "Welcome home Katie. Kick CANcer in the CAN." The hugs that followed were cautious, as everyone avoided the areas where Dr. Moore had removed tissue. Katie was embracing Fran when she heard a familiar whistle: the strains of "Hi Lili Hi Lo." She looked over Fran's shoulder and saw Brian standing a few feet away, flanked by her sisters Chrissie and Peg, and her brothers-in-law Eddie and Tony.

"Opa, it's sweet of you, but you didn't have to come. I'd have come to see you."

She kissed him.

"Not come to see my best girl? Are you serious? How do you feel?"

"I'm ready for a fight. I've still got to get radiation over the next several weeks."

"You're back with us. That's what matters."

———

WHEN KATIE AND Andy arrived at St. Johns Oncology Associates, the receptionist sent them to Frank Jonas, the practice administrator. He escorted them to a room with a long polished table and leather-covered office chairs.

"We use this for our initial consultations, but don't worry. We're more relaxed when we get to know you. Did you bring your records?"

Andy handed him a thick manila envelope. "This starts with our first meeting with Dr. Francis and goes through the surgery. I think you already have the imaging stuff."

"Let me give these to our records tech, and I'll check on the other. Would you like something to drink?"

Katie said, "Ice water with lemon if you have it."

"Coffee served just like my heart," was Andy's request.

"Black and cold? Coming right up," the man said with a laugh. Andy snorted.

He returned with the beverages. A middle-aged man with the build of a weightlifter and thick silver hair accompanied him.

"Good morning. I'm Eric Grueneberg."

"Pleased to meet you," Andy said. "You must've been an athlete in college. You've got quite a grip."

Eric gave them a half-smile. "I was a varsity wrestler at Cornell, but I never was much good at it." He turned to Katie. "How do you feel today, Mrs. Lyle?"

"Please call me Katie, Dr. Grueneberg."

"Okay. Please call me Eric."

"I've had some soreness, and I'm tired. I've had to sleep in an awkward position, so I haven't slept well at all." She motioned toward her left side.

"You'll lose the surgical soreness with the help of time and ibuprofen. Let's discuss what comes next." He launched into what sounded like a medical lecture, complete with talk of "gray units" and how he'd regulate the doses of radiation Katie received.

After Eric concluded, Andy asked, "Will these treatments do it, as far as getting rid of Katie's cancer?"

"Maybe yes, maybe no. It depends."

"That sounds pretty uncertain. Are there still questions or dangers?"

Eric looked down at the table for a second. He rubbed the knuckles of his right hand against his chin. "Cancer is a disease with a lot of indeterminacy. Individual cancers evolve. As we understand life, cancer isn't alive at all, or maybe I should say, it's alive, but it's stupid and obsessively single-minded."

Katie gave him an incredulous look. "What do you mean?"

"Sorry. That's a poor choice of words. I meant to say that cancer cells have only one purpose. They exist to reproduce and they overpower any normal cells that get in the way."

"All right, but how will radiation stop that?"

"Radiation is most effective in attacking cells that divide rapidly: skin, blood, but particularly cancer. It disrupts cancer's DNA, so it doesn't divide and crowd out other cells."

"I guess that makes me feel a little better."

"It should do the job. There are other lines of defense as well."

"Such as?"

"Chemotherapy and immunotherapy. It if spreads, we may have to use one or both of those methods. I'll discuss those in detail if it comes that that."

"Can you do those treatments here?"

"No, but I've got a friend I'd strongly recommend to handle the chemotherapy. His name's Clark Burton, and he's got a clinic in Tampa. We've been friends since medical school."

There was another question Katie needed to ask. She composed herself by looking at a Venetian waterscape on the opposite wall. "Just one more thing for now. How will these treatments affect our ability to have more children?"

"You have a son, correct?" When Katie nodded, he continued, "Radiation won't target your reproductive organs. But I have to be honest with you. If we do chemotherapy, that might make it impossible or at least inadvisable for you to conceive."

She looked at her hands. Andy put an arm around her shoulder. "Darling, we still have Timmy."

The conference concluded, with treatment to start in three days. Frank walked them to the front desk. "We'll do everything in our power to help you. I have two kids about your age, and I'd move mountains if I had to, to save them."

Katie looked at him and mouthed a silent "thank you."

———

A FEW HOURS LATER

The visitation to Luke that night was a voice-disturbance, a woman, a voice familiar, yet not. "Luke."

He was wide awake, despite the fact that he'd consumed half his usual nightcap. *This is more like what I'm used to.* "I'm here. Where are you?"

"I just met a man named Theo. I think he was one of my husband's patients, a few years after I died."

He couldn't help the "Uh" that accompanied a sudden exhalation. "Nikki?" *She's never spoken to me before.*

"Yes. I've come to warn you."

"Warn me? Warn me of what?"

In the long seconds of silence that followed, his mind reeled back almost forty years, to the day his sister-in-law died, drowned in a boating accident. He said, "Why have you chosen this time to speak?"

"Your race is almost over."

"I've hoped that for some time. There must be some other special message. What is it?"

"There are dangers ahead. You cannot lay down your burden until you overcome them."

The Delphic quality of Nikki's declarations stirred a low-grade anger, an emotion he'd never experienced during previous such disturbances. "You've told me nothing. What you say could mean many things. How can you expect me to know?"

"It can't happen until you lay down your self-delusion. Why do you think I mentioned Theo?"

Luke's mouth felt as though he'd swallowed a spoonful of cold ashes, a sensation bland but with a bitter aftertaste. "What has he said to you?"

"He knew I'd secretly loved you for years. That was a secret I took to my grave. Nate and Artie never knew it."

The smoldering fire in Luke's soul died instantly, as surely as a campfire inundated by a deluge of water. Chilly fingers tightened around his throat. Nikki's use of the diminutives for his brother and niece locked the words he wanted to say in his throat.

She continued. "Theo also told me you've always had a fear of admitting your own weaknesses. We both know what they are. You can never be healed until you bring them out into the light."

Very well. It's out in the open now, at least between Nikki and me. But what does she not know? Did Theo Loukretios tell her everything? He coughed. "You said 'Artie,' even though that's not the name she uses now."

"Yes, I know that. But calling herself 'Diana' instead of 'Artemis' doesn't change who she is. You must teach her to be herself."

"I can try. It may not be possible. Your daughter's a very strong person."

Nikki's voice rose to a pitch she'd never used with him in life. "Do you think I'm a fool? Do you think she could hide her feelings from her mother? She thinks she can conceal her anger from herself by becoming a different person."

"She also has her grandmother's gift. Perhaps you should talk to her directly."

"I've thought about it. I even asked Nate what he thought I should do. He believes she still harbors anger at me."

Can you blame her? You abandoned her. "All of us have those barriers, even with those we love. I do know she shed tears for you. That's something she wouldn't do for her father."

Another period of silence followed, this time lasting several minutes. Luke thought the disturbance might be over until Nikki said, "She respects you above everyone else. Will you at least try to convince her to listen to me?"

"I'll try."

He heard a muffled sound – was it a sob? – before his sister-in-law spoke again. "For the sake of my hopeless love, make her understand the hopelessness of her anger. When she can do that, she will be ready to take on your mantle." There was a catch in her voice as she said, "Farewell, Luke. Now I must go."

"No, wait, please. I still need to know . . ." The knowledge that he was speaking into a void flooded over him.

Luke couldn't sleep for hours. Just as his brain gave up the struggle and he dropped off, one more question intruded: What else was Nikki trying to warn him about?

PART II
BATTLEGROUND

Normal cells are identically normal; malignant cells become unhappily malignant in unique ways.
- Siddhartha Mukerjee, *The Emperor of all Maladies*

16

Luke was at his desk when he felt a psychic jolt, as if he'd awakened with a sudden recollection of something long forgotten.

He remembered his dream of the previous year, the visit to his dying father, the memory of something that never happened. What disrupted his thoughts was the way the dream had ended, with an argument between the two brothers over the inheritance.

Why did I dream about that? It couldn't have come out of memory. He stared at a painting on the opposite wall of his office, a depiction of the Tower of the Winds in Athens. He'd bought it in 2000 when he and Diana visited their ancestral homeland, a purchase inspired by something Andreas had told him in the 1930s: It was where Socrates was confined before his execution.

Know thyself, that's what he taught his students. Well, I've had lots of years to figure out who I am. I'm still not sure I know. In truth, the thought didn't bother him. Searching for clues to his own identity seemed a waste of time.

A discordant thought interrupted his musings. In settling Andreas's estate, Luke had renounced his right in favor of Athanasios. At the time, he'd rationalized this gesture as an acknowledgment that his brother had put his own schooling on hold during their father's final illness. What was upsetting to Luke was the realization that what he was actually doing was showing his brother that he could make it on his own without money from the family. *What you wanted more than anything else was to establish your moral superiority over Nate.*

His admission brought a moment of spiritual emptiness. "Okay, I've admitted it. I should just let it go now." He took his eyes off the painting and forced himself to return to work.

As he reviewed patient files, another dream-disturbance intruded. The movie that unreeled in his mind showed a young couple riding in a car, traveling down an expressway through an unfamiliar landscape. *Where are they going?* He couldn't see any road signs; even the terrain was alien to him. It was as if Luke were an observer, spread-eagle across the windshield, looking at a silent movie, a panorama of a man and a woman. There was a glare on the windshield, so he couldn't easily read their lips. It was evident that they were very much in love, but their faces also revealed fear lurking beneath the surface. *It's the fear that's the problem. I have to find out what they're afraid of before I know what to do.*

A sudden clamor in the hallway broke his concentration. *Damn it! I was on the right track, I know I was, and now I'm lost again.* He heard a woman weeping and the voice of another woman consoling the weeper. *Diana. They're back.*

He went to the door. The young woman was Ellie Catania, a nurse only two years out of college. Diana was holding her, a strong right arm around the shoulders, comforting words whispered in a husky voice. "Would you mind coming into my office?" he asked.

They sat down on a leather sofa opposite the built-in bookshelves along one wall. Luke pulled up an armchair. "Ellie, was this the first death you've witnessed? You're relatively new with us. We do as much as we can to spare our new employees this kind of unpleasantness until they've got their feet firmly on the ground."

Ellie shook her head, tears streaming down her face. "No, sir, I saw people die when I did clinical rotations in college." Her nose was running, so he handed her a box of tissues. She blew her nose, and the tears continued.

"Who was it?"

Diana said, "Joanna Faris. You know, that young woman who was referred a month ago. Melanoma."

"Why didn't you call me?"

"There wasn't time. When we got to the hospital, she'd already been in a coma for about six hours. There was some foul-up with their communications, and no one thought to call us. She died two hours ago."

Luke put a gentle hand under Ellie's chin and raised it until he could look her in the eye. "Ellie, I understand you're upset, but this wasn't your first time. It's just the nature of our business. Are you going to be okay?"

"I think so."

"It'll never be routine. Every death hurts. That won't change. Do you want to talk about it?"

She blew her nose again. "Uh, it was, uh, so sad. She was such a sweet, loving girl."

"I know. I dealt with her regularly until this last week."

"I had to watch her husband, her mom and dad go through the whole thing. Oh God, the looks in their eyes . . ."

"You and Diana did as much as you could. But we're human. We can't make everything right. Sometimes the best we can do is to admit we're helpless too."

"They told us that just before she died, her sister came in with a little girl in her arms. Joanna and Pete, that's her husband, had a baby girl. Now that baby will never know how much her mother loved her."

She started crying again, this time with sobs that shook her whole body.

Luke looked at Diana. Her eyes brimmed. She covered them with a hand for just a moment. She shot him a look with a question in it. He nodded.

"Ellie, it's something Luke and I don't like to talk about it, but I had two children who died," Diana said. "That was over twenty years ago, and there's been pain in my life every day since then. You told me you and Joanna were friends, right?"

"That's right."

"You can do something that people often forget about. You can be there for her parents. Right now, they're in a cold hell, the kind of place no one knows about until they're there."

"I'll try."

"At first, there'll be such a crowd of people offering sympathy that you'll have to fight your way through them. But three or six months from now, most of them will have gone away, and Joanna's parents will be lonelier than ever. That's when they'll need your support most."

Ellie squeezed Diana's hand. "Thank you for letting me cry on your shoulder. I'm going to cry some more when I get home, but I'll be all right."

Luke asked, "Do you need one of us to drive you home?"

She shook her head.

After Ellie left, Luke took a bottle of Pinot Noir out of a portable wine cellar and poured two glasses. He and Diana sipped these luscious potables as they sat in his office.

"Noble Pinot Noir," he said. "Almost as noble as the finest fruits from our homeland."

"True. It's not Greek, but it's still good."

"I had a dream this afternoon, but it didn't run enough times for me to figure it out." He recounted his vision of the couple in the car.

Diana said, "I'm sorry we interrupted you."

"Couldn't be helped. Do you have any idea what it means?"

"No. You're the interpreter, not me."

"You have the power. You just don't like to use it."

"Why should I? Your powers are stronger than mine."

He sighed. "Do you remember that day last spring when I went for a walk and a message from Sonny broadsided me?"

"A little. Refresh my memory."

He repeated Sonny's words. "I think this latest dream has something to do with, 'your time is coming.' That's why I'm trying to get you accustomed to interpreting. You may have to do it without me someday."

Diana snorted. "I doubt that, you old goat. You'll live as long as Zeus."

"Or Hades. Well, Nate and I weren't the only brothers who fought. But I'd really like to know when the fight will end."

After they finished their glasses, he walked her to the bus stop. "You still have that Taser in your handbag?" he asked.

She smirked. "Yep. On bad days, I want some dirtbag to put a move on me so I can see how effective it is."

She was laughing as she rode away.

Luke closed the office and headed home. As he walked the last few blocks from the DuPont Circle Metro station to his residence, he was buffeted by a cold breeze, a reminder that winter, and death, lay somewhere ahead. *Yes, but how far? Will I know it when it arrives?*

———

AFTER POLISHING OFF a light dinner his housekeeper had prepared, Luke went to a closet and searched until he found a photo album that hadn't been opened in years. When he took it off the shelf, it stirred up enough dust to trigger a series of sneezes. "Damned allergies," he muttered.

Luke browsed through it until he found a page with a faded color photograph: a young married couple with the wife holding a baby in a pink jumper. He smiled. Nikki had enclosed the photo in a Christmas card to him in 1951 when he was in Japan awaiting deployment to Korea. What made him smile was the adoring look the little girl was giving her father. "She was daddy's little girl then and for a lot of years after that."

The estrangement between Nate and his daughter emerged in the late 1960s, after Nikki's death. When his niece turned twenty-one, she'd gone to court and legally changed her given name from "Artemis" to "Diana." Her marriage to Hector Karras, a Vietnam veteran from a working-class Baltimore family, was another shot across her father's bow. Thereafter, she'd only communicated with him when Luke served as an intermediary. At his funeral, Diana and her family had fled as soon as the service ended, leaving Luke to stay behind and render courtesies to the other mourners.

I thought Sonny helped her get past that. But I think there's still something missing. Luke gave an involuntary shudder as the recognition hit him: He wouldn't gain his release until he'd convinced Diana to bury her anger towards her parents.

17

THE INTERCOM IN his office buzzed. "Helen Ferguson is here to see you."

"I'll be right out."

Luke grinned at the sight of the petite auburn-haired woman chatting with the receptionist. "Helen, my dear, it's lovely to see you." He kissed her on the cheek. "To what do I owe this pleasure?"

"I apologize for dropping in on you without warning, but I've been on the phone all morning, inquiring into job prospects."

His eyebrows jumped. "You folding up your practice?"

Helen smiled. "Not closing, moving. Bob's getting a transfer, and I won't be able to work with you anymore."

Bob was Helen's second husband, a rear admiral in the Navy.

Luke said, "I'm happy for Bob but miserable for us. I'm losing the best combination of psychologist and social worker I've ever seen. Where is Uncle Sam sending you?"

"Kingsland, Georgia. Bob's going to command a Trident sub squadron. He loves being at Annapolis, but he's been itching for sea duty for a long time now."

"I've never heard of Kingsland. Where is it? Savannah?"

"No, it's about thirty-five miles north of Jacksonville, Florida. We're going down next weekend to look at houses."

Jacksonville. There's something I'm supposed to remember about Jacksonville. What? "How about a farewell lunch to celebrate your move?"

"I ought to spend the afternoon making calls, but, yes, that would be nice."

Luke's inability to remember what he was supposed to disturbed him during the Metro trip across town. He knew he was vulnerable to the forgetfulness that commonly plagues the elderly, but that wasn't what bothered him. It was a nagging sense that Jacksonville was part of a puzzle; forgetting something meant that one or more pieces were missing. *Well, it'll either come to me or it won't.* This rationalization gave little comfort.

They went to a bistro in Foggy Bottom and were seated at a table that overlooked the Emergency entrance to GWU Hospital. Luke said, "I'd offer a toast, but I'm not up on my nautical terminology."

"Bob's favorite is 'fair winds and following seas.'"

He lifted his glass. "And to life in the sunshine."

Sadness began to weigh on Luke as lunch progressed. It became evident enough for Helen to ask, "What's wrong?"

"A bad case of conflicted feelings, that's all."

"Well, that's my specialty. Spill it, mister."

He paused and looked out the window at the leaves being blown into the gutters, driven by the relentless force from the change of seasons. "I love you, Helen. I've loved you for years. There were times, when we were on a case together, I wanted to ask you to go with me and find a nice private hotel room."

In a tender lover's voice, she said, "I know that. You remind me of a song. Oh, what was it called? I think it was 'I Loved You Once in Silence.' Did you think you could hide your feelings from me? Why didn't you ever try to do anything about it?"

He looked down at the table. "I supposed it was because I knew what would happen if I did."

"Were you afraid I'd say 'no?' You don't know me very well if you believe that."

"That's not it. I knew that if we made love, you'd look at my face, but you'd see Nate. I couldn't stand the thought of that."

"He wounded us both. We can forgive, but could we forget?"

He struggled for words. Helen reached across the table and squeezed his hand. "I'll answer my own question. No, I think not. That's the trouble with you, Luke. You've got too much damned wisdom, and love can't break through that barrier."

The rest of the meal passed in near-silence. When they left, she hailed a taxi. She gave him a long parting kiss on the mouth before saying "We'll meet again."

After the cab pulled away, Luke took a long walk, forcing himself to head into the cold wind, crunching underfoot the leaves that blew across his path. The walk took long enough that Luke was able to re-play the thoughts that fed his sense of responsibility. *Responsibility... Hell, it's guilt.*

Helen's first husband, Theo Loukretios, had started suffering unexplained muscular twitches and fibrillations in 1975, when he was in his early thirties. Tests led to a diagnosis of ALS, better known as "Lou Gehrig's disease." His doctor referred him to a neurological practice whose members included Dr. Athanasios "Nate" Vangelis. Theo's health struggles became a battlefield for the tryout of some experimental drug therapies, their effects making the last three years of his life a prolonged misery.

On one occasion during Theo's treatments, Luke happened to be in Baltimore, delivering a guest lecture at Johns Hopkins. A visit to his brother's office afterward led to a meeting with the Loukretios family. He'd stayed in touch with Theo and Helen and, after Theo's death, with Helen.

After Nikki Vangelis's death, Nate had affairs with a number of women, most of whom, like Helen, were in emotionally vulnerable positions. Helen became a notch in his gun belt, an off-and-on romance that ended only with Nate's sudden demise. Helen had subsequently taken a job at a hospital where Diana was a nursing supervisor.

The ugly revelations about Nate's affairs that came to light, revelations that embittered Luke and Diana, had all but destroyed Helen. *While my swinish brother was screwing my wife, he was doing the same to Helen.* Helen had plunged into depression. It had taken months of listening by both Luke and Diana to arrest the plunge and drag her back into an active life.

God, there were times I wanted her so badly, I could get aroused just thinking about her. Was I any better than Nate because I kept my impulses under control? Have I been living a lie all those years since?

Unlike so many of the questions that had bedeviled Luke since meeting Helen, this one got a quick answer. As he walked past the National Air and Space Museum, he suffered a reprise of the spike of acute pain that had accompanied his last message from Sonny. It was a different voice this time, the Tidewater-accented tones of Constance Woodward Vangelis. He groped his way to a nearby bench and sat down.

"Luke, my dear, you have to let it go."

"Let what go?"

"Trying to revisit the chance you missed with Helen. You made the right choice. Why do you have such regrets?"

"I don't know. I think it's because I know I could never make any woman happy. I think I failed with you."

Above the noise of traffic, he heard in his mind her laughter, not the laughter of mockery that had tormented him after her death, but the sound of gentle mirth. "No, if you'll just put down that Greek stubbornness, you can see how wrong you are. Remember when we were newlyweds? Our desire for each other was so hot it almost consumed us."

"We lost it somewhere along the way."

"You lost it. I never did."

Luke had no defense against these crushing words. He sat in silence, waiting for what she'd say next. After several minutes of waiting, he asked, "Why are you telling me this?"

"I can't reach Helen, but you both have something important that must be done. Unless you can trust each other enough to work together, you can't help her, or her son."

"Help who? Helen? Phil lives in Los Angeles, and, as far as I know, he's doing fine. He doesn't need help."

"Not Helen's son, the son of the one you must convince to trust you. It will soon be the right time."

A chilly gust mussed his hair, as if his wife were borne off by the wind. There was nothing but a sorrowful stillness in his mind.

———

AN ENVELOPE ARRIVED at the hospice just after the New Year. It was addressed "Dr. Lukas Vangelis – Confidential."

When Luke opened the envelope, a business card dropped out. It read,

ST. JOHNS ONCOLOGY ASSOCIATES
HELEN FERGUSON, PH.D., MSW
BUSINESS MANAGER

Diana usually took a vacation in January and went someplace where, as she put it, "I can get a reminder that winter doesn't always include snow and ice." She'd made no definite plans for this year's vacation yet. Luke showed her Helen's card, which was the only prodding she needed. She booked plane tickets and a week at a hotel in St. Augustine with a waterfront view.

When she returned, Luke asked, "How does Helen like Florida?"

"So far, so good. I know you don't like resort-y places, but there's something to be said for the area where she lives now."

"How's that?"

"It's easy to reserve tee times and time on the tennis courts. We both need to take better care of our health."

"So, she's happy?"

"Yes, you could say that. She's got a good job. She really likes the people she works with. She told me we ought to consider relocating. There's no lack of business."

Right. After what we said at her last lunch, that's just trouble waiting to happen. Bet she gets lonely when Bob's at sea. Stay away from that, Luke.

"Could we be happy there?"

"I don't know. I told her we'd think about it."

"I'm going to wait until the situation is clearer before I think about moving."

"When will that be?"

"When I get a definite message."

18

Katie and Andy sat in front of the television, watching Rick Blaine and Victor Lazlo joust over the disputed letters of transit in *Casablanca*. While his parents held hands and watched the movie, Timmy slept in a folding playpen, dreaming the dreams of a ten-month-old.

As the closing credits rolled, Katie asked Andy, "What kind of risk would you take to get me out of a jam?"

"Anything you need, babe, anything I could do. Why do you ask?"

She smiled a mother's smile at the sleeping baby. "You're my first love and always will be. But for Timmy, I'd. . ."

"You'd do what?"

"Sell my soul. Doesn't that sound stupid? I worry a lot about him taking a wrong path in life. I know there's no reason, not now, but what may happen years from now, when he's a teenager and doesn't listen to us?"

"We have our families. They'll be there for him. We have so much happiness that I think it's a waste of time to worry."

A frown crossed her face. "Have you heard anything from your mother since that court case?"

"Well, you know she didn't send a Christmas card. That's unusual. I didn't think we said anything to Jack that was very hateful. He must've given her some cock-and-bull story about how mean we were to him. I guess he didn't get the big fee he was hoping for."

"Would you do something for me this year?"

"Does this have to do with Mom and Jack?"

She nodded. "Try to make up with them, if you can."

"You're not making it easy on me. Honestly, what can I do? And why is it so important just now?"

"I don't know. But if Lisa and Fran can get along with Marilyn, you ought to as well. I know your dad and Tommy think like you do, so maybe it's a guy thing. Maybe it's harder for you to forgive. I just want our families to be at peace."

"I'll try."

When they went to bed, Andy dropped off quickly. Katie stretched out, turned on first one side, then the other, but couldn't find a position where she could sleep. More than an hour passed as she tossed.

A loud "Waaaah" hailing from Timmy's crib broke the stillness.

Andy stirred up, but Katie put a hand on his leg. "No, you've got to go to work in the morning. Go back to sleep. He probably just needs changing."

There was no evident reason for Timmy's upset. Even in the pale glow of a night-light, she could see he wasn't squirming, the usual sign of a wet or soiled diaper. He'd had a bottle and probably wasn't hungry. He lay on his back, crying and holding his arms up, as if to say, "Mommy, pick me up." She reached into the crib and lifted him, settling his head against her left shoulder. His tiny hands reached up and grasped for her, as if her presence was a lifeline. *What could be wrong?* Katie had never gotten into the habit of singing lullabies, a failing she blamed on her lack of a decent singing voice. But her desire to quell her son's fears was strong, so she hummed the melody to "Morningtown Ride," which she remembered her father singing to her at bedtime. As she tried to puzzle out her son's behavior, his cries got softer. Within a few minutes, he was once again asleep.

———

THE NEXT DAY, she got a call from St. Johns Oncology Associates, a reminder to come in for a follow-up appointment. Her radiation therapy had ended just before Valentine's Day, leaving her tired but hopeful. *This is probably just a routine exercise.*

Before her appointment, she went to an imaging lab and underwent another bout with high-tech medicine, a process that involved injection of a radionuclide, followed by a computerized scan. When Helen Ferguson called back, she asked Katie to bring Andy with her, explaining this was standard operating procedure for cancer patients. Katie sensed a hesitation in Helen's voice; she recalled what Helen's predecessor had said at their first meeting about how far he was willing to go. *What does that mean for me?*

Cold reality slapped them in the face when they arrived and the receptionist ushered them into a small office. Eric entered after a short wait. The look on his face told the story.

"Katie, Andy, I wish I could be more positive, but things don't look as good as we hoped."

Katie said, "Are you telling me that the radiation didn't work?"

"No, the surgery and radiation did get rid of the cancer on the surface." He paused.

"It's spread? What does the scan show?"

Eric turned to a computer connected to a projector. The first image flashed on the screen. "Okay, I know this is probably mumbo-jumbo, but the dark areas are normal tissue. Notice those red areas. Those represent malignant lesions."

"Where is this?"

"The liver." Eric's face was impassive, but his eyes showed uncertainty.

"You said the odds were ninety to ten in our favor if we caught it early. We didn't, so what are the odds now?"

He took a deep breath. "Fifty-fifty."

Andy broke in. "Fifty-fifty. What does that mean? Katie living or dying is a coin toss? Is that what you're saying?"

Eric took a tissue from a box on his desk and wiped the beads of sweat along his hairline.

"I wish I could be that definite. It's a fifty-fifty that Katie can make it to five years, which was our original goal." He clicked the mouse again, and another image filled the screen: an octopus-like protrusion, dark purple, with a spherical inner section displaying brown wormlike splotches. "That comes from electron microscopy of the original malignancy. Those 'arms' are where the tumor is trying to get access to a blood supply. Since all the blood in your body passes through the liver on a regular basis, it's hit the jackpot."

"What do we do now?" Katie asked.

"For our next line of defense, I'm going to call on that old friend I mentioned to you last year."

"Dr. Clark?"

"Almost. Clark Burton. He's a medical oncologist, a specialist in chemotherapy. Lately, he and I've done some joint explorations in immunotherapy, another promising area. Clark is in Tampa. There is one problem: You'll have to go to his clinic two or three weeks at a time, and then recuperate for the next round."

"There are some bad effects, aren't there?"

Eric grimaced. With a nod, he said, "We're trying to poison the cancer. Unfortunately, we also poison healthy cells. What we hope is that, as we kill off the cancer cells, normal cells can repair some of the damage. You'll have hair loss, at least temporarily, plus bleeding from the gums and damage to your nails. With enough time, the body can make things right. We just have to give it a chance."

Katie looked at the ugly image for what seemed an eternity. Then she said, "I guess we have no choice." She put her hand up to her eyes and struggled vainly not to cry. "I-I j-j-just w-w-want to know what my chances are of seeing Timmy grow up. You can't tell me."

Eric shook his head. "I'll do everything I can. But I'm human, not divine, despite the aura we doctors cultivate. We won't give up the fight unless you want to."

"I want to live. I have faith in you."

As they left, Helen came up to them. "Let me handle making the arrangements. That's my job and I'm good at it. You concentrate on fighting cancer." She reached out and squeezed Katie's hand. "I have lots of friends in this business, and we'll call in any help we can get. We'll go the full distance with you."

"What can I do?"

"Pray. Pray, and give as much love as you can."

Katie didn't respond at first. She looked past Helen and saw, on a wall of the corridor that led to the waiting room, a photograph of Eric and a woman, obviously his wife, both with heads covered, praying before an eternal flame. She couldn't remember the name of the place, but she knew it was Israel's memorial to those who died in the Holocaust. She reached out and squeezed Helen's hand.

———

KATIE CONCENTRATED ON bucking up her spirits during the ride home. When they arrived, Bonnie handed Timmy back to them. "What did the doctors tell you?"

She looked her mother in the eye. "I've got to have chemotherapy." Seeing that Bonnie was on the verge of tears, she said, "It's just an extra measure of caution. The surgery and radiation treatment got most of the cancer. This is just the knockout punch."

Andy said, "We're pretty confident. Dr. Grueneberg gave us a lot of reasons for hope."

On that note, Bonnie departed.

19

KATIE'S NEXT APPOINTMENT included a meeting with the hitherto unseen Dr. Burton. Eric opened the appointment with an apology.
"I know it's odd, scheduling an appointment for Saturday afternoon,
but it's the only time we could get Clark here without disrupting his
regular schedule."

"I'm sorry I wrecked your weekend, Doctor, um, Clark, I mean."

The tall man grinned. "Eric and I don't stand on ceremony. I'm
familiar with your chart, but I don't know how much you already know
about what we're going to do."

"I used to teach biology. I know a lot of the terminology. Be as thor-
ough as you can. I'll ask questions if I don't understand something."

"Do you prefer words or pictures?"

"Actually, both."

Clark launched into a presentation about the uses of chemotherapy in fighting cancer. The slides he showed, academic at first, became
very personal with pictures of patients in various stages of treatment.
Katie said little, thinking, *Until I know this guy better, I'm not going to let
him see how he affects me.*

At the end, Andy said, "Eric told us this might keep us from having
any more children."

A shadow seemed to pass over Clark's eyes. "We won't know for sure for some time. My advice to you is to focus on contraception. It could be bad news if Katie got pregnant, and the fetus was abnormal."

"I'm Catholic," Katie said. "Abortion is out of the question. We'll talk to my gynecologist."

Andy said, "Dr. Grueneberg, uh, Eric, also mentioned another method, immune something or other."

Clark nodded. "Immunotherapy might become part of Katie's treatment regimen."

"How does that differ from what you're doing?"

"Your immune system is the body's first line of defense. Immunotherapy uses drugs to goad the immune system into attacking and killing cancer cells."

"Wouldn't that be better than trying to poison the cancer?"

"That's a good question. We may be able to use immunotherapy later. There are a limited number of pharmaceuticals that work against metastatic melanoma. Also, the side effects can be quite severe. Katie could be incapacitated for a long time."

Silence fell in the conference room. Katie appeared to be looking at the last slide Clark had put on the screen. In reality, she focused on the digital clock on the wall, counting the seconds, coming to a realization of how lead-footed the passage of just a few seconds could be. *How did Shakespeare put it, 'Tomorrow, and tomorrow, and tomorrow…' I wish I could remember the rest of it, but the only thing that comes back to me is 'the way to dusty death.'*

Eric's voice disrupted her thoughts. "Are there any more questions?"

They looked at each other and then shook their heads in unison.

Eric pulled out his cell phone and sent a text message. In less than a minute, Helen Ferguson entered the room, dressed for a Saturday on the golf course.

"Helen, you know Katie and Andy Lyle. This rubber-faced clown across the table is my colleague Clark Burton from Hillsborough Oncology in Tampa. You'll need to coordinate with his staff on the legwork to get Katie's treatments set up."

Clark rose and shook her hand. He wisecracked, "One thing I've always liked about Eric is how respectful he is toward his fellow professionals."

Everyone laughed, and Helen said, "Katie, are there any arrangements I can help you with?"

"I think we can handle the routine things. My mother and Andy's sister can take care of our son while we're at Dr. Burton's clinic."

Helen's eyes glowed. "I guess we're all good to go. Just remember one thing from your American history classes, what Franklin D. Roosevelt said: 'The only thing we have to fear is fear itself.'"

On these confident words, the meeting ended.

———

TO COMPENSATE HELEN and Clark for the disruption of their weekends, Marina Grueneberg gave a small dinner party that evening. Except for Bob Ferguson and three women, all of the party guests were doctors.

Helen often interjected droll comments during a stilted conversation that was heavily oriented toward medical shop talk. Tonight, she nursed an after-dinner Courvoisier and listened. Her background in social work and psychology focused her thoughts on the comments Eric and Clark made. As the evening progressed, two things became clear: Eric seemed to be driven by subconscious proddings he was reluctant to share, and Clark felt some tie to Katie that went beyond the doctor-patient relationship.

When Marina asked about "that young woman you're treating," Eric said, "Katie resembles Tina. Not a physical resemblance, it's just that, well, I, uh, . . ."

"She's got your sister's strong will, is that what you mean?" Marina said. "Tina has a pretty tough emotional shell."

Eric nodded. "Yeah, that's Tina all right."

Clark muttered, "She reminds me of my niece Caroline. They're pretty close in age. They even have similar speech patterns."

"Which niece is that?"

"Caroline is my brother Robbie's daughter. She's an Air Force officer."

Clark's use of his dead brother's name caused Eric to pause before he said, "She's upholding the Burton military tradition."

"Yep, particularly since her uncle just wanted to do his hitch and get out."

Helen continued listening in silence.

———

TWO DAYS LATER

Diana looked at the number before she answered her phone. "Hello. How are you doing, Helen?"

"I'm fine. I just thought I'd call and see how you and Luke are getting along."

"About the same as always. When are you coming back for a visit?"

Helen hesitated. *Luke hasn't told her anything about our last lunch. If I came back, it would be too easy for us to pick up where we left off.* "Don't know if we can make it anytime soon. Of course, you're always welcome at our house."

"Believe it or not, Luke has actually talked about moving. I think he's waiting for some kind of signal."

"I've got a question you can ask him. I need you to ask him about someone."

"Sure. Who is it?"

"My boss is Eric Grueneberg. He's got a friend from medical school, a specialist in chemotherapy named Clark Burton. I was at a dinner last night with them, and the conversation set off something in me. I'm not sure what it was. I just got an odd feeling that there's something, some tie, between them and you and Luke."

"That is strange. I met a general named Burton in Washington about two years ago. Wonder if the doctor is some relation?"

"Might be. If there's some old tie, it could help me work better with Grueneberg."

"Well, I'll see what I can find out."

The conversation moved on to the kind of spontaneous small talk common among old friends.

After Helen got off the phone, she decided to take a walk around the neighboring golf course. She anointed her body with insect repellent and headed along the cart path, thinking about Luke, wondering what they would say the next time they saw each other. She walked for over an hour, feeling the heat soak into her and listening to the croaking of frogs in ponds along the way. She returned home with her emotions no more settled than when she had set out.

———

WHILE REAR ADMIRAL Ferguson was on an official trip to the naval installations at Hampton Roads, Helen started making notes about her feelings. It wasn't a diary; rather, it was her means of analyzing her own thoughts and emotions. This was an exercise she avoided unless there was something in a case that caused her to look inward.

The center of her writings this time was Luke. She wondered about Diana's remark that he seemed to await a sign or a signal.

I know he relies a lot on these intuitions of his. He's almost feminine in his abilities to sense things, but this sounds like something different. Luke isn't a churchgoer. Is he expecting a divine revelation?

Her call sounded with "I Dreamed a Dream" from *Les Misérables*. She looked at the caller ID and smiled. It was her daughter, Alexis, calling from California. "Hello, baby," she said. "What's new?"

"Mikey's started talking. He said, 'Mama' to me this morning."

"That's wonderful, darling. Can he say something to his old grandma?"

"Just a second, let's see." A brief pause, then, "Say something to Grandma, Mikey."

At first, there were only the gurglings you would expect from a baby. The connection wasn't altogether clear, but the baby spoke clearly enough for the syllables, apparently nonsensical, to come through: "Gah-go-ook-ee-yun-day-go."

Helen shivered. She heard Alexis say, "Sorry, Mom. He's a little ahead of himself, trying to speak in complete sentences. I guess that's what happens when your daddy is a college professor. He'll get there soon enough. Say bye-bye, Mikey."

"Eye-eye." Helen heard Alexis's husband come up and take her grandson. Mother and daughter chatted a few minutes longer, then Alexis excused herself and rang off.

Helen put her phone on the desk and leaned back, eyes closed. Over and over, she replayed the baby's words. The random sounds, undecipherable to her daughter, sounded eerily like, "Doctor Luke is in danger."

Get a grip. Don't put too much stock in something from the mouths of babes. She started to write something, but the words wouldn't come. After several attempts, she gave up.

20

"LUKE, I HAD a phone call from Helen Ferguson this morning."

"Really? What's the occasion?"

"I thought it was just a social call. We haven't talked since I got back from Florida. She said some things that make me wonder."

"What kind of things?"

"She works for a doctor named Eric Grueneberg. Over the weekend, she met a doctor named Clark Burton who's working with Grueneberg on a case. It's really a tough one, at least psychologically. I could tell that much. The patient's a young woman with metastatic melanoma."

"Huh? What was that?"

"You're not listening. Eric Grueneberg and Clark Burton. Do either of those names ring a bell?"

He looked at her, his eyes half-shut, a look she'd sometimes seen when he was lost in thought. "It's been many years. I met them because Nate insisted on having me as a guest lecturer occasionally when he was teaching at Hopkins. Odd, isn't it, after all these years?"

She waited for a minute or two, expecting him to say more. Instead, he reached for some papers on his desk. Diana, knowing she'd get nothing more out of him, left his office. The mention of the two doctors didn't trigger a recollection of their encounter at the D-Day reunion.

———

LUKE DIDN'T SLEEP that night. He'd disciplined himself not to think about Helen. The message from her via Diana was unsettling. It still hurt, being unable to tell her about his true feelings until she'd drifted out of his reach.

In the months since the dream disturbances had started again, he'd waited for the next messages. Since Connie's cryptic words of last fall, he'd felt there was a blockage in his senses, something that barred him from taking the vital next steps to carry out his mission. He suspected that he'd failed to do something that would guide him to the next milestone. *If only I could figure out what it is.*

In the no man's land between wakefulness and sleep, the voice came to him again, this time from Sonny. "Helen is your pathway to the truth. She will guide you to the next steps." This message banished hope of even a temporary respite from his daily cares. With a sigh of resignation, he got up and made a pot of coffee. He was still hopeful that he would get further guidance. It did no good to worry about it. *At least I haven't completely lost contact with Sonny.*

———

THREE DAYS LATER, confirmation of Sonny's words came to Luke from an unexpected source: his brother.

It was a voice-disturbance, this time unaccompanied by a pain signal, as had been the case with Sonny and Connie. As Luke strolled through Rock Creek Park, taking shade from the midsummer sun, he heard Nate say, "You've backed yourself into a corner with Helen, brother."

These words brought him to a dead stop, emotionally breathless. Uncertain if his knees would continue to support him, he sat down on a nearby boulder. Runners and rollerbladers zoomed by, some making greetings he didn't return.

"Do you want to know the real truth?"

The ridicule implicit in this last remark restored his power of speech. "You're one hell of an authority about being in a corner with Helen, or maybe I should say, being in some hideaway."

Nate gave a throaty chuckle. "I was a poor substitute for you. Tell me, Luke, how it is you've lived as long as you have, yet you're still as emotionally oblivious as ever?"

"I've heard just about all I want to hear from you. Goodbye."

"Hey brother, you can't get away from me by wishing me out of existence. I haven't got a body you can kick, and as for you trying to damn my soul, we got past that long ago. At least that's what I thought."

Luke took several deep breaths, letting the scent of verdant foliage restore his emotional balance. Even though he wasn't moving, beads of sweat popped out on his brow. After mopping them up with his handkerchief, he said, "All right, we're past that. Why do you bring up Helen now?"

"It's because both of you are being dishonest as hell about each other. Helen still wants you so badly. She'd hop into the sack with you if you just crooked your finger at her."

"Even if that's true, what about me? Got any more psychoanalytic insights?"

"I know you forgave Connie and me, but you haven't forgiven me for having an affair with Helen at the same time."

Luke rubbed his forehead. What Nate said went beyond just discomfort. *What is he getting at?*

"You putting on a mask, Luke, doesn't stop me. I can read you like a cheap paperback."

"Thanks for shoring up my self-esteem."

"That's irrelevant to this discussion. When I died, Helen was pregnant with my child."

"What?"

"It was a baby girl. She lost it to a miscarriage."

"Why do you bring this up now?"

The background sounds along the walking path were swallowed by white noise. Nate said, "Because having my child was as close as she'd ever get to having *your* child. That was really what she wanted."

Luke's shoulders sagged. "And that means . . ."

"It means you have to trust her. She kept that from you all these years because she's beyond it now. Unless you can trust yourself enough to work with her again, you won't be able to reach your goal."

As Luke pondered these last words, a cool breeze from the river blew across his tormented features. After several minutes, he got up and resumed his walk.

———

ANDY ASKED, "WHAT do you think about this new guy, Burton?"

Katie said, "He's different from Eric. Clark has that 'I'm from old money, screw you' look, but Eric looks like he's been stepped on a few times in his life."

"Do you trust him?"

"Eric does."

"Is that good enough for you?"

"It has to be. I don't think we have the energy to do a lot of digging into their backgrounds."

"I just want to be sure they aren't hiding anything from us."

Katie gave him a resigned look. There seemed to be no easy answers.

21

AUGUST 2006

Luke's belief that Helen would be his source of guidance was correct. He was wrong about the timing.

Despite his vivid memories of the furies of war, betrayal, and the scars they left, he still believed that most humans were rational creatures. This belief had helped him maintain his emotional balance, but disregarding the power of irrational actions had already scarred his life. It happened again, on a calm summer night.

In the neighborhood around the Library of Congress and Seward Square, few passersby took any note of a light-grey brick building with a black door, marked by two signs. The entrance was deliberately unobtrusive, with only two signs that indicated what the building was used for. The first had white capitals on an olive-green background: ELENI HOSPICE. Just below it, a smaller sign announced: No prescription drugs stored on these premises. The hospice only kept a small stock of painkillers in a locked cabinet, in the event of an emergency when a pharmacy wasn't available.

The midsummer sun was sinking behind Virginia's green hills as Luke left the office. He had locked the second of two deadbolts on the front door when a red-eyed man whose face resembled the complexion of a smallpox victim came up the stairs from the street. "Hey, mister, you got any painkillers?"

Luke turned, saying, "Sorry, my good man. We don't keep any in our offices. But I'll be happy to take you to a pharmacy on my way to the Metro."

He'd barely gotten these words out when the man drew a switch-blade. The blade snapped open, an evil glint in the dying sunlight. "Like hell you will! You keep the good stuff in there, and that's what I want, not some overpriced shit that I ain't got a prescription for. Now open that damned door!" He pushed the knife blade against Luke's Adam's apple. A sallow, gaunt woman who'd been lounging against a nearby sycamore tree came up on his right. Luke didn't see the gun in her hand.

"I told you there's nothing here. Put down that knife and let me take you to a drugstore."

"If you don't want me to stick this all the way through your throat, motherfucker, you'll open that door *now*."

The woman said, "If he don't kill you, I will. Move your ass."

Luke turned back to the door and unlocked it. When he stepped inside, a silent alarm began a countdown. *Now how can I stall these fools for ninety seconds?*

The knife wielder twisted Luke's left arm behind his back and pushed him through the foyer. "Okay, there's a closet in the main hall-way where you keep the stuff. Unlock it."

With the knife still at his throat, Luke went down the hall, reached the closet, and opened it. Still stalling, he fumbled with his key ring and tried three other keys before he came to the correct one. He opened the locked cabinet and stepped back.

The man grabbed a plastic pillbox labeled "Oxycodone. By pre-scription only." Then the woman smashed the barrel of her pistol against Luke's skull. As he crumpled, the man kicked his head two, three, four times. The woman whacked him again, this time across the face, breaking his nose. They turned and fled.

In a cloud of pain, his eyes and nose full of blood, Luke heard a peremptory voice from the front door. "Freeze, you sons of bitches. Drop those weapons and do it now!" There was the sound of a scuffle and a flurry of gunshots. Just before he blacked out, one thought filled his mind: *This is it. I'm done for, and I'll never know what I was supposed to do.*

———

WHEN HE REGAINED consciousness, the smell of alcohol, ammonia, and other assorted fragrances burned into his nostrils even before he opened his eyes. The beeping that summoned him back to the land of the living was a cardiac monitor. His head throbbed in two or three different locations, and his ears seemed to have stopped working altogether.

The first person he saw was a young woman wearing green scrubs. He could see her lips forming the words, "Dr. Vangelis, can you hear me?" but there was no sound. He shook his head. He had a question of his own: "W-where a-a-m I?"

"I'm Dr. Artinian, and you're at GWU Hospital. You've been out for several hours."

Thank God I'm pretty good at lip-reading. "W-w-what h-happened?"

"You're a lucky man. You've got a fractured skull, but you're alive. The police called the paramedics."

"Thank them for me." He passed out again.

When he awakened again, he had no idea of how much time had passed. Diana stood at the foot of his bed. "Luke, can you hear me?"

This time he didn't have to read her lips. "Y-yes."

"Can you talk to the police?" She gestured toward a middle-aged man whose wire-rimmed spectacles gave him a strong resemblance to Samuel L. Jackson.

He nodded. The man came forward and said, "I'm Detective Robbins of the Metropolitan Police. Do you mind if I record our conversation?"

"N-no. Y-y-you n-need t-to g-g-go s-s-slow."

The detective nodded. For the next twenty minutes, Luke reconstructed as much of the drug theft and assault as he could recall. It was an unproductive exercise; portions of his recall seemed to have vanished. At the end of the conversation, Robbins said, "Thanks for your help. Those two thugs decided to shoot it out when our guys got there. We just needed to hear your account of what happened."

Luke beckoned Diana. "W-w-what a-a-bout t-the h-h-hospice?"

"I've already contacted several others to make sure they can pick up our patient load. I've only kept the patients who don't have immediately life-threatening conditions."

"G-g-good w-work. Th-thanks." Sleep overtook him before he could say anything more.

———

WHEN HELEN HIT the red "End Call" button, the tears she'd held back for the duration of Diana's call broke through her defenses.

Bob asked, "Honey, what's the matter? Has something gone wrong?"

"I-it's Luke Vangelis. Two thugs trying to steal painkillers from his office beat him up. They almost killed him. He's got a fractured skull, and Diana's not sure he'll ever fully recover."

She could feel an unspoken question in his eyes. He reached over and squeezed her hand. "Would it help if you went up there?"

She gulped back her words two or three times before saying, "I think it might comfort Diana. You know, she was our matchmaker after your wife and my husband died."

A Navy courier plane was flying from Jacksonville Naval Air Station to Washington the following afternoon. Bob called flight operations and secured space for Helen.

———

"HELLO, LUKE."

At the sound of Helen's voice, Luke opened his eyes and tried to smile. It was a gallant but unsuccessful attempt because of the four teeth he'd lost in the beating. "Hello, Helen. Nice of you to come all this way."

"How could I not? I knew Diana might need support."

Diana said, "Your presence is a priceless gift. Luke is still trying to be the man in charge. Maybe you can talk some sense into him. I've done what I could."

Helen sat in a chair next to the head of the bed. "Luke, you've got to give up this belief that you're always the giver, never the recipient."

His response was a near-mumble. "Still got work to do. Need to ask you some questions."

"Such as?"

"Can't remember. I know you have the answers."

"You men," she said, with a feigned air of vexation. "Let it go."

He shook his head. "Too important."

Helen threw up her hands in mock disgust. "All right, you win. Just call me when you know what answers you need."

———

WITH FEWER HOSPICE patients, Diana had to make a decision as to which staff to furlough or lay off. As she sat in Luke's office, reviewing employee files, the question nagged her: How had the would-be drug thieves known where to search?

She was willing to do whatever was needed for Eleni Hospice to survive. Not normally given to indecision, her memories returned constantly to the years between her mother's death and her marriage to Hector. The struggle to complete her education, compounded by her hostility toward her father, had endowed her with sympathy for their nurses and social workers, all from humble circumstances. After the assault, she'd forsworn taking a paycheck until she had a better grasp of the situation, but that was only a short-term solution.

Five days after the attack, Ellie Catania came to her. She asked for a few hours off to attend a funeral. Diana agreed. Later, she used a break to check the *Post's* obituaries, where she found one for a man named Martin Catania. The death notice stated, "Died suddenly August 2, 2006." *That was the day of the assault.* A phone call to Detective Robbins confirmed her suspicions.

The next morning, Diana summoned Ellie to her office. She asked, "Was Martin Catania a relative of yours?"

The young woman's brow wrinkled. "Why do you ask?"

"Well, the fact that he was killed in a police shoot-out on the day when, coincidentally, my uncle was beaten within an inch of his life aroused my suspicions. How could a mugger know exactly where to look for our drug storage cabinet?"

Ellie's mouth dropped open. She covered it with her hand, only to burst into tears, jump up and flee the office. Diana pursued her into the ladies' room. "Ellie, I'm not blaming you for what happened. I just need to know the real truth."

She stammered an explanation, the gist of which was that her cousin Martin and her mother had dropped by the hospice one day when both Luke and Diana were out on calls. She'd given them a quickie tour of the premises, undoubtedly the source of Martin's insider knowledge. She swore she didn't know her cousin was a dealer.

Diana sent her home for the rest of the day. She could justify a decision to terminate, but she wanted to let Luke have the final say if he were up to it.

At his bedside, she delivered a recital of her conversation with the young nurse. Luke, who'd started weaning himself off painkillers, listened in silence, his eyes tracking every movement she made, but saying nothing. At the end of her monologue, he dismissed her with a few words, saying he'd "sleep on it."

In the event, it was Connie who aided him in making the decision. He awakened in the wee hours with an urgent need to pee. Unable to untether himself from the monitors that shackled him, he had to summon a nurse for a bedpan. This humiliation over, he lay back and closed his eyes. Before the Sandman showed up, though, he heard her, as distinctly as if she were sitting beside the bed. "Luke, you know what you should do. Why are you stalling?"

In his somnolent state, he couldn't tell whether his reply formed on his lips or only in his mind. "Not stalling. Unsure what to do."

"You need to forgive."

"Already done that. You and Nate both."

"The couple who tried to kill you."

For the first time, the ugly scene replayed itself: the knife at his throat, the woman with the gun, taking the drugs out of the cabinet, the beating. "How you know about them?"

"They told me what they'd done."

"They're in the same place?"

"We're all in isolation cells. They sent a message."

A long silence followed. "Make a difference to you?"

Connie didn't respond at first. "Yes. I'll tell you why. Who said death was a restful state? For as long as I've been here, I'm still a prisoner of the bad things that afflicted me in life. I know you forgave me, but I've never been able to reconcile myself to losing your good opinion of me. I'm isolated here. Maybe, if you can let me go without holding on to that last bit of anger against me, I'll know I've laid down the burden of one bad thing that happened in my life. There may be a chance of me getting out of this dreadful loneliness."

"Why didn't you tell me until now?"

There was a sound like a sob being choked back. "I've spent all these years learning about myself and about you."

"What you tell me I don't know already?"

"Two things. It's all right for you to admit you love Helen. Maybe even more than you loved me."

"Other thing?"

"You're like me, Luke. You're a prisoner, and you'll always be a prisoner until you complete your forgiving. That includes forgiving yourself."

Connie said nothing more. Finally, Luke said, "I forgive them. Free and full pardon."

There was only a whisper in reply, a word spoken so softly as to be nearly inaudible, an assurance of enduring love.

The next morning, Luke handed Diana a note stating his wish that Ellie not be fired, concluding with, "She didn't know she was doing anything wrong." She accepted the message with only a nod.

22

OTHERS SEARCHED FOR answers as well. As Luke battled the feeling he'd missed something vital, Katie wondered if she and her son would ever have a normal relationship. Timmy was more mature than was usual for a year-old toddler. He was making excellent progress in learning to walk and talk.

What troubled her was that he got frightened easily, particularly when strangers were around. When Katie and Andy were at home alone with him, or when his grandparents or Aunt Lisa were around, he was outgoing and affectionate. The presence of persons outside this small circle seemed to upset him.

The "night frights" resumed. Since the episode in June, there had been no others until the end of summer. Then, it seemed that every second or third night, Timmy would wake up crying. When Katie picked him up, he always grasped at her, as if to reassure himself she was really there.

This latest phase had gone on for a couple of weeks when Katie brought the matter up to her parents. "Mama, Daddy, did I ever go through a phase when I got scared a lot?"

"Every little child has times like that, I think," Art said. "Of course, maybe he notices that you look different, and he can't understand why."

"You mean, not every child has a mother with no hair?" Her blonde locks had been the first casualty of the chemotherapy. She gave a gentle laugh.

"It could be pain. Is he teething?"

"That may be part of it. But it only seems to happen in the dark, which shouldn't be true if it's teething pains."

Andy's mouth tightened.

"Dad Art, the problem is that Timmy only stops crying when Katie is the one who attends to him."

Bonnie's brow wrinkled into worry lines. "Let's just hope it's a phase. I remember, honey, for a while you were like that, except it was your daddy you wanted to be around. You didn't like me then."

Katie answered, "The last episode, two nights ago, was really strange. I got up, so did Andy. He said he'd see if there was anything in Timmy's room that might scare him, but he couldn't see anything. It was what Timmy said that bothered him."

"What was that?"

"It sounded like just two words, 'Mommy stay, mommy stay.' He said it two or three times while I was holding him. Of course, his words aren't all that clear. Andy and I could have misunderstood him."

"Well, you probably should mention it to the pediatrician the next time Timmy goes for a checkup. Maybe he can give you some advice."

"I'll do that. I just don't want my son to grow up thinking that his mommy will ever abandon him."

———

TIMMY'S LIMITED VERBAL skills left him unable to explain his night frights. The videos that played in his mind would've seemed unique to an adult at first, but not frightening. Each set of images opened in the same way: He, Mommy, and Daddy were on a beach, with the sun rising out of the ocean. They were collecting shells, with Mommy pointing out to him scalloped shells, cowries, and a sand dollar. Their search always culminated with the discovery of a chambered nautilus washed up on the shore. Timmy had no words to describe what he saw, but the images imprinted themselves below the surface of his consciousness.

Just after this remarkable find came the scary part. A lady dressed in black appeared, seeming to walk upon the waters, with the sun at her back. When she reached them, she extended her hand and took Mommy's hand. Mommy kissed Daddy and leaned down to give him a kiss, then the two women turned to face the sun and walked away, across the waves toward the eastern horizon. When Timmy looked up at Daddy, he noticed tears on his father's face. At that moment, he knew, even without speaking, that something dreadful had happened.

These dreams always ended with him waking up and calling for Mommy. When he felt the reassuring touch of Katie's arms lifting him out of his crib, he fell silent and went back to sleep. Then the dream reappeared, this time with a different ending. As he and Daddy stood on the beach and watched Mommy walk away, a strange man and woman came up to them. Timmy knew without being told that strange people walking up to him could mean danger. This was nothing like that. Instead, one of them took each of his hands and led him back in the direction that would take him home. Even the man's battered and bloody face didn't scare him. Daddy was with them, but it was the presence of the strange couple that gave Timmy peace.

23

LUKE'S INJURIES HAD, for a time, driven memories of the visitation from Eleni in the spring of 2004 out of conscious recall, leaving a faint imprint of something odd in his mind, similar to the impressions left by a typewriter with a worn-out ribbon.

He'd been someplace strange, a foreign city he'd never seen. *Where? When?* These simple questions echoed in his mind like shouts into a deep canyon. He also recalled his mother's words to him about "end of the road" in the vision. *What road?*

Since his wife's and brother's betrayals, Luke had struggled against lapses into wrath and self-pity. Now he felt those emotions stirring within him. His battered brain couldn't give him enough clues to quell the gathering emotional storm that thwarted his progress.

In his prime, Luke had enjoyed reading spy novels. The artistry of Graham Greene and John Le Carré picking their way through the topsy-turvy morality of espionage won his admiration. In an effort to sand down the rough edges of remembrance, he was working his way through *Tinker, Tailor, Soldier, Spy* late one night in his study when another visitation interrupted him. This was jarring: It involved both of his parents.

Luke knew it wasn't a dream. He was in the process of downing a sip of ouzo when he heard Andreas say, "Lukas. Your mother and I must explain something to you."

"Papa? Mama? Where are you?"

"Stay where you are. Don't look around."

"Why are you here?"

Eleni responded. "We're here to help you on your journey."

"Journey to where, Mama?"

"To where *he* is."

Luke wasn't conscious of his sudden sharp intake of breath. "Where who is?"

"The one who will follow."

"I've lost the way, Mama. I mean, I don't have any idea of who he is and how to find him."

Andreas answered, "You will know in time. We will guide you. But we know you're not ready yet."

This last remark, delivered in the emotionless monotone Luke remembered his father using to deliver words of reproof, made his mouth tighten. "I'm not ready. Why does that matter?"

Eleni said, "My son, we know you're angry about the idea of leaving your old life for a new one. But your father and I did it, at a terrible cost. If we did, you can also."

"What do you mean, Mama?"

"Come with us. You will see. Just close your eyes."

He obeyed his mother's instructions. Within only a few breaths, the scene changed. He was no longer in a townhouse in America on a late fall night. He could feel the warmth of an Aegean sun on his face, smell the salty air, and hear voices all around him, speaking in tongues unfamiliar, yet strangely comprehensible.

———

SEPTEMBER 1922, SMYRNA

Rumors had raced across the city, shock waves from a man-made earthquake. For weeks now, there had been lurid stories about a Greek army in disarray, routed by the forces of a destroying angel named Mustafa Kemal.

Only a week earlier, Andreas had discussed the news with Arif, boss of the drovers who brought the agricultural wealth of Izmir province to Vangelis Exports. The two men stood at the back of the building, watching as a line of trucks, oxcarts interspersed among them, unloaded.

"It looks as though the Greek army will be leaving us," Andreas said.

"Well, that means law and order's out the door," was Arif's pithy verdict. "Who knows what comes next? With the Sultan deposed, the brigands will have their way. Already, some of my men are talking about leaving to join Kemal's army."

"I didn't think I'd ever miss the Ottomans. Now those days seem like a golden age."

Arif turned his head, hawked, and spat. "I agree. At least we knew which officials to bribe."

A clear voice cut through the noonday din, the call of a *muezzin*: "In the name of Allah, the Merciful, the Compassionate, come to prayer, come to progress. *Allahu akbar.*"

Most of the teamsters and warehouse workers halted their work and headed for a nearby plaza for prayers. Andreas looked at the scanty force of men still on the loading dock. "Ever since the Greeks invaded, a lot of our workers went with the army. I guess they thought they'd strike it rich somewhere in Anatolia." He looked at Arif. "Aren't you going to pray?"

The Turk shrugged. "Why? It seems the joys of heaven are reserved for Christians and Jews, while Muslims are condemned to the torments of hell. I've heard that Kemal doesn't give a damn for religion. If that's true, more power to him."

That conversation remained in Andreas' memory. Now it replayed with the addition of another sound effect: dull thuds in the distance, followed by a loud banging nearby.

He shuddered, awakening from his dream. As his mind struggled for a grip, the pounding started again. Sitting upright in bed, he realized that someone was pounding on the front door of Vangelis Exports.

Eleni woke up just then. When she heard the sounds, her eyes widened. "Who on earth would be knocking at this time of night?"

"Papa. Mama." Two small, frightened voices in the night, their eighteen-month-old sons Athanasios and Lukas, stirred as if having a bad dream.

"Look after the boys. I'll go see who's at the door."

Eleni nodded. Andreas got up and donned a robe. He moved quietly from the bedroom through the darkened parlor, a small dining room, and the kitchen. Opening a door, he stepped out onto the balcony. The smell of distant fires assaulted his nostrils. Two streets away, along the quay, there came the mournful murmur of retreating troops, the tramp of feet, clatter of horses, and harsh shouted commands. The stench of horse manure seemed overpowering, as did another aroma, the smell of human fear that arose from the throngs in the street. Looking down, the flickering light of a gas lamp showed that the man pounding at the door was Eleni's brother, Nikos.

"Nikos, stop that racket! You've already disturbed the boys."

Nikos looked up. "Let me in. I've got some bad news."

"Just give me a minute. I'll be right down."

Andreas went to the back of the apartment and descended a staircase that led to the back of the offices on the first floor.

When he opened the front door, he sucked in his breath. Nikos had a dirty bandage wrapped around his head; blood was seeping through. His cheeks were smudged, as though he'd rubbed them with ashes from the fireplace. "Water, for God's sake. I'm dying of thirst."

Andreas took him to his private office and poured a glass from a carafe he kept in an icebox. "Would you like coffee? I can brew some upstairs."

"There's no time. The army is pulling out, and I'm going with them."

"To where?"

"Khios. The damned Turks are in the outskirts. They'll be here by midday."

"Is that the bad news?"

Nikos gulped. "No. Papa and Mama are dead." He took another swallow of water. "While they were loading the cart to flee from the Turks, a truck driver coming down the street lost control and ran into the cart. It killed both of them."

"Are you sure?"

"I had to identify them. They're buried at St. Maria Theotokos, but there's no time to worry about them now. You and Eleni have to leave."

"Come upstairs with me. It'll be better if you tell Eleni yourself."

"I can't. My unit is embarking now. I have to get back to it."

"Where can we go?"

"To Athens. Don't you have an uncle there?"

Andreas nodded. Nikos drained the last of the water, got up, and left without saying goodbye.

———

ANDREAS, ELENI, ATHANASIOS, and Lukas waited in a queue of refugees, in flight from the fires that had started during the night. Lukas's Uncle Ioannos, a doctor in a village on the outskirts of Smyrna, was with them.

The old man said, "The damned British are taking their time. If they don't move faster, the Turks will get here in time to butcher us all."

"Did they start the fires?" Eleni asked.

"What does it matter? I saw Turkish soldiers shooting Greeks and Armenians in the streets as they tried to run away. They burned schools and churches with women and children inside. I'm not of a mind to stay around and wonder what will happen next."

The sea shone like burning copper. In the town, separate volcanoes of flame were merging into a giant conflagration. Churches, mosques, shops, houses, all burned together. *The flames don't care if they burn Turks, Greeks, Armenians, or Jews.*

A young British naval officer and several sailors came down the line. "Those of you in this group will have to board a warship. It'll not be as comfortable as you might like, but at least you'll be safe."

Eleni saw Yochanan, a heavily loaded pack on his back, passing at that moment. "Yochanan! Are you going with us?"

The Jew came up to them and dropped his burden. "No. I'm heading to the railroad station."

She looked at him with alarm in her eyes. "Railroad? Where will you go?"

"To Kusadasi. I've heard there's a freighter there that will soon be leaving for Haifa." He knelt down and kissed Athanasios and Lukas, who clung to their mother like drowning men to a raft.

Andreas dropped the suitcases he was carrying and embraced Yochanan. "Go with God, my friend."

Yochanan turned away, so his friends wouldn't see his tears.

No sooner had the Jew passed out of sight than an automobile darted out from a side street and screeched to halt. Two men jumped out. Eleni recognized them as both chums of Nikos. In truth, she considered them little better than brigands.

One of them came up to Andreas. "You there, Vangelis. Why are you running away with someone else's money?"

Andreas' face had a look of consternation. "What on earth do you mean by that?"

"The money your father-in-law lent you. Nikos told us you'd never repaid him."

"I repaid Demetrios every lira I owed him."

"That's a lie."

Andreas stepped toward the young man, his fists clenching. Before he could act, the other man struck him on the back of the neck with balled fists. Andreas crumpled to the ground.

The two men grabbed one of Andreas' two suitcases, which held a large canvas bag with gold coins, taken from the safe in the offices of Vangelis Exports. They slung the luggage into the back of the vehicle, jumped in, and raced away.

As Ioannos and another man helped Andreas to his feet, he didn't react at first. After a moment, he looked at Eleni. "My God. Those two bandit accomplices of your worthless brother just took all our money. What will we live on now?"

She gave him a tearful glance. "God will provide. We still have our lives and our sons." *My parents are dead. I didn't even get to say goodbye to them, and you're worried about money?*

Before either could reflect on this latest catastrophe, the naval officer returned. "All families with children, please come with me."

They followed him to a launch moored at the quay. The boat pulled away from the shore and motored out into the harbor, finally drawing up to a British battleship. They ascended a shaky metal stairway to the main deck, where a Greek-speaking officer took their names and added them to a manifest. Eleni turned and gave a last glance at the city where she had enjoyed so much happiness. *The world is dissolving in flames. Is this the Last Judgment?*

———

THE SCENE VANISHED. In an instant, Luke found himself alone in the familiar surroundings of his study. He murmured, "Yes, yes, I understand." No response came, yet he felt his parents' approval, as surely as a pat on the head conveys a message of love to a small child.

He took a sheet of paper and a pen out of a desk drawer. After writing a few sentences, he folded the paper and sealed it in an envelope. On the front of the envelope, he wrote, "Patience. Assurance." He put it in the desk drawer, turned out the lights, and went to bed.

24

LUKE AND DIANA made the decision to close Eleni Hospice at the end of 2006. Since their lease had two years to run, Luke went to the office every day, although he spent most of his time reading his favorite authors in Greek.

Diana went to work for another hospice near the National Arboretum. She insisted on escorting Luke home from the office every day. More than once, she found him asleep at his desk when she arrived.

———

"I'VE GOT SOME good news. A firm has offered to pick up our lease on the building." Because of Luke's reluctance to sever the last bond with the hospice named for his mother, Diana had gone to a commercial real estate broker without his approval.

His knit brows signaled a low-key expression of displeasure. "Why did you do that? How can we serve our patients?"

I should've known this could happen. He isn't even focused enough to get mad at me. "We've transferred all our patients to other providers. You remember I talked with you not long after the attack."

"Hmmm. I don't recall that, but I guess I've got to trust you." His comment ended with a wince.

"What's the matter?"

"Just a headache."

"You'd better skip the glass of ouzo tonight. Alcohol and ibuprofen don't mix."

He snorted. "That could be a permanent solution to a lot of things."

"True, but it would violate our commitment."

"Commitment?"

"The one we made to Athanasios and Connie."

Luke rubbed his brow. "Oh yes, before we found out what they were doing."

He's groping. He doesn't remember the talks with Sonny or the fact that we didn't know the truth until they died. Is it dementia or something else? "It's time to go. Pick up whatever book you're working on now, and let's get you home."

———

LUKE NEVER REQUIRED much sleep. For most of his life, he'd flourished with four or five hours a night. After the early stages of his recovery, his old habits reasserted themselves. However, the beating had undermined his concentration, so that his thoughts were, for the most part, a series of phantoms, wisps of smoke blown away by the wind.

In six months, he'd recovered enough memory to recall the dreams and voices, the sources which directed him. But their substance was a mystery, even the recent vision of Smyrna in flames. The voices were dormant, the damage to his skull had driven them too far below the surface to retrieve.

The return of the headaches was a blessing. Waking visions sometimes accompanied the dreams and voices. The first of these came during a stroll which took him from the office toward the Mall. When he saw a sign that read, "I-395 South Beltway Richmond," it became as clear as sunshine on a cloudless winter's day. *This is the path I must take.* In subsequent weeks, other visions appeared, always a picture of a road sign.

"I-95 Richmond I-295 Petersburg."

"I-95 Fayetteville."

"I-95 Savannah."

I'm to go south. Is this the clear call I've been waiting for? And what about Diana? Does she follow the same path? She hadn't talked about a move recently. Whatever messages she was getting, they didn't draw any outward reaction from her.

As the headaches became more frequent, he consulted a neurologist, who referred him to a colleague at Yale-New Haven Hospital. He made an appointment, deceptively telling Diana that he was taking a few days off to visit an old friend.

Luke cared little for long-distance driving, preferring to take the train if possible or to even fly if necessary. This time was different; he felt the need to be in control again. Despite the winter weather, he set forth in his '94 Crown Victoria. He diverted around New York City, approaching New Haven on the Wilbur Cross Parkway.

It was dusk as he neared the heart of the city. He passed a hospital with a statue of an angel in front. *St. Raphael. Funny, in my trips to New Haven, I don't ever recall seeing this place before.*

The brain scan revealed that, while the major damage from the assault was healing, there were areas in the brain where blood clots might form. The neurologist prescribed a blood thinner and told him to call if there were complications.

———

THE DREAMS RESUMED after he returned to Washington. The image that recurred, night after night, was the statue of an archangel, a healer and the patron of travelers: St. Raphael.

The direction he'd sought for almost three years became clear with a two-part message. Part one was another of what Luke, in his thoughts, referred to as "road sign visions." The sign in this one read, "I-95 Jacksonville I-295 St. Augustine." Part two came the following night: his mother's voice. "She is there. She will guide you to him."

———

"HELEN, IT'S LUKE. How are you doing?"

"No, you fool, it's how are *you* doing? You're the one who got beaten within an inch of your life." She laughed, a lilting melody in his ears.

"Diana and I need your help."

"You know you've got it. What is it?"

"I need you to scout some business locations for me. To be specific, locations for a hospice."

"Are you going to relocate Eleni Hospice?"

"Not exactly. I've sold Diana on the idea of starting a new one, St. Raphael."

"Hmmm. Why are you adopting a new name?"

He recounted the visit to New Haven and the sudden inspiration, adding, "And if you know a good lawyer, I'd appreciate that too."

"All right, I'll check around. What's your timetable?"

"Probably early next year. Diana has developed strong bonds with some patients at her present job. I'm afraid we both share the family characteristic of believing we're indispensable."

"No, there's nothing uniquely Vangelis about that." He heard her snicker. "Lots of us are like that. In any case, you'll have to meet my boss down here."

"I will, in time." The conversation concluded with small talk. When Luke hung up, he leaned back. Closing his eyes, he repeated a simple prayer, "Lead us not into temptation. Lead us not into temptation."

25

TIMMY WAS A few days shy of his second birthday. He'd gotten over his susceptibility to sudden fears, no longer showing an obsession with separation from Katie. When she was in Tampa for another round of chemotherapy, he intensely focused on the actions of people around him. To his parents' relief, he displayed few signs of "the Terrible Twos."

His great-grandfather was a boon companion. Timmy loved Brian's bottomless well of stories about the family. Andy had more than once observed that no small amount of blarney went into these tales. Years earlier, at Bonnie's urging, Brian and Christina had written reminiscences about their lives. Timmy never tired of hearing about Opa and Oma.

Timmy's precociousness showed in his love of jigsaw puzzles. The Thompson family heirlooms included an impressive collection of these. One afternoon, Brian and Timmy were working on one that showed a map of the United States when Bonnie arrived to take her father back to his apartment.

She walked in just as Brian pointed to an empty space on the map. "Timmy, can you find the state that goes here?"

The boy stuck his nose close to the map then looked at the pile of unused pieces. "That one."

"Great! Now put it in the right place."

Timmy complied. "Opa, can you tell me a story?"

"Of course. A story about what?"

"That." He pointed to the newly-filled space, the state of Illinois.

"A long, long time ago, there was a big town called Chicago. It had millions of people, but the fairest one was a girl named Katie. She had red hair and the most unforgettable eyes you ever saw. They were grey and could look right through you. People said she could tell what you were thinking. Everyone loved Katie, especially Brian, her big brother."

He paused to catch his breath and saw Bonnie in the doorway, a hand was in front of her mouth, alarm in her eyes. He motioned for her to sit on the sofa next to him.

"Opa."

"Yes, Timmy."

"A story. You promised."

"Oh yes. Brian loved Katie, and he'd fight anybody who said bad things about her. He was about your age then, but he could whip the meanest boys in his neighborhood, 'cause he loved his sister so much."

"Is Katie my mommy? Her name's Katie."

Brian put a scarred, weather-beaten hand on Timmy's hand. "Maybe so. Now Brian could fight any human, but he couldn't beat the banshee."

"Who's the banshee?"

"Banshee's an evil spirit that comes at night and cries when someone's about to go."

"Go where?"

"Go away. One dark night, Brian heard the banshee crying outside his window. He ran out into the dark, ready to fight whoever it was. When he came back inside, he found that somebody had taken Katie away."

"Who took her?"

"We don't know. Brian looked for Katie many years before he found her again, or part of her. That was when Mommy came along. But it took many more years to find the rest of her. He didn't find her until he looked into your eyes and saw Katie there."

Timmy shook his head. "Katie's a girl's name. I'm a boy."

"That you are, boyo, but you've got part of little Katie's soul. She lives on inside you."

Brian paused again, fearful he'd frightened Timmy or used words beyond the ken of a two-year-old. His great-grandson looked up at him, small face shining with wonder. "If I lose her, can I find her again?"

"Of course, boyo. That's your gift."

————

THAT NIGHT, TIMMY had the kind of dream that, a year earlier, would've scared him into crying out for his parents. This night, it was a different variant of one that had played earlier. A boy and a girl were walking on a beach. Timmy knew he'd seen the beach before. The boy was older, with hair the color of fresh rust and a body that radiated tough self-confidence. The girl looked to be about Timmy's age. When he could see her face, he saw that her eyes were of a penetrating grey color.

They wore strange clothes. The boy had on a white shirt and blue pants that ended just below the knee. Grey stockings and square-toed black shoes completed the ensemble. The girl was clad in a style of garment his grandmothers would've called a frock.

As they wandered along the beach, focused on searching for seashells, a threat arose from the waves: a fiddler crab of monstrous size, with a claw big enough to snap either of them in two. The huge crustacean crawled toward them with malevolent intent.

The girl stood frozen by the horror of this confrontation. As the crab approached, the boy dashed to a campfire burning a few paces away and seized a firebrand. He shouted defiance as he interposed himself in front of the girl, waving his flaming stick like a fencing foil.

The monster crab retreated in the face of this unpredictable attack. The boy came to a sudden stop when he heard the girl's shriek. A gaggle of other crabs had come ashore and seized her. He raced toward them in vain. Before he could reach her, the assailants dragged her beneath the waves. He plunged forward into the sea until a large wave knocked him down. He got up, saltwater streaming from his hair and clothes.

As the boy staggered toward nearby sand dunes, his chest and shoulders heaving with a grief too deep for words, the monster crab renewed its attack. A momentary panic crossed his face until the creature halted. A man and a woman – the same couple he'd seen in his earlier dream -strode toward him. The man raised a hand and roared a challenge to the crab, which fled back to its native domain.

Before any of the three could move, they reacted to something, apparently a sound. At the spot where the girl had been dragged into the ocean, she rose again – but with a difference. It was Mommy, unmistakably, clad in the same fashion as the young girl. She smiled, waved at them, turned, and walked away down the beach.

Timmy didn't wake up. He slept a peaceful, dream-free sleep for the rest of the night.

———

AT ABOUT THE time his great-grandson was dropping into undisturbed sleep, Brian awakened. Combat experience in three wars had schooled him in being ready for a "stand-to" at any moment. He scanned the bedroom for lurking enemies. Seeing none, he got up, picked up the rosary from his bedside table, and went to the living room where he dropped to his knees, ignoring the screams of protest from his joints.

After praying the rosary, he improvised a plea of his own: "Blessed Mother of God, may the spirit of my dear sister strengthen the souls of my beloved granddaughter and her son. May they face whatever lies before them with the courage of my sister who now abides with you and all the saints in glory. In the name of your most holy son, our Savior, amen." He got to his feet, walked to his recliner, and sat down. With an inner comfort he hadn't felt since Katie's cancer diagnosis, he soon fell asleep.

———

IN FOUR YEARS of marriage, Ginny had persuaded Tom to change his lifestyle. She and her first husband had enjoyed foreign travel, so she convinced Tom that he needed to relax, telling him that his sons could keep the business rolling without him there. Their travel habits included a Caribbean or South American cruise every fall or winter and a cruise to Alaska, Europe, or the Far East in the spring or summer.

At about the time Brian was telling Timmy about the banshee, Ginny and Tom were checking in for a flight to Hong Kong, their point of embarkation for a cruise around Southeast Asia. Tom, who seldom talked about his Vietnam experiences, went along with Ginny's suggestion without quibbling.

She asked, "How long will it take us to get there?"

"Okay, it's three hours to Dallas/Fort Worth, an hour layover, another three hours to Los Angeles, a two-hour layover, and a fourteen-hour flight to Hong Kong."

"I don't think I can sit still that long."

"You're not supposed to sit longer than an hour or two without getting up and moving around."

"Should we have booked First Class?"

"Twice the space at five times the price."

"I'm thinking about you. Those knees of yours aren't getting any younger."

"Flying to Vietnam on a C-141 was worse. Once we get to the ship, I'll be fine."

The first two flights went off without incident. Things changed in Los Angeles. At the boarding call for First Class passengers, Ginny said, "Oh God. Look who's getting on the plane."

Marilyn and Jack Pilcher were handing over their boarding passes to a gate agent.

Through gritted teeth, Tom said, "He's doing right well, Attorney Pilcher is. I wonder how much of Lupton's settlement he took as his cut."

"They haven't seen us. Maybe they won't."

Luck was with them. Coach passengers boarded the 747 through a separate jetway, allowing the Lyles to enjoy an anxiety-free, if cramped, Pacific crossing. Luck ran out when they boarded their cruise. They encountered the Pilchers in the passageway where, as it happened, both couples had cabins on the same deck, or rather the Lyles had a regular stateroom while the Pilchers occupied a suite near the bow.

Ginny tried to steer Tom clear of contact with his ex-wife, but without success. During an encounter in one of the lounges, Marilyn asked Tom, "How is Katie doing?"

"What do you mean, how is she doing?"

"I know she's taking treatments for cancer. Audrey McKenzie told me about it in an e-mail."

Tom glowered. *You didn't send Andy and Katie a Christmas card last year or the year before, although you always get Timmy something for Christmas and his birthday. You didn't send us a card either, but I don't give a damn.* "You might consider picking up the phone and giving her a call."

"Tom Lyle, don't play games with me."

"Have it your way. It's serious. Metastatic melanoma is really nasty. Katie's getting excellent care, though. She's seeing an oncologist in Jacksonville and one in Tampa. They give her hope. Now, if you'll excuse me, I have to make a pit stop."

He rose and went to the men's room. During his absence, Marilyn asked Ginny, "Who are Katie's doctors?"

"Uh, well, the one in Jacksonville is named Grueneberg. I can't remember his first name. The one in Tampa is either Clark or Burton. I'm not sure which."

Marilyn smiled. She relaxed and sipped her martini.

———

ERIC LOOKED AT Katie and said, "We've made good progress with the chemo. Clark thinks we can keep immunotherapy in reserve as a fallback plan."

Katie's gave him a puzzled look. "Does one rule the other out?"

Clark spoke up. "No, but you've got to handle it with care."

"How does it differ from chemo?"

"The proteins that feed cancer can sometimes be combatted by mobilizing your body's white blood cells, if you will. There are natural proteins called interleukins that your body produces. We give you concentrated doses of those proteins. It doesn't cure cancer, but it may help prevent the spread while the chemo attacks the cancer where we know it exists. The downside is it makes you very weak for a while after each treatment."

Andy said, "How many trips to Tampa would that take?"

"Probably no more than two."

Katie looked at Clark. "You're really going out of your way to help us. I mean, literally, all those trips from Tampa."

He smiled. "I have my reasons. Do you have any more questions?"

26

AS 2007 DREW to a close, Brian read the signs: the blood in his urine, the pain that was now his constant companion, the weakness that made him drag through day after day and making him want a rest that never came. *It can't last much longer. Damn, what I'd give to be the Brian I used to be.* He looked from the balcony of his townhouse toward the wetland that marked the start of the coastal marshes. *I think my fishing days are over.* He took a deep breath, inhaling the smells of marsh life, freshness mixed with the scents of death and decay. The mixed aromas didn't bother him. *Even after losing Christina, I've been happier here than anyplace else I've lived. I only want Katie to lick her damned cancer.*

The countdown started in October when his doctor ordered a battery of tests. When he called Brian for a follow-up visit, the old soldier was blunt. "Cut the crap, doc. What is it?"

"Pancreatic cancer. This is a fast-moving variety, so there's no time to lose. I've contacted Shands in Gainesville, and you've got a high priority for treatment."

"Why should I? Why should I put myself through the rigmarole of bouncing back and forth between doctors and hospitals, getting stuck like a pincushion, and yoked to a bunch of high-priced drugs? I'm ninety years old, and I've lived on borrowed time since 1944. My wife and most of my friends are gone. I'm ready. I want to go like a man, not like a sniveling little turd. When Death comes calling, I'll give that scythe-wielding bastard a one-finger salute and say, 'let's get on with it.'"

"Well, what do you want me to do?"

"Help me stay in control. I'll take the pain, but I don't want to die cringing. I want to die on my feet, or at least as close to it as I can manage."

"Well, that's a curious ambition, or, should I say, that's the first time I've heard anyone describe it that way."

"You're a young man. You'll see a lot more who think like me if you stick with the VA. World War II, Korea, Vietnam, Iraq, Afghanistan, the basics of war never change. You're not in danger of running out of business any time soon. As for Brian Thompson, well, I guess what I'm saying is, I want you to help me lie."

"What do you mean?"

"My granddaughter is battling melanoma. If she's worried about me, she can't concentrate on her own fight. Help me put up a front for my family."

The doctor took a deep breath, exhaling slowly. "I'll catch hell from the Administrator for misleading your family."

"What's that thing doctors sometimes say, 'First, do no harm?'"

"What does that have to do with your case?"

"Nothing can harm me now. I'm going soon. It could do a lot of harm to my little Katie if she's worrying about me. Give me covering fire."

———

THE CHRISTMAS GATHERING of the Thompson clan was subdued. The battle to save Katie, visible in her altered appearance, was on everyone's mind. More shocking, though, was the fact that, at the Mass,

Brian had to have Art and Bonnie bracing him up during the Eucharist. By force of will, he stood when most worshipers knelt, but the physical toll meant that he now had to be guided by someone else.

Another tradition fell by the wayside at Christmas breakfast. Brian had always offered thanks. When it was time for him to speak, he turned to his eldest grandchild. "Katie, would you do the honors?"

Visibly on the edge of tears, she recovered. "In the name of the Father, Son, and Holy Spirit, Amen" she began. Brian crossed himself with a visibly shaky hand. Bonnie's mouth trembled.

There were five great-grandchildren in the gathering. Each of them took a turn sitting with Brian. When Timmy sat down in Brian's lap, he said, "Opa, do you know what I want for next Christmas?"

"Your mom told me you wanted to go to Disney World."

"What I really want is a jigsaw puzzle."

"That's not what little boys usually want."

"I love doing puzzles with you, Opa. I want one that's my own." "Alright, you can have your choice. Be patient. If you are, you'll have a lot of them to choose from. Just give me a few weeks. But you've got to promise me one thing."

"What?"

"Spend as much time with Mommy as you can. She needs you right now."

"I promise."

Out of the mouths of babes. "I'm counting on you."

———

ON NEW YEAR'S Day, Luke brewed a pot of coffee and wrestled with his never-forgotten fear that he'd missed some important message. The fear had faded for a time, only to resurface since the first anniversary of the assault. Last night, there'd been another dream-disturbance. The setting was obviously someplace south of Washington; he could see palm trees in the background. An old man was walking in a cemetery. He approached a large headstone, and the picture got blurry, like looking through a camera lens that was slipping out of focus.

Luke asked himself a series of questions. *Who is this? Where is this? What is he doing?* He suspected that the cemetery meant this was a riddle about death. Beyond that, nothing else was clear.

The scene replayed, again and again, each time a little clearer. At last, the blurriness went away, and Luke could see the man standing, looking at the headstone, which bore the inscription CHRISTINA MUELLER THOMPSON 1921-1996. The man's head moved slightly, and Luke could see him looking at another inscription: BRIAN ALBERT THOMPSON 1917-. As the old man stood there, a young woman joined him, putting an arm around his shoulders.

The young woman was the one in his dream-disturbance, showing the couple riding in a car, from two years earlier. He'd never grasped the full meaning of his earlier vision. What seemed clear was that the man was visiting his wife's grave, and the young woman was a relative or caregiver.

Suddenly, he recognized the old man. *Brian Thompson. But what's the connection between him and the young woman?* Again, the scene replayed, this time from a different angle. The young woman turned to the old man. Lip-reading, he made out her words: "You miss Oma, don't you, Opa? It seems like she's been gone such a long time."

The old man replied. "I'll join her soon. But I want you to promise me one thing."

"What's that, Opa?"

"Fight as hard as you can. I'll be back with Christina. But you need to stay here for Andy and Timmy."

"I promise."

———

HELEN FERGUSON WAS wading through a stack of insurance forms when her cell phone buzzed. She looked at the number. "This is Helen, Diana. What's going on?"

"I'm at work and I trust you are too. But I think I've persuaded Luke to get off the dime and get serious about moving down there. That is, if you think there's a market for our services."

"I'm sure about that," Helen replied, utterly deadpan. "You know what they call Florida: God's Waiting Room. You'll have plenty of clients when you get set up."

"He wants me to do most of the arrangements. It's odd for Luke to act like that. You know he's always been a control freak."

"Maybe we ought to be thankful he's changing."

"There's one more thing. Do you have any contacts in the Veterans Administration?"

"Yes, but what for?"

"Luke met a World War II veteran a few years ago in Washington. He told me the fellow lives in Jacksonville now, and he wondered if you could check on him."

"You know how strict the laws are on medical confidentiality nowadays. Is it important?"

"Luke seems to think so."

"I'll see what I can find out. Who is this mystery man?"

"His name is Brian Albert Thompson. I'm told his close friends call him Bert."

"Brian Thompson. If I learn anything, should I call you or call Luke?"

"Call me. I think I need to filter the information."

When Diana hung up, Helen got up and walked around her office. She wondered why Luke considered it important to locate Brian

Thompson. She also wondered how she would react if she were close to Luke again on a regular basis. A silent prayer formed in her mind, a prayer that she could keep the strength of her love for Luke in a place where Bob would never see it.

27

SINCE THE CLOSURE of Eleni Hospice, Diana's work schedule had become a frightful mess. Her performance as a hospice nurse at her new employer was so outstanding, her services in such demand, that she went home exhausted at the end of each working day. This left her senses dulled and no longer as sharply attuned to the disturbances she'd once shared with Luke. With her uncle spending most of his days reading in his study or strolling the streets of Washington, the advance of her emotional dryness was palpable.

A major part of her responsibilities included supervision of the hospice's dementia patients. The years of experience she'd gotten at Eleni Hospice had endowed her with a sensitivity to the very different worlds in which her dementia patients lived. Now, her worries that Luke's beating had caused enough disruption of his brain circuitry to bring forth a full-blown case of dementia nagged her. These fears blossomed into an unwanted tiff one evening during her usual courtesy visit.

Luke was waiting on his front stoop when she came up the walk. He said, "I think I've got a better fix on things now."

"How so? A better fix on what?"

"What happened a few years ago makes more sense now."

"Luke, I'm afraid I'm too tired. I don't follow."

"Well, maybe a strong cup of coffee would help that."

While the coffee brewed, they talked about current events, particularly the prospects for the upcoming presidential primaries. When Luke brought two mugs into the living room, the fragrance of hot Blue Mountain made Diana close her eyes for a second and take a deep breath. *How can I handle this the right way?*

She decided on one of their usual ice-breakers, the one they always used to introduce a new revelation. "Heard any good conversations lately?"

His eyes gleamed. "Florida is definitely in the picture. I heard from Brian Thompson again. You remember him, don't you?"

"Of course. The D-Day veterans' gala. I'm sorry to hear he died."

"No, he hasn't yet, although his time's coming. I mean, that visit to the cemetery was a major clue."

She hadn't gotten this revelation, and talk of a cemetery was baffling. "What cemetery? Arlington?"

Luke shook his head. "This was down in Florida someplace, maybe Jacksonville. He told us he lived there."

"Okay, I recall that." *But a cemetery visit? Is he delusional?*

"It was the young woman with him. She's involved in this."

"Was that the daughter we met at the dinner?"

A vexed look crossed his face. "This is no time for word games. No, this was someone much younger. She looked like she was in her thirties."

"Luke, this makes no sense. I don't know anything about a visit to a cemetery." *Oh God, not another delusion.*

"It was a cemetery, as sure as we're sitting here. Or have you gotten so busy with your new job that you don't have any more time for conversations?"

The sting in his words was so sharp that she almost physically recoiled. In an effort to recover, she gave him a wry smile and said, "I'll admit to being tired. Maybe if I get a good night's sleep, I'll remember."

In a sterner tone than she'd heard him use in many years, he replied, "Yes, I'd recommend that. Don't forget what our *real* job is."

Diana gritted her teeth and looked down. *Maybe he doesn't realize how much that hurts.* "I won't forget."

The rest of the visit passed with inconsequential chit-chat.

When she left, she walked two blocks through the wintry night to a bus stop on Wisconsin Avenue. She sat down inside the shelter, which gave only minimal protection from the elements, turning Luke's biting comment over and over in her mind, wondering what she could do to get past her uncle's apparent loss of confidence in her. By the time the bus arrived, she had an idea of where to go. It was almost eleven o'clock when she got home, and she decided to let it go until tomorrow.

———

ONE FRUSTRATION DIANA had regarding her spiritual gifts was that she didn't know how to seek guidance. She had to wait for someone else to open a conversation.

The next day was exceptionally busy, as was the day after. Two nights after the brusque discussion with Luke, she heard from her mother. Nikkoletta Pappas Vangelis had died when Diana, who was then known as Artemis, was eighteen. Her grief, compounded by her growing hostility toward her father, had thrown up emotional barriers against any reconciliation with her mother's memory. Even after she recognized her own spiritual role, nothing happened. Her mother was, she believed, permanently lost to her.

She lay alone in the dark, her mind refusing to power down long enough for her to fall asleep. At first, she didn't recognize the voice that came in the night, until she heard, "Baby darling, is something wrong?" It was her mother's way of offering comfort.

"Mama? Mama, is that you?"

"Yes, my child. You're angry about something. Has someone hurt you?"

"Oh no, it's not a major thing. It's Uncle Lukas. He's behaving strangely. But why have I never been able to reach you until now?"

"Because the door was never open to me until now. Here in the world of the unquiet dead, we are all equally restless until something lets us break down the hatred, the anger, the sorrow that we left behind."

"I've never been angry with you, Mama, only hurt. You didn't say goodbye."

"You won't say it, but I know you're still angry with me for killing myself. I did my best to make it look like an accident, but your father always suspected the truth. He loved his sailboat more than he loved either of us."

Diana's emotional resolve collapsed, and she broke into sobs. "Oh, Mama, why did you hate Papa so much you had to kill yourself to get away from him? Did you think about who else you hurt?"

"Perhaps I thought that, by killing myself while we were out sailing, he'd finally understand the things I couldn't say to him."

"I don't understand. I missed you so much, and no one gave *me* any comfort. No one except Uncle Luke, that is."

"I know you've always looked up to your uncle. Was it because you thought the fact that he had no children of his own meant that you were a chance to satisfy his paternal instincts? Your admiration for Lukas is commendable, but even with what your father did to us, he's still your father. You owe him at least a minimal amount of respect. Besides, I know a lot more about your grandfather than you do, and I know how hard Athanasios had to work to get him through the Depression years."

"Alright, I'll try. Why did you marry Papa in the first place?"

She heard Nikkoletta's silvery laugh, and she felt herself smiling. Nikkoletta said, "Your father always thought he had done me a favor by marrying me. One thing I never told you was that I had a fiancé, an Italian boy named Carlo, who was killed in World War II. When I met your father, in his college days, I was still in mourning for Carlo. Nate asked me out several times before I agreed. I guess he thought that because my family had very old-country values, with wives deferential to their husbands, when I agreed to marry him, I'd treat him like the crown prince he considered himself to be. Andreas had moved up from running a fruit stand to being one of the most prosperous fruit wholesalers in Boston by then, and Nate thought his father would leave him a wealthy man. But of course, your father didn't want to run a fruit company. Then, your grandfather died suddenly, without grooming another successor to take over the business. The fruit soon turned rotten, and Nate didn't get the wealth he thought was his rightful inheritance."

"There has to be more to it than Papa and his resentments."

"Lukas was already in medical school by then, and your father felt the need to prove he was as good as his twin brother."

"I guess I have to trust you on that."

"I have to make a confession of my own. After I died, when I was still helpless to reach you, it worried me that you did so much work with veterans returning from Vietnam. I was afraid something bad would come of it, and something did. Poor Hector. I suppose I shouldn't judge him so harshly. The war turned him into a killer, and he ended up bringing the war home with him. You and my poor grandchildren got the worst of it."

There was a long silence in the dark bedroom. "Can you see Andrew and Athena?"

"Yes, sometimes. Someday, when Hector and Nate are released from their isolation, I'll see them also."

A sense of deep peace settled over Diana. "That means I can hope we'll all be reconciled someday. What do I need to do?"

"Help Luke. He still doesn't understand."

"He doesn't understand what?"

"It's all right for him to admit he loves that woman."

"Helen."

"Yes, Helen. But it's even more important for him to understand that he has to forgive himself. There must be some things he still can't let go. I can't reach him, but you can."

"I'll do the best I can, Mama."

"Remember me without too much anger, my child. You will always be in my heart, whether we are together or apart."

In the silence that followed, Diana knew her mother's visit had ended. She started sobbing again. This time, they were sobs of profound joy, not of deep grief. She soon fell asleep.

28

CLARK BURTON MET his father's flight from San Francisco at the airport. He extended his hand when the general walked up to him and was shocked when George put his arms around him in a bear hug. *That hasn't happened since I was a kid. Is it just old age? Does he have some idea of what's bothering me?*

"Dad, let's go to the house. It's late, and you've had a lot of stress. It's a four-hour round trip to Gainesville."

"All right. What do you know about Brian's condition?"

"I've talked to his VA doctor. He estimates Brian may have a month to live."

"That's why I didn't want to take a chance, although Brian Thompson is as tough as the hide of a bull elephant. Well, at least there are no regrets in our friendship."

The next morning, George wasted no time in getting to a point Clark didn't enjoy discussing. He asked, "Have you heard from your boys lately?"

Clark's eyes rolled. "Rob tells me that Lori has a live-in girlfriend. I always thought she wasn't the best choice for his wife. I guess that confirms it."

The breakup of his older son's marriage three years earlier had scandalized elite circles in their hometown of Nashville.

"Don't let that get next to you. Rob needs to learn about forgiveness. It took me a long time to forgive your mother when she ditched me for that accountant in Colorado Springs. When I finally visited her, just before she died, she was so doped up I don't know if she could understand me. Don't let the time for saying, 'I forgive you' slip away. What about Jeff?"

The mention of Clark's younger son made him smile. "He says he's going to seminary when he gets out of the Army next year."

"Has he picked a denomination yet?"

"This month, he says he's Episcopalian. I guess it's family tradition coming out."

"Your Grandpa Bob would be proud of him, a priest having a great-grandson who followed in his footsteps. I hope your grandfather has forgiven me for causing bad blood in the family."

"It wasn't your fault, at least not all of it. He didn't know about Mom." *That's the first time Dad's ever admitted how much it hurt because of Grandpa's refusal to forgive him.*

"True, but I think he held me responsible for encouraging Robbie to go to West Point. I think Maggie was probably right. Robbie should have gone to Albright or Dickinson."

"Vietnam would have still been there when he graduated."

"Yes. I just don't like thinking about all the stuff I taught Robbie about duty, honor, and country. I wonder how much of it was bullshit. I was in agony every day Caroline was overseas during the Gulf War and later in Iraq. It would've killed her mother and me if anything had happened to her."

This last comment brought an awkward silence. After they finished their coffee and got on the road to Gainesville, Clark wondered why his father, approaching eighty-nine, would come all the way from California for a last farewell. As they passed the exit for Florida's Turnpike, he voiced this thought.

George looked out the window before speaking. "You know Brian and I have had a special friendship for decades. That's why I've asked you to go out of your way to help his granddaughter. But you don't know why. It was something I meant to tell you. Since you were fourteen when your mother and I split, I never got around to it. Brian Thompson saved my life at Bastogne. He took a sniper's bullet that was meant for me."

"Wow. If he hadn't done that--"

"You and your sisters wouldn't be here. I was able to make it right for him, but it took a long time."

"What do you mean?"

"I recommended Brian for a Silver Star after that incident, but with the war coming to an end, recommendations went astray. Almost twenty years later, I was able to use some pull to get it for him. You remember back in '63 when I was at the Pentagon, don't you?"

"That was a great time. It was right before you got a brigade in Germany."

"Brian was with the Old Guard at Ft. Myer. I was on a first-name basis with Maxwell Taylor, and that moved things along. I had to get statements from other survivors in the company, but Brian eventually got the honor he deserved."

"That's a great story."

"Was what I did enough? Every good thing that's happened to me since 1945 wouldn't have if that hardheaded Mick hadn't taken a bullet for me. Well, that's the rest of the story."

Clark nodded. For the rest of the trip, there wasn't much conversation. It seemed to him that George's comments about "no regrets in our relationship" may not have been entirely truthful.

When they reached the VA Hospital, Clark called a private number to reach Brian's doctor. This got them escorted directly to Brian's room with no delay.

Clark noticed that his father hesitated after his first step into the room. Brian's eyes were closed, his breathing shallow. The regular beep of monitors testified that, for now at least, he was still on this side of the river.

George approached the bed and said, "Attention, Sergeant Major Thompson! If you can't get up, you can at least lie at attention."

Brian's eyes opened, and he turned his face slowly toward them. "You damned Johnny Reb, can't you get it through your thick head I'm not taking any more orders?"

George laughed. "How about if I respectfully request your attention?"

To Clark's astonishment, the old sergeant gave a horselaugh, following by a bout of coughing. An IV drip in Brian's left arm was sending what he knew was heavy-duty painkiller through the clear tubing. *At least we've gotten better about muffling the pain, although we can't make it go away entirely.*

There was a soft knock at the door. A middle-aged man entered and extended his hand. "I'm Fred Temple, Mr. Thompson's doctor here."

"George Burton. Brian and I served together in the 101st Airborne, back in The Big War."

"How are you doing, Fred?" Clark asked.

"About as well as you'd expect, Clark, given the territory."

"What's new?"

Dr. Temple shrugged. The bags under his eyes spoke volumes. He said, "Mr. Thompson, you have some family members in the waiting area. I've given them an update on your progress, and they'll be along in a minute."

"Doc, if you said anything about progress, you're a damned liar," Brian said. "We both know the truth." He chuckled.

Bonnie and Katie appeared in the doorway. "Doctor, is it all right for us to come in?"

Temple nodded.

Clark said, "Ladies, this is my dad, George Burton."

"I'm Bonnie Warren, Brian's daughter." Daughter and grand-daughter kissed Brian on the forehead. Bonnie asked, "How do you feel today, Daddy?"

"Not so good. But when you've had ninety years of good days, you've got to expect some bad ones to come along."

Katie said, "Opa, Timmy has made up his mind. He wants that jigsaw puzzle that shows a map of the U.S."

"Of course. Would you hand me that pad and pen on my nightstand?"

She gave them to him. Brian scrawled a note: "To Timmy from Opa. Hope you and Mommy enjoy this. Love, Opa."

Katie's eyes brimmed. "Timmy will love this note. He wanted to come with us today, but I said no."

"You did the right thing. There's no reason why he has to remember me as a helpless old man."

George snorted. "Mrs. Warren, your father is about the least helpless man I know. Don't listen to his bad-mouthing."

George and Clark chatted with Brian for a few minutes while Bonnie and Katie sat down on opposite sides of the bed. Brian beckoned to Bonnie and whispered something in her ear. When the two said good-bye, Bonnie walked them to the door.

"Daddy told me you came from San Francisco to see him. Thank you so much."

"I had to. Command responsibility and all that." He turned to his son and said, "Take good care of that young lady. I know you'd do it anyway, but I've got an order from Brian."

"I will, Dad."

29

Three weeks after his ninety-first birthday, a priest gave Brian the last rites. While some family members hoped the old soldier might yet hold out against the cancer, most recognized it was time to say good-bye. His descendants came in twos and threes to give him a farewell kiss and hear any parting words of wisdom.

Katie and Andy waited until the last of the mournful procession into the hospital room had come and gone.

"Aren't you worried?" Andy asked.

"No. Opa won't go until I tell him good-bye. I wish Daddy would get here with Timmy."

Art showed up ten minutes later. Katie and Andy took their son by the hand and followed Art into the room where Bonnie and James, Brian's youngest son, waited. The muted lighting gave the deathbed the effect of an altar guarded by two statues. They approached with muffled footsteps.

"Daddy, Katie's here."

Brian's eyes opened. He managed a smile and greeting, uttered in a half-croak. "How's my Katie-Poo today?"

She kissed him on the cheek. Andy hoisted Timmy over the bed's guardrail so the boy could reach out with one pudgy fist to touch Brian's cheek. "Wanna do a puzzle, Opa?"

"I'd like to, big boy, but I can't stay awake long enough. I'm sure your Mom and Dad will later. Give Opa a kiss."

Timmy's aim was off. He wound up kissing Opa's nose. This brought another fleeting smile.

Andy said, "Let Mommy stay here a few minutes. You and I can go get ice cream."

Just before they left the room, Brian muttered, "Take good care of your Mom, big boy."

The door closed. Bonnie fought back her tears. "Stay with us, Daddy. Keep fighting."

Brian's eyes were closed, and his voice was little more than a whisper. "I can't fight any more. This is a massacre, not a battle."

His breathing became slower, more labored. His eyes opened, and he took a deep breath. The old sergeant's commanding voice emerged through parched lips. "Pull me up."

Bonnie and James supported his shoulders and lifted him until he sat upright in bed. He patted Katie on the hand. "Keep fighting, Katie. I've had enough combat."

His eyes closed. He took two deep breaths, exhaling slowly, and then there was nothing. The multiple monitors in the room flatlined. His daughter and son lowered him to the bed and crossed his hands over his chest.

Katie sobbed her last farewell. "I love you, Opa. I'll miss you forever."

Katie composed herself, left the deathbed, and walked to the hospital cafeteria. When she saw Andy and Timmy enjoying cups of ice cream, her momentary self-control fled, leaving her unable to speak.

They came to her and hugged her. She regained her voice and said, "Timmy, Daddy's going to take you home now. Mommy has to stay and take care of Grandma and Opa."

"Okay, Mommy. Tell Opa I love him."

She turned away, so her son wouldn't see her crying.

———

IT WAS LATE afternoon before she got home. When Timmy ran up to her, she said, "Let's you and Daddy and I go out to the deck."

They sat down, and she took Timmy's hands. "Opa has left us. He's gone to heaven now to be with Oma and Big Daddy and his sister, little Katie."

Timmy's bewildered look testified to his incomprehension. "Where's heaven? And when is Opa coming back?"

Okay. I should have expected this. We need to take him to church more often. "He won't come back, darling. We'll have to go to him. Opa is there with Jesus, and he'll be there forever. But Opa still loves you, and he'll watch over you."

"I miss Opa. I want to see him."

She clutched him to her breast, not trying to hide the tears. "So do I, sweet boy. Mommy and Daddy miss him too."

———

LUKE AND DIANA had spent several weeks reviewing online listings of commercial properties around Jacksonville. They narrowed the list to a dozen possible locations, and Luke e-mailed Helen to ask for her input on neighborhoods.

When Diana came to his townhouse the following Saturday morning, Luke greeted her with a frown. "What's up with Helen?" he asked.

"I don't know. Why are you asking me?"

"I've sent her at least five e-mails. She hasn't answered any of them."

"That's not like her. Let's take a look at your 'Sent' box."

When he opened his e-mail account, Diana quickly spotted the problem. Luke's e-mails were addressed to Helen at her old workplace account. Each was marked "Undeliverable."

"Luke, it looks like you haven't updated your address book in ten years. You sent every one of those e-mails to St. Matthew's Hospital. Helen hasn't been there since 2005."

He looked at the stack of e-mails and said, "That's odd. I could've sworn I changed her address." He opened his address book. "Well, there it is. I added her new address but didn't delete the old one. Old habits die hard."

"Just let me call her."

"Go ahead."

She located Helen's cell phone number and hit the "call" button. When the call went through, she said, "Good morning, Helen. This is Diana. Do you have a minute? What? Who? Yes, I think I remember the name. Let me put you on speakerphone."

"Hi, Luke. I was just telling Diana I can't talk because Dr. Grueneberg is picking me up any minute now."

"Some special occasion?"

"No, it's a funeral. Odd thing is, we didn't know the old gentleman, but the family asked us to come. I've got a question for you."

"Shoot."

"Does the name Brian Thompson ring a bell? I think I remember Diana telling me you knew a man by that name."

"Hmmm. Brian Thompson, Brian Thompson. Oh yes, now I remember. I ran into him at a D-Day reunion some years ago."

"He was the patient who died. I just thought you'd like to know."

"Thanks for telling me."

"There's the doorbell. I've got to go. One of you can call me tomorrow."

Diana put the phone in her purse. "Helen sounded upset. That's odd, since she said they didn't know him. As I recall, Brian was *really* old."

"He was older than I am. You're right. It's sad, but not a surprise, I'd think."

"Back to work. Do you want to look at more listings?"

"I guess not. Why don't we go out for lunch and then take a walk around the Tidal Basin?"

Luke repaired to his bedroom and donned a light windbreaker. *There's something here I'm missing. When I saw Brian at that reunion, I got a strong feeling that he might be a channel, a pathway to something new. Won't be surprised if I get a message from him soon.*

———

WHEN BRIAN WAS laid to rest, Katie stood with Timmy holding one hand, Bonnie the other. An honor guard bore his flag-draped coffin to its final resting place.

As the sweet, slow, sad notes of "Taps" drifted over St. Matthias Cemetery, Timmy asked, "Mommy, who's that?"

"Sssshhh, darling."

When the final notes sounded, Timmy repeated his question, pointing to the head of the grave.

"Darling, it's not polite to point. But there's nobody there."

"But there *was*, Mommy. There was a man, but now I can't see him anymore."

The now-vanished figure Timmy had seen was a young, powerfully-built redhead. In fact, it was the boy, now grown to manhood, he'd seen in the dream about the monster crab. Before he could say anything more, mourners flocked around the bereaved family to offer condolences. Andy's sister Lisa collected Timmy and took him away from the crowd until the mourners dispersed.

———

HELEN CALLED LUKE that night, seeking to pin him down on the idea of relocation. After Brian's funeral, she was still shaken by the sight of Katie Lyle. She'd never seen Katie as upset about her own struggle as she was about losing her grandfather.

Luke was dozing when the phone rang. " 'Lo."

"Luke, is that you? This is Helen?"

"Oh hello, Helen. What's up in Baltimore?"

"Baltimore? I'm calling from Florida. I haven't been in Baltimore for over two years."

"No need to get snippy. I just forgot."

"I'm sorry. Are you on vacation?"

Helen recognized that Luke was confused. After a few awkward seconds, she said. "No, I live here now. Don't you recall me telling you about the Navy transferring Bob down here?"

"Well, congratulate him for me."

He's either half-asleep or tipsy. She'd called with a specific intention. Given his inability to follow a simple conversational thread, there appeared to be no point in prolonging the conversation. She mentioned that she'd tried to call Diana but had gotten no answer.

"She was probably playing bridge with some of her friends. Diana's dependable. She'll call you back."

"Oh, in that case, I'll just wait for her call. Good night."

" 'Night."

———

AFTER THE MUDDLED phone conversation with Luke over relocation, Helen went for a nocturnal walk through Mimosa Estates, trying to sort out her emotions.

At first, anxiety predominated. Since leaving the Washington area, she'd sensed that there was some force drawing Luke to Florida. If that was true, the assault had disrupted it. *I've never known Luke to be as slow and indecisive as he is now.*

Her worries were amplified by an intuition that there was some specific reason why they were needed nearby. Whatever the reason might be, it wasn't going to become clear until they were here. *What if they don't feel that need? What if they stay there?*

She'd shoved the grief she felt at seeing Luke in Intensive Care below her own emotional horizon, but it was still lurking in the background. *Luke's always been a monument to good health, but he acts like he's fallen off a cliff. Is he dying?*

It wasn't until she returned to her house that another reason, perhaps the strongest one of all, bubbled up, refusing to go away until she confronted it. With Bob away on yet another of his many days on the road – or under the sea – her physical needs were going unmet. *Might as well admit it, Helen... you're horny.* She undressed in front of the full-length mirror in the master bedroom. Decades of tending to her bodily health meant that she was exceptionally fit. *Fit, hell, well-preserved.* It didn't do a thing to quench her drives or to calm emotional storms that raged whenever she remembered how Nate Vangelis had treated her. *What's really driving me over the edge is if I never make love to Luke, I'll never know what kind of life I might have had with him instead of his brother.*

It took a sleeping pill to push her into a few hours of restless slumber.

———

AFTER KATIE RETURNED from her latest visit to Tampa, Clark called to give Eric an update.

"I don't want to be a Pollyanna," Clark said. "Things are too unpredictable with melanoma, but I'll say I'm guardedly optimistic. There's one thing that bothers me."

"What's that?"

"Katie's always been a fighter. Every time she's been here, she's reminded me that she has faith in us, and that keeps her fighting. This time, she was in a serious funk. I tell her that no one can fight cancer and not get depressed sometimes, but she wasn't the Katie I've gotten to know."

"True. She was really upset when I saw her at her grandfather's funeral."

"Anything we can do to buck her up?"

"We need to emphasize keeping her hope alive, particularly her hope of seeing her son grow up."

"That's a good point. I'll have to play that theme the next time I talk to her."

After Eric hung up, Clark set to work on a stack of professional journals in his always-towering "to be read" pile. He was perusing one magazine's table of contents when a stray thought lanced into his mind: *Better a live dog than a dead lion. Who said that? Machiavelli? I think Katie's lost a lion in her life. Does she need something different?*

He riffled aimlessly through the publication, but no answers came.

30

"I THINK IT'S time we made some serious moves toward relocation."

Luke's latest policy declaration caught Diana by surprise because it was simple and straightforward with none of the rambling and disconnection from reality that had worried her for the last year and a half.

She looked at him and saw something that looked like a smile crossing his face. "Alright, but why now? You know Helen has been trying to convince us for quite a while."

There was an unaccustomed softness on his face. Even the scars from the beating seemed less threatening. "There's been something holding us back, something that has gotten in the way of us going ahead. I think I've figured it out. In all our brooding and anger about your father, we've never shown him much understanding. Was our forgiveness not sincere? Maybe that's been a roadblock for both of us."

"A pretty serious roadblock, I'd say." *Has he had another one of those visions I don't get?*

"Yes, but we've got to clear it. I think the time's right."

"More mysterious messages?"

"No, just a hunch. Shall we try our old approach?"

The old approach was what Sonny had taught them: meditative visioning. They'd learned to abide in complete silence, emptying the mind, and waiting. Diana nodded and moved her chair next to Luke's. They took each other's hand and closed their eyes.

A stillness of indeterminate length descended over the living room, overpowering the noises outside. Through the peaceful darkness, Diana heard her father's voice: "Luke."

"Yes, I hear you, Nate. What is it?"

"It's time for a final reckoning between us." Nate's voice was calm, but there were still traces of the hectoring tone Diana remembered from her childhood. *Why is he talking to Luke? Does he not know I'm here?*

"Yes, my brother, it's time. Go ahead. I'm listening."

Nate continued. "You always hated me because I was Papa's favorite. I know you were Mama's favorite, but it's not my fault you lost your favorite parent. You've blamed me for a long time for evils I didn't cause; some you even contributed to yourself.

"What evils, you ask? There was the little matter of Papa's estate. You thought it was unfair that I got to pick the better portion of it. But who helped him while you were off fighting a war he never understood? Who helped him make the business a success? You need to remember that Papa was just giving me my due by making sure his estate would help me to follow in your footsteps in going to medical school."

Luke's mouth wrinkled. "Of course. You were the one who did more to help Papa recover what was stolen from him in Smyrna. Papa and Mama told me what happened. I ask your forgiveness for all the times I judged you harshly."

The knowledge that Luke had some *gnosis*, a secret knowledge from her grandparents, disturbed Diana. But it was obvious her father was focused on communicating with his brother, so she remained silent.

Nate said, "You blame me for Connie. I guess I can understand that, but there's one question you need to answer. How many days did you leave her alone while you were busy being a big-shot doctor, a leader in your field? She wanted a child more than anything, but she understood that I couldn't help her to reach that goal. She wanted it to be your child, *your child*, you who could never recognize the source of all the tears she cried for thirty years. Maybe we should have made a trade – Connie for Artie. That way, you would've gained a perfect disciple for a daughter, and I would've gotten the wife I should've had all along."

The snide words at the end of her father's latest remark stirred the embers of resentment in Diana's mind. She quenched them when she heard Luke say, "Perhaps you're right about Connie. You need to leave your daughter out of this."

"This is no time for more of your disapproval. I don't care what you call her or what she calls herself. She's not 'Diana.' She's 'Artemis.' That was the name Papa gave our lost sister. She always blamed me for Nikki's death. Would her opinion of me be any different if she knew what a kindness I was doing for a poor sad girl who always wanted things she couldn't have? Of course, it was a pity she lost her boyfriend in World War II. If he'd lived, they could've married and settled down to lives of happy mediocrity. That would have suited both of them better than anything else."

Diana was half-expecting Luke to retaliate with a sarcastic broadside. Instead, there was a hint of laughter when Luke said, "Is happy mediocrity worse than unending combat? Have you told Nikki any of this?"

"I've seen her, her and her Wop boyfriend. Of course, there's no marriage, no happy families here, but they get to spend all the time in the world together if you get my drift. She could've asked me for a divorce. Why didn't she? I think it was because she knew that, as long as she wore my name, she could pretend to be an upper crust lady, not a transplanted peasant girl. If she'd wanted a divorce, she could've had it. Her actions – or maybe her inaction – spoke louder than words."

Luke still refused to be baited. "You know divorce was not possible. It would've destroyed Nikki long before she took her own life. I think we may never agree on that, but we can disagree without hatred. What about Papa and Mama? Have you spoken to them?"

The long pause that followed made Diana think that Luke's last response, his refusal to lash back, must have touched something deep in her father's spirit, touched something he didn't want touched.

"What about Papa and Mama? No, I haven't seen them. I've been waiting for you to give me permission. You see, there's still a barrier here. It walls me off from everything I want to reach. I can see Nikki, but I can't talk to her. She can't see me. Apparently, she's never noticed my absence. I can't see Connie either."

Despite the communications they'd had with her father under Sonny's guidance, for the first time, Diana heard him admit to something that was a secret terror: It was the idea that loneliness might be an eternal state, that there might not be a full reconciliation, even in death.

Nate's tone of voice changed. "I know you think I must be in hell, but you're wrong, at least not hell the way the priests taught us when we were young. If this were hell, could you or Artie communicate with me? No, this is just somewhere I don't want to be, out of contact with everyone I ever cared about. I know what you're probably thinking, this is what I deserve. Damn it, that's no answer. You know how I know? Because I've seen the drunkard who killed Mama go by more than once. He's always hanging out with some of his ne'er-do-well Mick friends. If that's what he gets for killing a mother, why can't I reach anyone else?"

Luke asked, "What do you need from me?"

"Alright, there, I've admitted it: There's something I want and can't have. For the first time since before the war, I'm asking you for something. You see, I've learned that what's keeping me away from all the people I want to see is that barrier between us. It's been you who stood in my way all along, you and Artie. I'll give you this much: If you release me from this prison I'm in, I'll go to all the people you say I hurt and ask them for forgiveness. I'll make everything right that went wrong in my life. Is forgiveness too much to ask of a brother?"

Her father's hostility had been so evident, Diana expected Luke to respond in kind. Instead, she heard him say, in a sorrowful voice, "I release you, my brother. For what we endured together in life, let there be no wall between us." He squeezed Diana's hand. "Your daughter wants to say something."

"What is it, daughter?"

"I also release you, Father, on one condition."

"What is this condition? Is it your pound of flesh, Artemis?"

She bit her lip. "No, the condition is, when you are released, you must find Hector and my children." She swallowed. "Tell Hector I forgive him, and give Andrew and Athena as much love as you can."

For the first time, Diana heard something like contrition in her father's voice. "Yes, I will. You have washed the black stains off my soul. Farewell, my beloved child."

Her voice broke as she said, "Good-bye, Papa. Go with my love."

There was the merest whisper, like the sound of a passing breeze. Diana and Luke both opened their eyes. For the first time since the deaths of her husband and children, she said, "Now, in the fullness of time."

"Yes, in the fullness of time, you are free. Perhaps, someday, I shall be free as well."

31

KATIE'S PROGRESS WITH her chemotherapy was sufficient enough for Eric and Clark to decide to defer immunotherapy. Before her next trip to Tampa, they discussed the reasons in a conference call with her.

After a discussion of pros and cons, she said, "What you're telling me is that you don't think I need the immunotherapy."

Clark said, "Not at this time. When we get more evidence that chemotherapy has gotten the upper hand, we'll do a round of immunotherapy as a way of activating your immune system to attack whatever remains of the cancer."

"Let's go through this again. Why do you think I should wait? I'm in the middle of the fight right now. I told my grandfather I'd use every weapon I could get my hands on."

"Let's think about the downside. Immunotherapy will leave you drastically weaker for some time. It could weaken you so much we might not be able to do more chemo if we needed to restart it."

"So, you're asking me for some more faith in you?"

"That's about the size of it. I guess I owe you an apology. We don't always explain what we're up to. We're still learning how to use the weapons we've got."

"Okay, I'll trust you. Do you want to know why?"

"Sure."

"Because you just admitted you're not infallible."

Eric broke in. "Clark, watch your damned mouth. You've broken a guild rule, and we can't have that."

This sally was so unexpected and out of character. There was an instant of silence, followed by raucous laughter from all three of them. Katie was still snickering when she hung up.

Andy asked, "What was that about? Why are you laughing?"

She leaned over and kissed him. "I just got proof that doctors can be real live human beings. That's good news."

She recounted the conversation.

"So, they want to keep on with the chemo, but not the other thing."

"Not yet on the immunotherapy. Clark made it sound like the cherry on an ice cream sundae."

"Ice cream, Mommy?" Timmy had wandered into the kitchen while his parents were engrossed in their discussion.

She bent down and picked him up. "Ooof. Pretty soon I won't be able to pick you up, the way you're growing. But yes, ice cream. Let's go to the Double Dipper."

As the three Lyles walked hand in hand the few blocks to get ice cream, Katie thought about the special meaning autumn had always held for her. It was the season when they celebrated Andy's and Art's birthdays, the time of football games, Sunday afternoon cookouts with friends, and of lazy days on the river. A chilly breeze blew in from the ocean, reminding her that the worst of the summer heat was gone. Another stronger breeze blew leaves off the oaks and beeches that lined the roads.

"Pretty leaves," Timmy said.

"Yes, honey, they are."

"Why aren't they pretty like that until they fall?"

She squeezed his hand. "It's because, while they're still growing, they're always green. Green is the color of life. Red and gold are lovely colors, but they're a sign that life has gone out of the leaves. But, before they go, they put on a show for us, to remind us how beautiful life is."

"It's sad when the trees don't have leaves. They look so sad."

"Sweet boy, that's just how they get ready to give us new leaves and new life in the spring."

"You promise, Mommy?"

"I promise."

———

AS THEY SAT in the ice cream parlor, Audrey and Phil McKenzie walked in. Audrey had been Marilyn Pilcher's best friend since elementary school. They spotted the Lyles and came to their table. "Do you mind if we join you?"

Andy battled his impulse to tell them to buzz off. He said, "Pull up a chair. What's new?"

"I talked to your mom last week. She and Jack just got back from New York. They have season tickets to the Metropolitan Opera."

There's no culture in Atlanta, so they had to go to New York. I'll bet Jack found some way to claim the airfare and hotel as business expenses. "Oh really? Other than that, Mrs. Lincoln, how was the play?"

Audrey was so wrapped up in her narrative that she missed the nasty crack and its implied slam against Marilyn. "They saw a new production of *Das Rheingold.* The Met's doing all four operas in the cycle this season."

That figures. Mom would make one hell of a Valkyrie. "Do they have any major trips planned for the near future?"

"They're going on a river cruise in Russia in August, and we're going with them."

Phil, who rarely said anything when his wife was purveying gossip and other assorted small talk, said, "I'll bet Jack's managed to schedule a private meeting with Putin. That would make their expenses deductible."

Touché. I guess Phil doesn't have all that much use for Jack either. "Katie's parents did that in the late nineties. They said the cabins weren't exactly what you'd get with Royal Caribbean."

"How are your parents doing, Katie?" Audrey asked. "I was sorry to hear about your grandfather's death."

"Mom's doing all right. We're fortunate that Opa had everything planned. We didn't have to worry about making arrangements. He was very tired, and now he's back with Oma again."

Timmy spoke up. "I wanna see Opa. I wanna to do a puzzle with him"

Audrey said, "Your Opa's in heaven now. And if you give your life to Jesus, you'll get to join him someday."

Way to go, Audrey. Remind me about Mom's lifestyle and drag Jesus into the picture for good measure. "Finish your ice cream, Timmy. Mommy and I have to go home, so I can cut the grass."

Back at home, Andy said, "All these years, I've blamed Mom for being a social climber. If she grew up with friends like Audrey, it's no wonder. That is one clueless woman."

Katie said, "One thing about fighting cancer I don't like is that it's made me thin-skinned. Audrey didn't ask me or you how I'm doing."

"Like I said, clueless. Also self-centered."

———

"MOMMY, WHAT'S CANCER?"

Oh, God. We haven't told him much about my treatments. Is he old enough to understand? "Why do you ask, honey?"

"I heard Big Tom and Grandma Ginny talking about Opa. They say he died of cancer."

Katie nodded. "Cancer is when bad things start growing inside your body. Sometimes nothing can stop them, and people die because of the bad things. That's what happened to Opa."

"You have cancer, don't you?"

She looked away for a long moment. "It's different with Mommy. Opa was very old. He was worn out and couldn't fight back against the cancer. Mommy's still young, and she's got very good doctors."

"Can I get cancer?"

"Heavens no, sweetheart. Why do you ask a silly question like that?"

"My tummy hurts. Is that cancer?"

She beamed, a smile so radiant it made Timmy's eyes widen. "That's just 'cause you ate too much pizza at supper. That's pain that'll go away soon. Let's get you some Pepto-Bismol."

After Katie and Andy said bedtime prayers with their son, they turned out the lights and left the room. In the pale glow of a nightlight, Timmy looked up at the shadows on the ceiling. He folded his hands. "Opa, help Mommy. Make her not have cancer."

———

THE DREAM OF the boy, the girl, and the monster crab came back that night, this time with a strange new twist. In the earlier version, Timmy hadn't heard any words. This time, the boy's voice roared defiance at the huge crustacean: "Go away! Leave my sister alone!"

The voice was familiar and beloved. In the peculiar logic of dreams, Timmy didn't recognize Brian's voice. Likewise, when the girl was attacked by the swarm of crabs, her cries for help were not those of a young child.

"No! No! My son needs me! I can't go with you!"

Timmy knew his mother's voice, but his sleep was so deep, his mind didn't process what he was hearing.

The sequel, resumed, playing as it had before. When the strange couple repulsed the monster crab's renewed onslaught, though, the man came to the boy and took his hand. Mommy rose from the sea, came to them, and said, "My darling, wherever I am, I will always love you and always reach out to you." Then she took the boy's hand and led him away.

32

Soon after accepting the idea that the time was right for a move to Florida, Luke ran into an obstacle: the heartfelt pleas of Sisters of Mercy Hospice, Diana's employer. They begged him to not deprive them of her services until they had time to find and train a replacement. He let matters slide until an extraordinary occurrence forced him to a decision.

The message from Brian Thompson came as no surprise. Since he'd heard of Brian's death, he thought further contact was possible. When it came, it was not in the way such messages usually came to him. It was neither a dream-disturbance nor a voice-disturbance. What happened was a visit from a dead man, in his own living room.

He'd fallen asleep in his recliner after his usual nightcap, a juice glass of ouzo. His bladder woke him at about two o'clock. When he came back to turn out the lights, the visitor was sitting in a wingback chair no one had used since Connie died in 1981. His friends knew the ground rules. But dead men have their own rules.

He'd gotten a strange sensation when he opened the bathroom door. Without hearing or seeing anything, Luke could tell someone else was in the house. He crept to the master bedroom and got his equalizer, a Smith & Wesson .38. Checking to make sure it was loaded, he returned to the living room.

"You can't scare me with a popgun like that, trooper," the visitor said. "I'm a South Side Mick, and I don't run from anything. Besides, I'm dead."

I know the guy. He wore Army dress blues, with six rows of decorations on his tunic and service stripes up the ying-yang. Luke's eighty-seven years and the beating he suffered in 2006 slowed his recall. After a few seconds, a recollection of the conversation with Helen six months ago lit up his memory circuits. He said, without cracking a smile, "Brian Thompson, right? Bastogne, 1944, I think it was, and Seoul some years later. I'd heard you'd left us, but I wasn't sure if anything could put you six feet under."

"Cancer did it. But that's a trivial matter. You can just call me Brass-balls. We're friends."

"Well, my friend, what do you need me for? Healing?"

"No, it's not that. I've already been healed. You're a hospice doctor, aren't you?"

"Uh-huh. You got a referral for me?"

"Yep. It's my granddaughter. She lives down in Florida. She's been very sick. It's gone on for three years now."

I don't want to blow him off. Why do I think I already know about her? Brass-balls' face was scrunched up. Men in dress blues didn't cry, but it looked like he might. Luke said, "If she's in Florida, how can I help her from here? Besides, I don't practice anymore, except for occasional referrals."

"It's time for you to move. Florida is nice in the winter, none of this snow-and-ice crap like you get here, or in Boston or Baltimore."

That brought Luke up short. *There's no way he can know why Boston and Baltimore are important to me. Play for time while you try to find out more.* "I don't have practice rights in Florida. I can't just move down there and start another hospice from scratch."

"The name Helen Ferguson mean anything to you?"

Brian must've seen the surprise on Luke's face because he started laughing. "I know you two are friends. She's, uh, a special person in your life. I find it hard to believe that she's never suggested the idea to you."

"Okay, let's say I move. How do I locate your granddaughter?"

"Not to worry. She'll find you when the time's right. You'll know what to do."

Luke put a fist up to his lips. Continuing to stall, he said, "Give me a few minutes to think about this. What else do you know about me? Why am I the right person to help your granddaughter?"

"I've talked to some of your family here. You're a few years younger than I am. You were born overseas and came here when you were just a boy. We have something in common. I lost my father when I was seven. You lost your mother when you were just a lad."

"Right. I was four when she died."

"You started college before the big war and enlisted in '42. The Army kept you in college until you graduated, then sent you to school to become a surgical tech. You came into Bastogne with a hospital unit right after Patton's boys broke through and relieved us. That's how you were able to save my life."

"Correct. When else did we meet?"

"Twice. Once in '52. You'd been to medical school by then. You set a broken leg for George Burton, one of my former COs. Our last meeting was four years ago, not far from here. Not that it makes any difference, but Burton's dying too. He'll be here soon. Do you believe I'm on the up and up?"

"Okay, I believe you. Who told you all this stuff? My niece met you, but no one else in my family ever heard your name."

"A guy named Sonny told me. We met at an old soldier's gathering here not long ago. He's the one who suggested I contact you."

"What do you need?"

"Like I told you, somebody needs to look after my granddaughter. That's why you have to get down to Florida. You can't do it from here."

"You're on," Luke said. "What do I get out of this deal?"

"You'll find peace. That's what you've wanted for many years, isn't it?"

"Yes. Anything else you care to tell me?"

"Yes. My granddaughter's name is Kathleen Lyle, Katie for short, and she has a son called Timmy. Ultimately, Timmy is the one that matters."

"Timmy, you say? If he's just a boy, how can I help him? Can't you tell me any more than that?"

"I can't explain it to you. Trust me."

Luke bowed his head for a second. When he looked up, Brian was gone.

———

IN THE MORNING, Luke sat down in his study and began making notes on a legal pad. After half an hour, his thoughts hadn't progressed very far. He looked, for the sixth or seventh time, at what he'd written.

Things have changed since 2004.

Diana doesn't always have the same disturbances. Why not?

Appearances by Mama and Papa give hints but no direct guidance. Will I ever get it?

I'm ready to move, but am I too late?

Why did Brian mention his great-grandson?

Was Nate's visit really about me and Helen?

Why do the words "unfinished forgiveness" keep coming up in my mind?

He stared at the pad for a long time. There was a thread that connected all these questions, but he couldn't figure out what it was or how he might go about locating it. Finally, he made one more note.

Let Diana handle the move logistics. I need some answers.

33

WHEN DIANA STOPPED by to check on Luke that afternoon, she saw him scribbling on a legal pad. His request came as a surprise. "I think it's time we go with this Florida move. I need you to do the legwork down in Florida. Do you think you can get us a deal on leasing space? I've got some work to do here."

"What? Lukas Vangelis trusts someone else to undertake negotiations on his behalf?"

"You're not funny when you're sarcastic. Yes, I trust you."

"I'll have to request time off from Sisters of Mercy Hospice. Do I need to go ahead and give them notice?"

"Not yet. It'll be time when you get back."

"Okay, I work out a lease while I'm down there. Anything else?"

"Once you've got the lease, arrange for phone and internet service. You have signatory authority on all our financial accounts, so we don't need to make any changes right now. Oh, yes, I almost forgot. I'd like you to work out some arrangement with Helen Ferguson. She's got to have a foolproof system for referring clients to us who are, shall we say, special cases. Can you do that?"

"Of course."

"Draw out any money you need for travel and per diem. Text or e-mail me if you've got any questions. We don't need to engage in conversations that prying ears might overhear."

"Understood."

Before she went to bed that night, Diana started working on her assignments. She began by making a detailed checklist. When she put down, "Talk to Helen Ferguson," a bothersome thought intruded: *Why is it Luke doesn't want to talk to Helen himself?*

———

ANOTHER VOICE-DISTURBANCE CAME while Diana was in Florida. Luke had spent most of one afternoon at a lawyer's office, working on incorporating a nonprofit corporation named St. Raphael Hospice. The law office was on 15th Street NW. He decided to walk home. As he made his way through the clamor of DuPont Circle, he heard the voice. It was the maternal voice, paying another of her rare visits.

"There's something else you need to know. I know you don't trust yourself when you're with that lady out of fear you'll do something shameful. You must have faith. You can be her friend without being her lover. You've been called to help a young woman walk a rocky path. Help her and her son. There will be many traps set for him. Show him how to avoid them, and you will find the peace you seek."

The blare of a car horn interrupted the voice. "Hey, you damned fool! Stay out of the effing crosswalk when it says, 'Don't Walk.'" A young man was leaning out of the passenger's side of a sports car. As the driver hit the gas, the man shot Luke a bird.

Chastened, he stepped back to the curb. A teenager with a skateboard, also waiting for the "Walk" signal, said, "You got to watch out for dudes like that. He's the kind that thinks it's cool to scare the shit out of people."

Luke smiled. "Yeah, fella, I know the type. I've dealt with them all my life."

When he got home, he found an e-mail from Diana. She'd located a property away from the heart of Jacksonville, in a small town called Fernandina Beach. Other than the out-of-the-way location, it seemed perfect: adequate space that could be reconfigured without too much work, ample parking, a safe neighborhood. His terse response was: Go with it.

Things are going well. I hope we can move down there soon. With these encouraging thoughts, he lay down for a nap. When he woke up, he found it was almost eight o'clock. *It's too late for me to fix something. I'll just find a restaurant.*

His search for a dining spot took him far afield to the food court at Union Station. He sat at a small table to one side of the main concourse, watching as travelers hurrying to catch trains for Philadelphia, Richmond, and Charlotte wolfed down pizza, barbecue, and Chinese take-out. *I'll miss the old rat race. But I think now there's something I've got to concentrate on: a young woman and her son.*

The next revelation came that night. As he sat in his recliner, reading the *Meditations* of Marcus Aurelius, he heard suspicious noises from the garden. He picked up his cell phone and browsed through his contact list until he located the entry for the police department, then halted. *I need to find out what's going on first.* He quietly unlocked the back door and stepped into the darkness. To his surprise, the motion-detector floodlights showed no one inside the enclosure.

"Who's there?"

"Just an old friend here for a visit."

"Sonny?"

"I know you've got some serious unanswered questions. That guy, Brian, and I talked a little while ago. He said there was stuff he couldn't tell you, family business and all that. But there aren't any restrictions on me. What are your questions?"

Taken off guard, Luke's memory failed him. When several seconds passed, the voice in the darkness said, "If you want answers, now's the time to ask for 'em. I don't get to make these visits very often, so you'd better ask me while you can."

"Okay, let's see. Why did Brian come looking for me? We met three times when he was alive, but we weren't friends."

"Have you forgotten what I taught you about our connections? You and he are already connected. That connection runs from you to him to his granddaughter and her kid. It will become a lot more important very soon."

"He said she was in a lot of pain. Is she going to die?"

"I don't know. I'm one who testifies to the truth, not a fortune-teller."

"Why would he come to me if it's just illness? Something bad must be in the works."

"You've forgotten something. She's not the important one."

"Her son?"

"Yes. He carries the inheritance."

There was a sudden murmur, as if a breeze were stirring the lilacs in the garden. Sonny was gone.

Luke hadn't set foot inside a church in over thirty years. The dawning awareness of what lay before him was overpowering. He fell to his knees and lifted his face to the night sky. His hands raised to the distant stars, he whispered, "Thank you." This moment of gratitude was dispelled almost in the same breath by the seed of another thought: "I hope I'm not too late."

———

SONNY'S LATEST WORDS sent Luke back to the list he'd made after the spectral visit from Brian. He reviewed the questions, once again looking for the common bond among them. After a few minutes, it came to him: Since becoming a hospice physician, his attention had been drawn outward to an ever-increasing degree, leaving him out of contact with the old Lukas Vangelis. The man who planned to leave these familiar surroundings was not the man who'd come to Washington with such high hopes and grand expectations in the mid-1950s.

He went back out to garden and sat down in the darkness. He knew Sonny wouldn't be coming back. He also knew he had to get back in touch with himself.

As the night wore on, he reviewed the last thirty-odd years of his life, how he'd come to love the mission of caring for those whose hopes had fled. Year by year, he thought about the past, until, just as he reached the mysterious visit from Eleni in 2004, it came to him, not in a Damascus road moment, but with an equally blinding certainty: *I can't give comfort to others anymore, not until my forgiveness is complete.* In the ancient tongue of his ancestors, he said, "Lukas Vangelis, I forgive you. Now go in peace to the end of the road."

34

Eric seldom smiled, but his mood seemed upbeat as he began his regular appointment with the Lyles. "I won't say we're out of the woods, but I think the forest is less dense. There may be daylight ahead."

Andy asked, "How many more of these treatments are you going to put Katie through? She's put a lot of her life on hold for the last three years."

Eric's knit brow spoke volumes. "Six more months, perhaps. We can't be sure with cancer. The chemo has eliminated some of the lesions on the liver and reduced others almost to the point of undetectability. That's a good news-bad news story."

"What do you mean?"

"Cancer seldom tips its hand. That's what makes it dangerous. If there were a blood test, as there is for STD's, or a skin test, as there is for tuberculosis, it would be less scary."

Katie squeezed her husband's hand. "Darling, we've got to treat each day as a gift."

Andy's mouth turned down. He said, "When you work in building construction, you can know what you're dealing with, what materials and techniques work, and which ones don't. If medicine's 'scientific,' why can't it give us better information?"

Eric took off the rimless glasses he used for reading and started twirling them by one of the temple pieces. When he saw Katie's silent laughter, he gave an embarrassed smile and set them on his desk. "Sorry. I only do that when someone asks me a really tough question, which is what Andy just did." He drummed the fingers of his left hand on the polished wood. "Okay. Where science is concerning cancer is about where astronomy was between Galileo and Newton. We're on the verge of uncorking a flood of new information. At least we think so, but we can't be absolutely sure. Every patient like Katie gives us another brick in the wall."

Andy looked at his wife. "How does being a guinea pig make you feel?"

"Physically, not so hot. I never wanted to be a pioneer, but I guess I've got no choice."

He turned to Eric. "What's going to happen with this next round of chemo?"

"We're going to do 'chemoembolization.' That is, Clark's going to introduce a catheter through a small needle into the femoral artery and from there, via the aorta, to the artery in the liver that supplies blood to the tumors."

"How many treatments?"

"Three, each of about three hours."

"Then what?"

"Katie's going to have pain, fever, and nausea, along with a lot of fatigue for a month or so after this round. That's a good sign. These symptoms probably mean the tumor's breaking down."

Andy said to Katie, "Doesn't this make you nervous?"

"Sure, but if it's near the end of the road, I can take it."

Eric said, "That's the right spirit. May I give you a real-life example?"

"Please do."

"My father lived for three years on the run, a fugitive Jew in Nazi Germany. One of the worst moments of that whole period was at the end. Have you read *Slaughterhouse-Five?*"

Katie nodded. "Vonnegut was lucky to survive. I can hope for the same luck."

"We all do. My mother's family was all but wiped out in the fire-bombing of Dresden. This is where her memories diverged from my father's. For *Mutti*, it was pure horror. For *Vati*, the horror was real, but so was the hope. It meant the end of the war was near if they had enough grit to survive."

She reached and touched his restless left hand. "You understand."

"I wasn't there, but my sister and I grew up with those memories. It's unscientific to say this, but it's almost as if they were genetically transmitted."

Katie turned tender eyes to her husband. "I'll take any pain and suffering I have to take." She hesitated. "If only I could be sure that Timmy never has to go through what I've gone through."

Eric put a hand over his eyes for a few seconds. Then, he looked at them and took a deep breath. "The odds are good, but we can't know for sure."

On that note, the conference ended.

———

NOT LONG AFTER Clark finished Katie's first chemoembolization, a call from his stepmother Eleanor obliged him to make hasty arrangements for a flight to San Francisco.

When he arrived at the hospital, he asked her, "How is Dad?"

"This is no time for happy BS. George looks as bad as Val did the week before he died."

The mention of Eleanor's first husband, who'd died of cancer in 1970, drew a nod from Clark. "There aren't many easy ways to go."

His sister Terri and his niece Caroline met him in the intensive care waiting room. Caroline kissed him and said, her voice breaking, "Grandpa went into a coma around midnight." She wept on his shoulder.

"Can I see him now?"

"Aunt Toni is with him now. We'll go in as soon as she comes out."

Five minutes later, a nurse entered. She asked Clark, "Are you Dr. Burton?"

He nodded. "What's the situation with Dad?"

"He's out of the coma, but it may be only temporary. He's asking for you. He said he just wants a few minutes alone with his son."

She led him to a room with a solid glass wall, permitting the nurse at a control console an unobstructed view of the bed. His sister hugged him and stepped out of the room.

Clark bent over the bed. "Dad?" Even with the nosepiece providing a steady flow of oxygen, George's skin had the bluish hue of cyanosis.

"Clark." A pause, then, "Thank God you got here." Another pause. "Wasn't sure I could hang on."

"I'll stay as long as you want me to."

"How long was I out?"

"About twelve hours the nurses say."

"I saw Robbie. He said he'd wait until I was ready."

He's hallucinating, but you're in his world now. Play along. "How did he look?"

"As handsome as the day he graduated West Point. He left this." The general pointed to an object on the nightstand: a metal shard, smeared with what appeared to be dried blood. "Said the Graves

Registration people didn't find it when they were getting his body ready to ship home."

Clark's eyes widened. *From the artillery shell that killed Robbie. My God. Is it delirium or something else?*

George's rambling continued. "Saw your mother too. She said she wanted to make sure I knew she forgave me. Papa, Mama, Aunt Jess, Grandpa Bob, and Grandma Flo were all there. Didn't say anything, though."

On the spur of the moment, Clark asked, "Dad, what about Brian Thompson? Do you remember seeing him?"

"Saw him this morning. He said to tell you to take care of Katie."

Okay, so he's still got some connection to reality. That's what Brian told me last spring. "I will, Dad."

"Make sure you do. I don't want that tough old bastard chasing me all over hell because you didn't."

He slurred the last words, drifting back into unconsciousness. Clark sat with him for a few minutes before returning to the waiting room.

———

TWO MONTHS LATER

The arrangements for the move were almost complete. Diana had obtained a five-year office lease on favorable terms. The interior reconfiguration and telecom upgrades were all that remained before the hospice opened for business.

The day after the presidential inauguration, Luke and Diana drank coffee in his kitchen. "When are you leaving?" he asked.

"Noon. By then, the last of our million or so visitors will have left, and I can get on the road. I've got a reservation in Florence, South Carolina tonight. I should make it to Jacksonville by early tomorrow afternoon."

He turned a page in the *Washington Post*. His eyes narrowed. "What's so interesting?" she asked.

"Another friend gone. You remember that retired major general we met back in 2004?"

"Yeah, sort of. He was a patient of yours, wasn't he?"

"Temporarily. I set his broken leg in Seoul. Anyway, he died just before Christmas, a few months shy of making it to ninety."

"Well, I assume the Army will give him a royal send-off."

"This says they're bringing his ashes from California for burial at Arlington. Strange, isn't it? Both he and that old sergeant who was a buddy of his have died in the last year."

"You're a vanishing breed, Luke."

"We few, we happy few. We just keep getting fewer."

As the time for her departure neared, they strolled through the townhouse. Luke had sold it to a subcabinet appointee in the new administration and would follow Diana to Florida after the closing. "Lots of memories in these walls," Diana said.

"Not all of them good."

"Don't be pessimistic. Maybe the worst is behind us."

Perhaps. Something tells me there's one more test. Most likely in Florida, but I won't get my release until I get through it. "Well, it's almost noon. Better get on your way, girl."

"Whatever you say, old man. I'll call you tonight."

"Be careful. Some of the revelers are probably fighting hangovers."

She was laughing as she went out the door.

35

LUKE FELT A change in the wind. Guidance in using his extraordinary powers had always come in the form of clear messages. At least, they were clear in the sense that he could meditate until he made sense of them. Sonny's last message, though, seemed to him like the closing of a door. He expected no more communications until after the move to Florida was complete.

His expectation was premature. A message from an unlikely source came on a bright winter's day at Arlington National Cemetery.

He watched the Burton funeral party from a safe distance, hanging around on the fringe of the large group of mourners. He'd intended to go to the family gathering at Arlington's Administration Building. As he headed down the walk along Memorial Drive, a mild buzzing in his ears crescendoed until it was as if a swarm of giant bumblebees was circling around his head. By the time he reached the visitor center, it drowned out the roar of jets from the nearby airport. When he grasped the door handle, he felt a giant hand pushing full force against him, determined to thwart his forward progress. He sat down on a bench. An eerie silence replaced the infernal buzzing. In the silence, a familiar voice said, "No. Not now. The time has gone. Wait until the next moment comes."

Nate! Is he trying to stop me? I have to be here. Unwilling to yield, Luke took his cell phone and called a number on his contact list: "Arlington Burial Information."

A young man answered. "Burial Information. Do you have a name?"

"Yes. Burton, George. Major General George Burton."

There was the sound of keystrokes on the other end of the line. "Uh, the inurnment will be in the Columbarium, Section 63, at 3:00 p.m. Do you need directions?"

"Thank you, no. I know how to get there." Luke checked his watch. *2:42. The procession will be leaving any minute now.* He quick-stepped through the visitor parking lot. As he reached Patton Drive, the cadence of snare drums and the sound of a band playing a dirge came to him, borne on a breeze that grew colder by the minute. *Damn this wind. This feels like Bastogne all over, the kind of cold that goes right to the bone.* He wrapped his topcoat and muffler as snugly as he could.

He positioned himself near the south end of the Columbarium. The procession approached, band and color guard in the lead, followed by the caisson bearing a flag-draped casket and a young woman in uniform. She walked alone in front of a convoy of vehicles.

When the caisson stopped on Marshall Drive, Luke could see that she wore Air Force dress blues. She halted next to a two-starred red flag. Two members of the casket team opened the casket and extracted a wooden box and a folded flag. The young woman came to attention and saluted.

She held the salute until an older woman, a tall, bald man, and two middle-aged women approached. She turned to the man and he embraced her. Luke could see her shoulders shaking. He recognized her. *That's Caroline Segura, Burton's granddaughter. I remember her from the D-Day celebration.*

Luke stepped behind a lamppost as the foot procession followed the casket team. They stopped and unfolded the flag, holding it taut over a small table. A chaplain sprinkled holy water on the wooden box and began a series of prayers.

After the firing of volleys by the honor guard and "Taps," Luke moved toward the group as the casket team refolded the flag. He went only a few steps and stopped; the invisible hand blocked him. Frustrated, he was about to turn away when a moment of recognition dawned, like a match lit in a blacked-out room. The tall man was talking to a stocky, silver-haired man in a dark suit. The other man turned and passed down a line of mourners, offering hugs and handshakes to family members.

Luke squinted against the sun, already sliding toward the horizon. *I know them.* He looked at both men, the tall one and the stocky one, and smiled. *Déjà vu.* In confirmation, the voice he'd heard at the visitor center returned. "Now you remember, don't you? When the right moment comes, they'll remember you, but this is not the time. You missed your first chance, but there'll be another."

He left the cemetery and took the Metro to a hotel near the White House. *I missed my first chance. What chance is that?* The closing on his residence was in the morning. After the papers were signed, he'd board a train for, as he put it, his new "theater of operations."

That evening he went to the Lincoln Memorial for what he knew would be the last time, taking in a long last look at the mournful seated figure of the Great Emancipator. *Good-bye, old friend. I'll miss your wisdom.*

———

THE NEXT "SURGE," as he called it, came while he was on a southbound train. As he stepped out of his sleeper compartment, intending to go to the dining car, the buzzing came back, then Nate's voice. "Wait. He is too close. If he meets you now, you won't be able to deal with him later."

He stepped back and shut the door. "Who is 'he?' And why is it so important for me not to see him?"

"Your thinking is backward. It's important for him not to see you. You recognized him at the cemetery yesterday. But he would think you're someone else."

"So, he confuses me with you. Why does that matter?"

"He thinks he's winning the battle. He doesn't know it's already a lost cause. He has to accept that before he recognizes you."

"Have I missed something? What 'lost cause' are you talking about?"

"You'll know in good time. It's not the moment. I have one final message for you."

"Final? What do you mean by that?"

"Now you are free to seek the peace you've always wanted."

He went back into the compartment and sat down. After a deep breath, he half-murmured, "Is this the end of the road?"

"No. It's not given to me to know. This is as far as I can take you."

"What?"

"I won't speak to you again, as long as you are on the road. It's enough that you know you've removed every barrier that I can help you with. Our reconciliation is complete."

Luke felt as though someone had lifted a thousand-pound weight off his shoulders. He bowed his head. Before he could speak, Nate continued: "One thing remains. My daughter must understand and accept my confession. Her mind is closed against me. Help me, please, so my child can be free of the anger that still burns inside her."

"I promise to try. How will I know if I've succeeded?"

No answer came, only the rhythmic clack of steel wheels rolling over steel rails. Fifteen minutes later, he went to breakfast without incident.

———

DIANA NOTICED A renewed vigor in his step as he disembarked from the train. "You must be feeling better."

"It was too damned cold in Washington. This sunshine makes me feel better."

"The transport service delivered your car to the office, and the movers unloaded everything else at that storage facility I rented. What do you want to do first?"

"Go look at the office. After that, I suppose I'll start calling real estate agents."

"You're in luck. It's a buyer's market. There are some brochures at the office, and I've made some notes on neighborhoods you might want to look at."

"Thanks. What else do we have to do to get St. Raphael to take wing, if I'm permitted a joke?"

"The website will go live next Monday. I've got mockups of our service brochure at the office. When you're ready to go to press, we'll distribute those . . ."

She stopped, noticing that he had put his hands up to his ears. "Lukas, what's going on?"

He shook his head, mouthing, "I can't hear what you're saying." He cast anxious glances in every direction until he spotted a silver-haired man getting into a car about fifty feet away. As soon as the car pulled out, he lowered his hands. "Sorry. I've just had some episodes of buzzing in my ears. I guess I need to get my hearing checked."

"Well, let's change the plan. Forget the office. You're in Florida now, and you need some seafood. How about lunch at the beach?"

"I'm with you on that. Let's go."

36

THE HEADACHES RETURNED not long after Luke arrived in Florida. Unlike the earlier episodes, characterized by brief but intense pain, these chronic aches centered in the back of his head, low-grade but never completely absent.

It was becoming difficult to conceal from Diana the things that started to go awry with his health. The constant pain and recent episodes of buzzing in his ears were bothersome enough to pose the question of what they meant.

Luke thought his brief separation from Diana had caused some of her unspoken but visible anxieties to dissipate. Once they were again back together at work, his efforts to put up a front required more conscious effort.

She reacted one morning when she noticed his unsteadiness pouring a cup of coffee. "What's the matter?"

"Nothing serious. That occasional buzzing I get may indicate some problems with my sense of balance."

"It's more serious than that. If you don't come clean with me, I'll make an appointment with a specialist."

He eased himself into a chair. "Alright, since you say so. This is the hour of truth and no consequences. Things have changed."

"Another blinding flash of the obvious. What sort of things are you talking about?"

He gave a report of the manifestations he'd encountered during the funeral and the train ride, mentioning that he'd recognized Nate's voice. At the end of his narrative, he said, "Your father told me I'd missed one chance but that there would be another. That's what still puzzles me. I don't know what chance he was talking about."

Diana gave him a sad look. "We'll have to wait and see. Oh, and Grandmama came to me in a dream last night."

"Did she say anything?"

"Yes. I heard her praying, at least that's what it sounded like. Most of it was in Greek, and I couldn't follow her, except for one phrase: 'Maria Theotokos, keep my sons from the fire.' She repeated it two or three times."

He looked down at his hands. "When I was a little child, sometimes I would hear Mama at her prayers. She always asked God not to cast us into the fire. Her belief in 'the fires of hell' was quite literal."

"Hell has different kinds of fire. There's none worse than seeing children you brought into the world lying on slabs in the morgue."

Luke sipped his coffee. "In my case, it was ice, the ice that formed on too many of my relationships. I spent too many years not believing in the forgiveness of sin. I'd have taken whatever pain I had to take to be certain that I'd really brought warmth into at least one person's life."

"If I didn't have faith that we did, I think I'd kill myself."

"Well, if you can go forward, with nothing more than that to lean on, I guess I can keep on trying."

———

LUKE RETURNED HOME at the day's end struggling with the surprise he'd successfully concealed when Diana told him about her dream of

Eleni. *She never knew Mama. How can she be so sure it was her? Who told her? Does it mean Mama won't come to me anymore?*

He'd long since abandoned any belief in Hell as a fiery state reserved for punishments after death. *Hell is here. I lived in it after Nate and Connie died. Sonny pulled us out of Hell. Why is Mama worried about us being in the fire?*

After a while, he decided to go out for a little night air. His buff-colored stucco cottage had a rear garden bordered on three sides by privet hedges. He took his glass of ouzo and went into the darkness. Late-winter breezes carried a salty smell from the Atlantic. Traffic on the nearby oceanfront highway passed in a steady stream, but the noise didn't penetrate his fugue.

This time, it wasn't a paranormal experience, rather a dredging-up of memories buried in a vault labeled "Nightmares."

Mama always prayed for Nate and me at bedtime, just before she went to help Papa close the store. That night, she prayed that prayer Diana heard. Then she went out and that drunk ran her down on the way to the store. Did she know she was about to die?

He answered his own question. "Yes, Mama knew. Diana got a warning of some kind."

Thunder boomed in the distance. Luke got up and went back inside, resolving to ask Diana about any warning signs she might have picked up.

————

A FEW WEEKS LATER

Eric picked up a folder from his desk and passed it to Katie and Andy. "This is the treatment plan for your immunotherapy. I know we talked about doing it here, but it was my decision to have Clark do it in Tampa. It's better if he's got the resources of his clinic if he needs them."

She sighed. "One more trip. What's the chance this is the last one?"

"I'd say about fifty-fifty. We may be able to deliver the knockout punch with one round, but it may take two. Clark and I think this is the right time."

Andy looked up from the folder. "Let me get this straight. Katie has to get these doses every eight hours for up to five days?"

"That's correct. Then she has a nine-day rest period, after which she does the second portion, with the same timetable."

"So, we're looking at three weeks or so."

"If we're right, we should see the remaining tumors vanish. She'll have a long recuperation and a lot of weakness. Please make sure you read the cautions closely. If she shows mood changes, it's probably due to the aldesleukin therapy. It's good stuff, but it hits with quite a wallop."

Katie fiddled with a ballpoint pen as she gave the multiple disclosures a close reading. She looked up several times during her scrutiny but asked no questions. With a look at Andy, she said, "I can live with this. Can you?"

"Anything to make you better, babe."

She signed the forms and handed them back to Eric.

37

THE ROLL-OUT OF St. Raphael Hospice was slow enough to frustrate Diana's no-nonsense outlook. In the first two months, only three patients arrived at the hospice's doorstep. All three were the result of contacts made before Luke moved south. In an effort to raise their profile, Diana donned a business suit and began making calls at doctors' offices and clinics in the Jacksonville area. These calls resulted in the arrival of a half-dozen new patients by the end of March.

Luke took a hands-off stance toward her promotion efforts. The headaches continued, but the buzzing hadn't recurred since the day of his arrival. He decided its appearance had been a warning signal, an aural hint to keep his distance. *The buzzing was to warn me away from someone or something, but what? I think Nate was trying to warn me against committing a serious misstep, but what kind of misstep?*

He was alone at the office when Helen called. She said, "I know you're in business, but I can't refer patients if you don't send me some information I can show our patients. All I have is some brochures from your practice in Washington. That's not much help down here."

"Hasn't Diana called you? She's been making the round of doctors and hospitals."

"Let me check my appointment book." A pause then, "No, there's nothing on the schedule."

"I'll take care of it. Talk to you later."

———

DIANA PAID A visit to St. Johns Oncology the next day. She brought a gift, a brand-new smartphone, complete with a docking station.

"What's this?" Helen asked. "Don't we have enough ways of getting in touch with each other?"

"Helen, you know we're not just another hospice. We've always relied on your good judgment to send us only those patients who need our unique services."

"I don't need a special phone for that."

Diana's eyes twinkled. "Until now, no, there's been no need. But there's a first time for everything. Everyone needs a back channel for certain occasions. This is a sure-fire tool."

Helen snapped, "Damn it, Diana Karras. Stop talking to me like you're the Oracle of Delphi."

"I'm sorry. Let me tell you why I brought this."

"All right. Why?"

"In the not-too-distant future, you may have to do some covert contacts, a little creative disobedience, if you will. This is a way that lets you do that while protecting yourself. May I demonstrate?"

"Go ahead."

The demonstration took several minutes, after which Diana gave Helen a discreet warning to keep the phone in a secure place and not allow anyone else to use it.

As Diana gathered her bag to leave, Helen asked, "Why haven't you given us a call before now?"

"What? Luke assured me he'd take care of it."

"Obviously, he didn't. I had to call him."

Diana looked away for a few seconds. "God, I was hoping it was only temporary. I guess I was wrong."

"Wrong about what?"

"Luke's been putting up a front for a while. I'm afraid his condition isn't as good as he makes it out to be."

Despite the closeness of the personal and professional relationships Helen enjoyed with Luke and Diana, she knew little about the source of their extraordinary abilities. Both uncle and niece had couched talk of hospice cases in mundane language. She heard nothing in Diana's language that hinted at anything more than the results of normal human aging. Luke's forgetfulness *was* disturbing, but what could she do about it?

To Diana, the admission she'd just made hinted at her own worries. The thought that Luke's powers might be slipping into an irretrievable decline threatened to dislodge one of the pillars on which her world rested. Since arriving in Florida, Luke had said nothing about the search for a successor. Years of experience in hospice care gave Diana confidence in her abilities while at the same time reminding her that the teamwork with her uncle was something she couldn't do alone. She bade Helen farewell and drove back to St. Raphael Hospice.

When she arrived, Luke had left for the day. She checked for voicemails, found none, and closed the office.

———

AS DIANA CONCLUDED her demonstration, Andy was reviewing the contents of an envelope addressed "Andrew Lyle – Confidential." It had arrived in the office mail at Lyle & Sons not long after Katie returned from her round of immunotherapy.

The envelope held a grab-bag of information about the hazards of immunotherapy. There were reprints from a variety of sources, mostly websites with provocative names. One document was an article printed from a blog called "Quacks and Snake Oil." It cited Clark Burton as a leading advocate of immunotherapy. After a lurid recital of the effects of aldesleukin therapy, it noted that Dr. Burton was the son of Major General George Burton, "relieved of his command during the Vietnam War for defeatism and incompetence." It also noted his long professional association with Eric Grueneberg, "brother of notorious New York leftist radical Tina Balser."

When Andy finished reading, he stalked into his father's office and tossed the packet on Tom's desk, saying, "Another shipment of steaming crap from attorney Pilcher, courtesy of Mom."

Tom began perusing the articles. He hadn't gotten far when Andy asked, "How in the hell could he get hold of the names of Katie's doctors?"

For the first time in his life, Andy saw a strange look on his father's face, a "Holy shit, did I do that?" look. Tom said, "Well, uh, you know, the only way he could've gotten those names is from, you know, Phil McKenzie."

"What the hell does that mean?"

"I, uh, was playing golf with Phil about three weeks ago, while you guys were in Tampa. He asked how Katie was doing. I, you know, tried to tell him what I could."

Andy's face was a clenched fist of disgust. Through gritted teeth, he muttered, "Yeah, Phil's like a plumbing line with no backflow preventer. No doubt he blabbed to Audrey, and she repeated it to Mom, chapter and verse."

Tom's mouth tightened. "I'm sorry. I'll make sure this doesn't go any further." He took the envelope and put it in a bin on his credenza labeled "Confidential – To Be Shredded."

Andy forced himself to speak softly. "I'm sorry for flaring off like that, Dad, but Katie is run-down from her treatments. I don't want to do anything that makes her sad or despondent."

Tom just nodded.

38

ANDY SUGGESTED A picnic at Little Talbot Island for a dual celebration: Independence Day and the end of Katie's immunotherapy.
Invitations to Katie's doctors drew polite regrets, but Andy's brother and sisters and Katie's sister, Peg and brother-in-law Tony, joined
Art, Bonnie, Tom, Ginny, and a gaggle of grandchildren beneath an
oversized pavilion that offered a vista of miles of pristine dunes and
shimmering water.

Katie's spirits were on the rise. She sat in a lawn chair in the pavilion's ample shade, sipping lemonade and chatting with her in-laws.

Ginny asked, "Are your doctors sure you won't need more treatments?"

"Doctors hate to say, 'I'm sure,' but Dr. Burton said these last two
treatments have had some of the best results he's seen."

"Doctors can be so wishy-washy, except when they're making out
your bill."

Andy came up at that moment. "Dad, Ginny, can I get you a refill?"
Tom declined. Ginny accepted.

He took her cup to a nearby ice chest. A jigger of Woodford
Reserve, smuggled in despite the park's no alcoholic beverages rule,
went in first. A half-dozen ounces of Diet Pepsi and a slice of fresh
lemon followed.

When he brought the cup to Ginny, she was listening to a CD, Frank Sinatra singing "Summer Wind." She thanked him and said, "This is the perfect song for a day like this. Isn't the breeze wonderful?"

Katie smiled. *It's nice to see Ginny in a good mood, not always talking about money and lifestyle.* She looked toward the nearby boardwalk, where Timmy and several of his cousins crouched, watching fiddler crabs, scuttling for bolt holes, trying to evade the beaks of hungry seagulls. The boys delighted in playing cowboys, riding herd on a darting flock of crustaceans. "Timmy, you boys stay where Daddy or Grandpa or Big Tom can see you."

At just that moment, Timmy stopped dashing back and forth. Katie thought something in the water – a school of flying fish or a dolphin – had caught his eye. Then she realized he was gazing at a couple strolling up the beach.

———

"WHAT DO YOU think of Florida, now that we've been here almost six months?" Diana asked.

"I'm still uncertain," Luke replied. "I thought the signals we got before the move meant some new challenge. So far, it's been our normal routine."

"Have you gotten any more messages?"

"No one's spoken to me about the 'missed chance,' nor about when the next one might come along."

"Let's not get impatient. Pushing against our limitations has never brought good results in the past."

Should I say something about the headaches? Maybe an indirect approach. "Next month will be three years since the attack."

"You've done pretty well, except you don't always let me know when you're not feeling up to par."

He was about to say something about the chronic pain when his gaze fell on something unusual. Amidst a throng of children cavorting just ahead, a small boy was looking directly at them. Luke gave the lad a smile and was about to bestow a friendly greeting. The boy turned and dashed for the nearby boardwalk. *Well, this broken nose and these scars do make me look a little bit like Frankenstein.*

———

TIMMY RAN UP to his grandmother. "Grandma Bonnie, there's a strange man and woman over there." He pointed to the beach-walking couple. The man gave a genial wave, a smile spreading across his scarred features.

Bonnie said, "Don't point, Timmy. It's not polite. Besides, they look friendly. Wave back at them."

The little boy's hand went up and moved half-heartedly back and forth.

At that moment, Tom called, "Lunch is on. Come and get it!"

As Bonnie went to round up the frolicking youngsters, the man and woman came up to her. "I'm sorry, Madame," the man said. "Is that young fellow one of yours?"

"He's one of my grandsons. I was telling him not to point at you. He knows better, but when you're almost four, curiosity still rules."

"I can't blame him for being curious. I must look like the creature from the black lagoon."

Bonnie smiled. "Would you like to come join us? We have plenty of food."

"No, but thank you for the invitation. My friend and I were just strolling along the beach, enjoying our day off."

"Well, I hope you both enjoy the holiday."

"And the same to you and your family, Madame."

When Bonnie returned to the pavilion, Katie asked, "Who was that gentleman you were talking to, Mom?"

"I don't know. We didn't get around to introductions. He called me 'Madame,' and he talks with a slight accent. He looks like an Italian or maybe an Arab."

Ginny said, "Looks like a May-December romance to me."

Katie replied, "You *do* meet all kinds of people on a public beach."

———

THAT NIGHT, LUKE sat for a long time in his enclosed garden. He loved smelling the salty air, but the citronella candles he'd lit to ward off flying pests overpowered the freshness of the ocean breeze.

Why are my feelings so confused? The headaches haven't been as bad today, but something about that boy on the beach is unsettling. He looked into the glass on his patio table. "Blessings from the wine-dark sea," he muttered. "I've never seen that boy, and he's never seen me. Why did we each have the reaction we did?"

He took a swallow of wine. From the darkness beyond the privet hedge, the familiar male voice spoke. "It's time for you to write your story. The ones who come after you need to know what you've learned."

"What about Diana? I've spent twenty-five years teaching her."

"She knows her father's and her husband's secrets, but not yours. She will have to guide the one who is to follow. Before she can teach him, you must finish teaching her."

Luke stared into the night. "Sonny, you're a hard master."

"Your salvation is unfinished until you leave a trail for those who follow."

After several minutes of silence, Luke went to his study and picked up a pen and a small notebook. He returned to the garden and sat for a long time thinking.

He put his hand up to his chin and stared, or so it seemed. In reality, he was far away, in the land of reminiscences, at a shelter for homeless veterans, listening to the words of the shelter director whose ravaged mahogany features belied his relative youth.

Sonny was talking about his own journey to forgiveness. "I went to Nam in '68, young and dumb, determined to kick me some yellow ass. I came home with one goal – to get even with the ones who'd ducked out behind student deferments or whose daddies paid off the draft boards to keep them out of the Army."

Luke knew he was wide awake. Still, it was astonishing how clearly he remembered the night he'd met Sonny and how Sonny's account had moved him.

"I did all right, making money. In some ways, my life was a lot better when I was playing my con games. Back in '75, I was making close to five or six hundred a week selling coke to kids in the slums. I had a rat's nose for trouble, so I never dealt with any kids in my old neighborhood. Most of the time it kept me out of trouble. When I got arrested, it didn't scare me. I was tough enough to whip any jailhouse punk in a straight-up fight.

"So what changed my mind? There were two people who get most of the credit. It was when I was doing my last stretch in the county jail that I met Frankie, the guy who helped me start this shelter. He told me about all the Vietnam veterans who were down and out after the war had blown their hopes to hell. It's funny, ain't it? The guy he talked to about starting a shelter was one of the few jailbirds in Baltimore who had enough drug profits stashed away to buy a place we could fix up. Frankie would have made something of himself, if life had given him a chance.

"What made me think about forgiveness? I guess it was when Frankie got killed in that carjacking in '79. When they brought his killer to trial, I didn't see some hulking thug who got off on killing people. I saw a scared little kid like I had once been. I didn't want to forgive him, but something kept whispering in my ear that it would eat me alive if I didn't. When I did, it got me started on my career as a counselor. I was able to take some college courses, and that gave me the book learning to go with my street smarts about helping guys in trouble.

"There was another person, this one a lady. Not a ho, broad, chick, fox, a *lady*. Her name was Diana Karras. She was married to Hector Karras, a guy I'd served with in Nam.

"When I talked to her, I asked her why a classy chick like her would get stuck with someone like Hector or me. She told me about her mother killing herself and her father being a self-centered bastard. I guess I don't understand why she should have had any sympathy for us. Nobody else did. I thought it was an act. What changed my mind? I guess it was one time I was in Doc Harvey's office when the symptoms of Parkinson's started showing up, and I saw a picture of her with Hector and her kids. He'd killed them in a bad flashback episode. My God, looking at the faces of those two dead kids day in and day out, I knew she was no phony.

"She told me the toughest job she'd ever had to do in her life was just getting through the average day. She knew she needed to forgive Hector, but she wasn't ready to, not yet. And she told me, 'Only the strong can forgive. The weak never try.'"

The recollection vanished in an instant, as if a cosmic power cord had been pulled.

Luke put his pen down. *Diana wasn't with me that night. I never told her about what Sonny said. Was I took shaken or just too gutless? I buried that memory so deep it took Sonny himself to help me dig it up.*

Taking pen in hand, he started writing in a leather-bound notebook. "My dearest Diana, there's something I've never told you."

———

TIMMY HAD GOTTEN a sunburn at the beach party. Katie gave him a butter rub-down to soothe the pain and put him to bed.

The dream of the crab attack came back that night. This time, instead of the crabs dragging Mommy into the sea, the strange man and woman blocked them, interposing their bodies. They put out their hands in a "stop" signal and spoke words in a strange language.

When the monster crab renewed his attack, they repulsed it in the same fashion, after which, the strangers walked away, leaving Mommy and the boy standing on the shore.

39

THREE AND A half years of treatment had depleted Katie's energies. Weariness undermined the active lifestyle she'd always enjoyed. The periodic bouts of depression were even more disturbing. Her family and friends, her lifejackets on the billows of life, still bore her up. She wondered, though, if the constant struggle hadn't increased the distance between them and her. Timmy was now enrolled at his Aunt Lisa's preschool. When invitations to birthday parties and cookouts arrived, Andy stepped in and played the role that should have been hers. Two unanswered questions that nagged her without respite: *When can I go back to being the wife Andy needs? When can I start being the mother Timmy needs?*

Andy's steadfastness, her tether to the world where life, work, play, and love went on as usual, was under attack from the economic challenges of a housing bust, financial crisis, and deep recession. The vitality of Lyle & Sons, unassailable during the first seven years of their marriage, was now under constant pressure. Dealing with canceled projects, the scramble for adequate financing, and layoffs among their workers meant that his nerves walked a fine line between control and meltdown. *I don't think Andy's slept more than four hours a night in the last year. I haven't either, but I'm accustomed to it. I just want to stop fighting and start living again.*

———

SINCE THE RESOLUTION of the Lupton case, Andy had kept his hands off the mail. Most days, he left mail chores to Mindy. But the Friday after the picnic at the beach, Mindy's boyfriend invited her to accompany him on a hiking trip in the North Carolina mountains. In her absence, Andy reverted to his old custom of going through the mail as soon as it arrived.

Near the end of his sorting chore, he picked up a vellum envelop. The printed return address read "Marilyn Niland Pilcher." It was addressed to his father.

He walked into Tom's office and handed him the letter. "Priority item, Dad."

Tom opened it and extracted a single sheet of paper. "Hmmm. This is interesting. I wonder, is it health problems or something else?"

"What are you talking about?"

"Jack Pilcher's law firm is breaking up. Jack's retiring at the end of the year."

"So?"

"I was never good at reading between the lines when it came to your mother, but this looks like an attempt to bury the hatchet." He handed the sheet to Andy. "What do you think?"

Andy read it. "Can a skunk lose his stripes?"

Tom shook his head, his lips compressed. "Why is it so hard for you to forgive your mother? If I can get over her treating me like a no-culture hick, why can't you let your grudges go?"

"I thought I had. It may take a while."

Tom sighed, leaning back in his rolling chair. He looked at the ceiling and said, "When Marilyn asks how Katie's doing, don't you think she's trying to change her ways?"

Andy shrugged. "Well, I've got to go check on our jobs in Orange Park." He left the office thinking, *Mom's just penitent because Dad's stopped sharing juicy tidbits with Phil McKenzie. What really bothers her is not being up on the latest gossip.*

———

KATIE SHIVERED, DRAWING her sweater more snugly around her. Once it had accentuated her lithe physique; now it hung loosely on her frame. She looked at her watch. *One-thirty. Timmy won't be back for another hour.* She fell asleep in her recliner.

She'd never been much of a dreamer until she started chemotherapy. When the dreams began, they seemed meaningless, processions of images disconnected from one another. In a discussion with Eric, she said, "God knows what Freud would make of my dreams, as disjointed as they seem."

The oncologist gave her one of his rare grins. "He'd probably tell you something like, 'Your id and your superego are fighting it out, while your ego is missing in action.' I think Freud was another Jew who never stopped looking for his Moses."

Recollections of that conversation put her mind at ease when she started to worry about dreams that made no sense. *They're probably due to chemical reactions caused by the drugs.*

The dream this afternoon was different. As it opened, she was in the living room of the house her family had occupied until 1984. The front door opened directly into the living room. As she lay on the floor watching *The Muppet Show*, there was a knock at the screen door.

"Mama? Daddy? Is that you?"

"*Nein, mein Schätzchen.*"

"Oma! Come watch TV with me."

Christina Thompson came in, pushing the walker that had been her constant companion for almost ten years. "Ket-tee, vere is your son?"

"I don't have a son, Oma. I'm only nine."

The old lady looked around in puzzlement. "Opa said your son would be with you. The time is coming."

"What time is coming?"

Just before Oma vanished, she said, "He will find you soon and put you on the right path."

"Oma, Oma, don't leave. Who are you talking about?"

She swam slowly into wakefulness, disoriented by what she'd just experienced. *This dream was coherent, but I still don't understand. Who is "he," and what is "the right path?"*

———

IN LATE SEPTEMBER, Katie went to St. Johns Oncology for a CAT scan. Eric had assured her that this was a routine check. He'd said, "Barring some unusual development, this is 'the new normal,' as they say. We just don't want to take any chances."

Katie still felt physically drained, but her appetite was returning. *That's a good sign.* When the CAT scan was completed, the imaging lab assured her they'd let her know the results by a phone call.

Three days later, she got a text message as she was driving home from the grocery store: "Katie please call me ASAP. Helen Ferguson (904) 996-5354." She pulled over to the side of the road and called Helen. After a brief conversation, she called Andy.

PART III
TRANSFIGURATION

The only way death is not meaningless is to see yourself as part of something greater: a family, a community, a society. If you don't, mortality is only a horror. But if you do, it is not.

- Atul Gawande, *Being Mortal*

40

IT WAS A bad sign when Eric ran late for an appointment.

The longer Katie waited, the more the dread welled inside her. When the delay reached forty-five minutes, Andy started fuming. "Does he have any idea of what it would cost me if I kept a customer waiting this long?"

Katie's heart-shaped face was placid, but her voice trembled slightly. "I think I know why he's late."

Before he could reply, the office door opened. Eric and Clark entered, murmuring quick apologies before they took seats facing the Lyles across the mahogany conference table.

Clark's presence was an unexpected, unwelcome surprise. Katie said, "Hello, Clark. It was kind of you to come all the way from Tampa."

His pate glistened beneath the fluorescent lights' chilly glow. He looked up from a red folder, his brow an array of deep furrows. Before he could speak, Eric said, "Clark just wants to be here to give you as much assurance as he can."

She looked at him and said, "Just tell us what you know, whatever it is."

With a swift nod, Clark said. "All right. The latest imaging shows new lesions on your kidneys. An additional round of chemotherapy *might* slow down the growth rate, but—"

"But not stop it." Katie spoke as calmly as if she'd been discussing repainting the house.

Eric nodded. "It's really bad. Remember that with all cancer therapies, we have to balance how well it works with the damage it does to your body. You're pretty weak from all the rounds you've done so far in dealing with the metastases to your liver."

She dabbed at her eyes. "How long do I have?"

Eric glanced at Clark, who said, "Predictions are nothing but speculation. Anything I tell you would be a guess."

"So give me your best guess."

"Six weeks, perhaps."

Her sigh was almost inaudible. "I'll be dead before Christmas."

Clark said nothing; the resigned look in his eyes was answer enough.

Andy jumped up, placing both hands on the desk. "You mean you're not going to even try any more chemo? What kind of answer is that?"

Katie placed a hand on her husband's taut forearm. "It's an honest answer, darling. It's the kind I want." Andy sat down, his lips taut.

Eric spoke up. "We don't think a cure is a realistic hope. We think it would be best to call in a hospice."

She nodded, looking at her husband with such transparent love that his lips, which seemed frozen in an expression of barely controlled anger, visibly relaxed. "Can we have a few minutes to talk about this?"

Both doctors nodded, rose, and silently left the room.

———

THE DOCTORS STROLLED down the hall to the staff lounge. Eric said, "You've really gone the extra mile to help Katie. Those long-distance conversations and the trips up from Tampa have to have taken a toll. We've been friends since medical school, and you know I'd do the same for you. Is there more to it than friendship?"

"It's a family debt."

"You mean Katie is related to you?"

Clark looked at the floor for a few seconds, and he slowly shook his head. "No, it's just that ever since Dad died, I've thought of him a lot, how he handled tough situations. There's not all that much difference sometimes between how generals think and how we doctors deal with crises. We can be pretty cold-blooded for our own protection." He pointed to an enameled lapel pin on his white coat, two crossed flags: stars and stripes and a solid red banner with two white stars. "I had a jeweler make this to remind me of Dad."

"I'm not following you."

"Katie's grandfather saved Dad's life." Seeing Eric's mouth drop open, he continued. "You went to Brian Thompson's funeral last year, right? He was Dad's company first sergeant at Bastogne back in 1944. He took a bullet meant for Dad."

Eric's dark blue eyes stared back through wire-rimmed glasses, like an accountant gazing at a column of figures that didn't quite add up. His eyes brightened and he said, "And your father always remembered that. That's odd. I saw Katie and Andy there, but I didn't catch on that you had any family tie."

"I'm tied by a promise. The last time I saw Dad, he reminded me of that debt. Even though Brian had died, Dad made it clear the obligation was still binding."

Helen came in to get a cup of coffee. Eric took her aside. "Mrs. Lyle's life expectancy is very short. I've recommended that we call in a hospice. Once I get her approval and her husband's consent, please make the necessary calls. I'll give you a referral letter."

She nodded and turned to go. In the silence that descended, her stiletto heels on the hardwood floor sounded like nails being driven into a board . . . or a coffin.

———

HELEN DIDN'T WAIT for permission. Upon her return to her office, she picked up the cell phone Diana had given her and dialed a number with a few flicks of her thumb.

"Lukas here," a monotone voice answered. "What's new?"

"There's a special referral on the way."

"Particulars?"

She took a deep breath. "It's a young woman. Melanoma, metastasized to the kidneys. Prognosis is terminal, a few weeks maximum."

"Who's the referring physician?"

"She's been under Eric's care for some time. Clark Burton has also been providing care."

"I see. How fast can you get me the paperwork? I'll need Dr. G's signature."

"Don't worry about a signature. It can be arranged. I'll fax it to you ASAP, an hour at most."

"Any more details I need to know?"

"She has a husband and a four-year-old son."

There was a long silence on the other end of the line. Finally, her interlocutor asked, "Do we need to take special precautions?"

"I think so. No one else needs to be involved except those we can trust."

"Understood. I'll have to bring Diana in on this."

"Of course. She knows the importance of discretion." With no further words, she hung up. She leaned back in her chair and put a hand over her eyes.

———

LUKE FROWNED AS he hung up. *This is what I missed. This is why I've battled the feeling of being too late. This is the reason for the dreams, the voices, everything that pointed me in this direction. There's no time for self-pity, Luke. The next time I see Brian Thompson, how can I explain that I failed in my mission to care for his granddaughter?*

He left his office and went to the reception desk. Anya, the Russian-born temp who handled calls and patient scheduling, asked, "Do you need something, Doctor?"

"Please hold my calls for a while. I have to work on a care plan for a patient."

"Yes, Doctor."

When he went back to his office, he turned his chair so it faced out the window. There had been rain last night, and a cold front had moved through, breaking the spell of summer heat. *A perfect day to go for a picnic or a golf outing, not to get a death sentence.*

The call from Helen was the first conversation the two had had since early July. Luke's concern over his failure and his repressed desire for her created an emotional whirlpool that threatened his ability to focus on Katie Lyle and her needs. Sooner or later, he'd have to bite the bullet and tell Helen the full truth.

He thought back to the beating. The two thugs who had assaulted him were willing to kill him. It looked as though, three years later, there would be another victim.

41

ON THE DRIVE home, Katie spent the time looking out the window. "Fall's always been my favorite time of the year. The ocean is so beautiful. I'll miss. . ." Her brave front cracked, and she broke into heaving sobs. "I'll miss you and Timmy most of all. I always had faith God would give Eric and Clark a cure. Now, I'm not sure what I believe." She looked at him with haunted eyes, as if she already saw things hidden from him.

Through gritted teeth, Andy said, "I have no faith in anything now. I don't have any hope either."

"I can't face our family or friends yet. I have no idea what I'll say to Daddy or Mama, let alone Timmy."

They drove on in silence, an unexpected death march toward the interstate exit for Fernandina Beach. When she saw the sign for Little Talbot State Park, she pointed to it with an unspoken question. They drove to the parking lot, got out of the car, and took the boardwalk across the dunes. Halting at a lookout on the seaward side, they gazed at the midday sun's rays throwing a thousand brilliant gems onto the rhythmic Atlantic waves. The salty air and cawing of gulls thrust a poignant dagger into Katie's soul, reminding her of her love of the sea.

"Remember how you asked me to marry you? It was right here as I recall."

His knotted features softened. "I'll always remember. Would you do it again?"

"In a heartbeat. Just one thing . . ." She halted as the tears welled in her eyes. "When you get lonely, just promise you'll bring Timmy here. Remind him his mommy always loves him."

Andy was undone. He took her in his arms as the tears on his face overflowed from a bottomless well of sorrow.

———

HE REGAINED HIS composure, and they headed home. Andy was still seething inwardly despite his best efforts at self-control. Through the course of her illness, he'd warred between trying to buck up her spirits and restraining his own worst fears. Through nearly four years of surgeries, radiation therapy, and regular trips to Burton's Tampa clinic for chemotherapy and immunotherapy, his love had sustained her, even when he wrestled against the demons of his family's continuing strife. The day's news had breached his last inner defenses.

She tried once or twice to start a conversation but gave up when Andy answered with the monosyllabic mutter he used when he wanted to say, "Please shut up."

He pulled into a playground about three-quarters of a mile from their house, parking well away from the monkey bars, slide, and seesaws where a throng of preschool children played under the vigilant eyes of their parents. He walked a short distance and sat down on a wrought iron bench, sitting with fists clenched and an unseeing stare, until Katie joined him.

"You want to talk?"

Her subdued voice cut through the static and white noise that fought for control in his mind. "Dirty sons of bitches!" he said, his voice rising.

She put a hand on his shoulder. "Darling, please don't shout. There are children right over there." She pointed toward a swing set sixty paces from where they sat. "Who's dirty? Why do you say that?"

"Eric and Clark. They *had* to have known. *Now*, they say there's nothing they can do."

She came to the edge of tears again. "Please, please, let's just go home. It hurts too much to talk about this in public." When he said nothing, she started crying.

Andy had never given free rein to his anger in such situations. For the first time in their marriage, her tears failed to divert him. He looked away from her and said, "When we saw them in June, everything was just fine. These guys are the experts in fighting cancer. I think they knew then that something was wrong, but were too proud to admit it. Maybe if they'd told us the straight truth then, we could've checked out some other treatments. But noooo, they just had to be the superheroes, and now it looks like our supermen have lost their ability to fly."

His last words dropped into a dry well of silence. When Katie spoke again, it was in a voice she seldom used with him, the authoritative speech of her school principal father. "Yes, you've got it all figured out, haven't you? Why don't you blame me? I should've known four years ago I had cancer. I was just waiting until I could play for everyone's sympathy."

He frowned at her. "Stop talking nonsense."

"I will if you will. Don't you think Eric and Clark feel bad about this? They're the ones who had to admit failure."

He sat back and looked directly into her eyes. His wrath subdued. He responded, "All right, so they've owned up to their failures. I'll concede that. A few sympathetic words, then it's, 'Let's talk about helping you die.' That's what it amounted to."

"What are they supposed to do? Try every longshot therapy they can find? Send me to Mexico or Thailand or wherever? Think about your grandfather. I don't want to die like that."

Andy bit his lip. "Big Daddy," Tom's father, had succumbed to lung cancer three months before he and Katie married. Images of the dying man, bedridden, fighting for every breath, tethered to a morphine drip in an Intensive Care Unit, flooded his memory. "Nobody wants that."

"That's what it's about," she said. "I want our time, the time I have with Timmy, with Mom and Dad, with our friends, to be as good as it can be." Her tears had stopped.

His knitted brow conveyed half-assent, half-skepticism. "I guess you're right. But I still can't help feeling that Eric and Clark have stopped looking at you as 'Katie Lyle,' and started looking at you as 'Cancer Patient A9695,' nothing more than an interesting source of observations."

Katie's face clouded, but she didn't cry. "So it's 'let's kill all the doctors,' right? I don't believe that. Maybe you ought to stop believing it too."

42

A placard with "St. Raphael Hospice" adorned the minivan parked in front of the Lyles' house. They'd called Lisa, asking her to keep Timmy until dinnertime, giving them a pause to digest the savage news. Andy muttered, "They sure didn't waste any time getting here."

An olive-skinned man, with a broken nose and several prominent facial scars, got out of the vehicle and walked up the driveway toward them. "Mr. and Mrs. Lyle?"

Katie said, "Yes. And who might you be?"

"Just call me Luke."

He held out his hand and she shook it, noticing that his breast pocket held a tag that read:

LUKAS VANGELIS M.D.
MEDICAL DIRECTOR
ST. RAPHAEL HOSPICE

She said, "Excuse me, you're not a hospice we're familiar with."

"We're new in this area, but we've been in the hospice business a long time." He handed her his card. "Please feel free to check our website. We have links to a number of professional references."

Katie looked into his eyes. At first glance, they seemed overcast, but when she looked back, they were as clear as an Arctic sky. His handshake was gentle, but she could feel the coiled strength beneath the surface. There was a reassurance in his voice that, even as her mind reeled from the morning's news, made her believe things might yet turn out right. "Would you like to come in?"

"I'd love to. I think I can be of some help."

When they went inside, Katie offered the doctor something to drink. While Andy fetched a glass of ice water, Luke took out a manila envelope labeled "Kathleen Lyle, referral from Dr. E. Grueneberg, St. Johns Oncology Associates." He handed her the envelope, saying, "Mrs. Lyle, the materials in here should answer most of your questions. While you're under our care, our people will give you any information you ask for. Let me assure you, first, that we understand your feelings."

Andy, who walked in just then, broke in with, "Oh really? And what do *you* think about all this? Can you give us something Katie's other doctors can't give?"

Luke looked briefly at the ceiling. "I think so. Let's review what we know already. Your wife's been under the care of Dr. Grueneberg for what, three years?"

"Four years," Katie said. "I've also gotten treatment from -"

Luke gently interrupted. "We already know about your treatment. You've seen Dr. Burton at Hillsborough Oncology in Tampa." He gave her a smile.

"Your information is very complete."

"Have you seen any other doctors?"

"Dr. Joe Francis is our family physician. Dr. Bruce Morton was the one who diagnosed me with melanoma and referred me to Dr. Ted Moore, who did the initial surgery."

Andy chimed in with, "What's the purpose of this game of 'Twenty Questions?' Can you do something for Katie the others can't do?"

"We can help her to a better life."

"Right. All six weeks of it."

Luke turned to Katie. "What do you want?"

"I want to live, *really live*, as long as I can."

"That's what I'm here to discuss, Mr. Lyle," Luke said, looking straight at Andy. "All of Katie's doctors are perfectionists, trying to bring perfection to a very imperfect world. Death doesn't fit into that view of things."

"Should it?" he retorted.

"It comes around for all of us. Our hospice operates on the premise that we can help patients live full lives until they die."

In the moment of silence that followed, Luke gave both husband and wife a look that signaled, "The ball's in your court." Katie didn't speak but responded with an inquisitive gaze.

Andy, unmollified, stalked off to the kitchen. Katie's face flushed with apparent embarrassment. She started to speak.

Luke held up a hand. "It's all right. What your husband is feeling now is a foretaste of what's coming. We're here to make it as easy as possible on you, on your whole family."

"So there's no hope."

"I think you'll see that there's always hope. It depends on what you hope for. Then, we can know where to find it."

For the first time that day, Katie smiled. "I'm willing to give it a try."

LUKE ASKED ANDY to walk with him back to the van. Andy's skeptical stance hadn't changed. "I don't think it was very professional of you to disparage my wife's doctors. They've spent a lot of time with us, doing their best to keep her alive. If that's the kind of person you are, maybe we need to call someone else."

Decades of experience had given Luke an ability to read the emotional states, not only of his patients but their families as well. "Mr. Lyle, I understand you're upset. That's all right. You can be as angry as you wish. I've seen it many times before." He sensed the significance of Andy's emotional shift to defending Eric and Clark. *I've got to gain his confidence.* "I wasn't disparaging anyone. I'm sorry I gave you that impression. Eric Grueneberg and Clark Burton are two of the finest doctors I know, and I've known thousands in the course of my career. But they're in the wrong business for your wife."

"What the hell do you mean by that?"

"Their business is to cure. Mine is to heal."

"That's just wordplay. It's the same thing."

Luke gave him a bleak smile. "I assure you, it's not just semantics. I think your wife understands that. You will too, in time."

Andy's scowl vanished. He took a deep breath and said, with a voice on the edge of choking, "She's been through so much already. God, she's only thirty-five. I just can't deal with the thought of being without her. Our son, Timmy, thinks the sun rises and sets on her. How can I explain to a little boy that his mommy is going on a long trip, and he can't go along?"

The doctor's eyes conveyed the calmness of a summer lake, undisturbed by wind or tide, radiating a quiet comfort. "It won't be easy, Andy. There will be lots of pain, for Katie and for you. As for Timmy, let me help him. I lost my mother when I was just a boy. I know how he'll react."

Andy's shoulders sagged. "How can you help him?"

"The main difference between 'curing' and 'healing' is that healing always comes with self-knowledge, with understanding, with a peace that medicine alone can't give. Before Katie leaves us, I promise you Timmy will have more wisdom than most seventy-year-olds I know. At least let me give it a try."

Andy held out a reluctant hand. Luke shook it, got into the van, and drove away.

———

WHEN ANDY RETURNED to the house, Katie asked, "Did you notice anything odd about Dr. Vangelis?"

"Other than the fact that he spoke with an accent, no."

"He was wearing a pretty expensive watch, maybe a Rolex."

"So, he's got expensive tastes."

"It's got some kind of gemstones around the face, but the funny thing was, it didn't look like the hands were moving at all."

"Well, even doctors can get absent-minded. He needs to get it repaired." He squeezed her hand, as if his touch might somehow make the old Katie return.

43

LUKE RETURNED THE next day, accompanied by a registered nurse whom he introduced as "Mrs. Karras," a cousin. She did most of the talking, explaining how the hospice's services would include daily monitoring of Katie's condition. Luke observed the back-and-forth between the nurse and the two Lyles, interjecting an occasional comment, mostly in response to questions about what to expect as the cancer progressed.

When the discussion wound down, Luke looked at Katie. "Do you have any more questions, Mrs. Lyle?"

Her smile was sad. "Nothing right now, but let's get something straight between us. We don't have a relationship, and we aren't going to have one unless you start calling me Katie, not 'Mrs. Lyle.' It makes me feel like I'm Andy's grandmother."

"All right, Katie. Since we're going to be on a first-name basis, meet Diana, my number-one nurse. She'll be the one who monitors your day-to-day care, handles prescriptions for pain medications, any blood transfusions you need, and the like."

Andy shot him a quizzical look. "So what's your role in all this?"

"I'm your guide. I'll answer any major questions you have, and I'll stay with you every step of the way."

"Well, I guess I have no choice but to trust you, Luke," Katie said.

"No, you have a choice. You can choose to give up."

"You mean, like suicide?" Her eyes flashed an alarm.

Luke shook his head. "No, you're not the suicidal type. I've been watching you and listening to you. You're not a quitter either. What I mean by giving up is to cut yourself off from everything you love."

"So where are we now?"

"On the same road. When can I have a chance to talk with Timmy?"

Andy frowned. "He's our son. We'll tell him ourselves."

Luke raised an eyebrow at this declaration but stayed silent.

———

ERIC HAD MENTALLY filed Katie's case under "Terminal" during the weekend. As he drove to his office on Monday morning, the ping of a text message sounded on his cell phone. He pulled onto the shoulder to check it out.

It was from Katie Lyle. "Dr G: Thanks so much for the hospice referral. Those folks you sent to us are terrific."

He texted back, "You're welcome," mildly vexed that he couldn't remember sending a referral to any specific hospice.

Eric entered the offices of St. Johns Oncology Associates, stopping at Helen's cubicle. He asked her, "Did we send out a hospice referral for Kathryn Lyle?"

"I called North Coast Hospice in Fernandina Beach. The referral letter is still with Ms. Lyle's chart in your inbox."

He went to his office and retrieved the Lyle folder. He found the referral letter, signed it, and placed it in an envelope for pick-up later. To his vexation, he couldn't remember the phone number. To make sure the hospice could accommodate Katie, he went to Helen's office and asked her for the number. She took a cell phone from a docking station on her desk, punched a few keys and handed him the phone.

"North Coast Hospice. How may I direct your call?"

"Admissions, please."

"Just a moment."

He drummed his fingers on the desk while listening to entirely too much of Barry Manilow singing "Mandy." After a minute and a half, a husky female voice came on the line.

"Admissions Office, this is Diana."

"This is Dr. Grueneberg with St. Johns Oncology Associates. I'll be sending you a written referral for Kathleen Lyle. She has Stage IV melanoma, and I want to get her into palliative care ASAP."

"We'll have our courier stop at your office and pick up the letter if that's all right with you."

"That's a lot of trouble, isn't it?"

"Not at all. He's making pickups on the Southside this morning. I'll have him stop by."

No sooner was Eric back in his office than he slapped his forehead. *Wait a second. Katie's message said the hospice had already contacted her. What gives?*

Before he could call Katie to resolve the matter, his cell phone sounded the signal for an "Urgent" call. It was the Emergency Department at Riverside Hospital: an elderly patient with lung cancer had just been brought in, coughing up blood. The imminent unplanned visit to Riverside drove thoughts of Katie Lyle out of his head.

————

AFTER DIANA HUNG up, she told Luke, "Dr. Grueneberg says the North Coast Hospice referral letter will be waiting at the office."

"Is it safe for me to pick it up myself?"

"I don't know. Let me call Helen."

She placed a quick call, exchanged a few words with Helen, and hung up. "The coast is clear. Dr. G's got an emergency and is out of the office."

Luke nodded, a mischievous glimmer in his eye. "Sometimes, playing courier is fun. I'll head over there in a few minutes. We need a little more time with Katie before Grueneberg and Burton come back into the picture."

———

WHEN LUKE MET the Lyles after Eric's referral, he recognized them from the picnic a few weeks earlier. It was a relief when they showed no signs of having seen him before. It might have brought up some complications that would've gotten in the way of winning their trust.

Likewise, Diana remembered the earlier meeting. She'd glanced at Luke and read the message in his eyes: Don't say anything.

On the way back to the office, she asked, "Is Andy the one you need to groom to follow you?"

"No, the Lyles' son is. Remember how he got scared when he saw us at the cookout?"

"Now that you mention it, I do."

"I felt a jolt at that instant, sort of like a reaction to hearing a familiar tune in an unexpected setting, or like a sudden moment of warmth on a winter day."

Diana hadn't felt anything similar. Feeling a little bit vexed, she said, "You didn't say anything at the time, as I recall."

"I wasn't sure then. Now I am. Do you remember the first time you had a vision of Smyrna?"

"Yes. That was-"

"Back in the spring of 2004, before the D-Day veterans' dinner."

"What does that have to do with the Lyle boy?"

Luke paused. *Do I tell her now? Yes. This is the moment.* "I had a vision later that night. This one involved Nate and me after we settled in Boston." He briefly recounted the religious school and the Biblical citation on the blackboard.

Diana's ears perked up. "You haven't said much about Boston in recent years. Why now?"

"It wasn't until the day I saw Timmy that I got a jolt, sort of a reminder."

By the time they reached St. Raphael, it was after six, and the parking lot was deserted. Luke unlocked the front door and beckoned her inside.

In his office, he took a Bible from inside a locked bookcase and told her to read Isaiah 11:6-9. As the rich prophetic words rolled forth, he smiled. She finished and closed the book. "So, seeing Timmy at the beach made a connection with what happened in Boston eighty years ago."

"Correct. That's when I knew he would be the one."

She nodded. "Sounds like a bit of female intuition."

"Since the gift came from Mama, I think you're right."

———

WHEN DIANA GOT back to her condo, she poured a glass of wine and took it to the den, hoping to catch the last few minutes of PBS Newshour. As soon as she got into the broadcast, she muted it. It was yet another group of talking heads, discussing what commentators called "Obamacare" and its prospects for making it through Congress. *Politics! Why can't people just focus on solving problems instead of taking credit or laying blame for things?*

As she sipped the wine, watching the silenced news program, she heard Eleni. Her grandmother's voice seemed to come from behind the television. "My dear grandchild, you are almost ready. Only one thing is lacking."

"I don't understand, Grandmama. Have I been unfaithful to my pledge?"

"No, your life has done me honor. You have always served others. What is not done yet is the hardest thing."

"What's that?"

"Take the ribbons off the portraits. That is all I ask."

Diana's fists clenched, causing her to spill wine on the hardwood floor. Against her will, she turned her head toward a bookshelf, which held two family portraits. One was made a few months before her father's demise: Hector, holding Athena on his lap, Andrew standing in front of them with Diana's hands on his shoulders. Hector's face was blocked by a piece of dark ribbon securely taped to the glass in the picture frame. *Why is it hard to breathe? Does Grandmama know what she's asking?*

The other was much older. It was made the year she graduated high school and showed Nate, Nikki, and her, looking for all the world like the average American happy family. Another piece of ribbon blocked out her father's face.

"My child, you've said nothing. Why so silent?"

Diana closed her eyes. "It's so hard, Grandmama. You sacrificed yourself for others. I can understand that. I would do it myself. But how can I forgive *him*, after what he did? Every time I try, I think of Athena and Andrew, what terror they must have known in the last minutes of their lives."

"You're wrong. They died without fear. Hector made certain they were sound asleep before he smothered them."

Her shoulders sagged, as if a heavy load had suddenly fallen on them. The crumbling of her rationalization left her with only one line of defense. "Could I have stopped them if I'd been at home that night?"

In a voice weighted down with what sounded like a bottomless sadness, Eleni said, "No, child. You would have died first and that would have frightened your children in the worst way. It was not your time to die."

"And Father. How can I forgive him for how he treated Mother?"

"You have to do it, to save yourself."

In the silence that followed this declaration, Diana wept. She cried for many things: for her dead children, for the parents who'd let her down, for her years of loneliness and misery. When her tears stopped, she stood up and walked to the bookshelf. She kissed the faces of her son and daughter. As the last drops of fury flowed out of her, she ripped the ribbons off both picture frames and carried them to the trash can.

When she returned to the den, she asked, "Is that enough, Grandmama?"

There was no answer, only a slight breath of wind that felt like a kiss on her forehead.

44

THE LYLES' NORMAL weekend routine included taking Timmy to visit one of his sets of grandparents. Instead, this weekend, Katie asked Art and Bonnie to come to lunch.

"Where's Timmy?" Her mother asked when she walked in, apparently nonplussed by the absence of her grandson's usual enthusiastic greeting.

"He had a field trip to the zoo with Aunt Lisa and some of her other students," Katie replied.

Her voice was calm. Looking at her father, Katie could see he wasn't taken in. He asked, "Will he be back soon?"

"Yes, Daddy. We aren't trying to keep him away from you."

Andy said, "Let's go out to the deck and relax a while. Art, how 'bout a beer? And what do you want, Bonnie?"

When everyone was comfortably situated, Art asked, "What is it you want to tell us? That's why Timmy isn't here, isn't it?"

Katie looked down at the deck, then looked up and scanned the yard, as if trying to make certain no one was eavesdropping. "Dr. Grueneberg has referred me to a hospice. The cancer's gotten into the kidneys. He and Dr. Burton don't see any way of stopping it."

Art's features sagged. He came to her, lifting her out of her chair as he'd once lifted his eldest daughter out of her high chair, and gave her a hug. "Are they certain?"

Katie nodded, her face taut from her efforts at self-control.

Bonnie stumbled to her daughter's side. She dropped to her knees and took out her rosary, clutching the crucifix as she began the ancient words of the *Credo*, followed by a succession of *Ave Marias* and *Paternosters*. Katie extended a hand, stroking her mother's hair, wordlessly offering whatever comfort she could give.

Andy, born-and-bred Baptist though he was, knelt next to Bonnie, enveloping her hunched shoulders in a strong, gentle arm as she assailed the gates of Heaven with her prayers. Katie and Art knelt next to them, completing the circle of sorrowful love.

When Bonnie's prayers ended, they all rose, Art grimacing at the pain in his arthritic knees. "Do you trust your doctors?" he asked.

"They've been honest with me. They're not holding anything back."

"As many new drugs as they've come out with lately, there *must* be something, somewhere that can stop this or slow it down."

"Even if there is, can we afford it?"

"To hell with the cost. If insurance won't pay for it, I'll shake every damned money tree I can find."

Bonnie nodded. "Whatever we have is yours. What good is money to us if we can't keep you?"

Katie didn't answer, but Andy said, "We need your prayers, Mom Bonnie. If you're on a first-name basis with any saints, please give 'em a call."

Bonnie tried to answer but couldn't speak.

Katie saw the pain on her mother's face and kissed her. As Bonnie choked back a sob, Art said, "I'm going to see what I can dig up on therapies. There may be something your doctors haven't uncovered yet."

Katie gave a gentle laugh. "It's worth the old college try, Daddy. Let's go have lunch and get ourselves in shape for Timmy. He'll be back around two o'clock."

45

WE'RE ONLY A *few days into this latest crisis, and I'm already scared shitless.* Andy almost voiced this thought as he and Katie watched "The Late Show." They held hands, sitting in silence.

A sudden cry from Timmy's room riveted their attention. Katie got up. "Stay here," she said. "He's probably having a bad dream."

Andy relaxed and tried, unsuccessfully, to follow David Letterman's chit-chat with a young British actress whose sexually adventurous videos with her boyfriend had become a YouTube sensation. His thoughts circled back to one thing: *My life is about to end. With Katie gone, how can I be the father Timmy needs? How can I concentrate on my work or do anything that gives me pleasure?*

He'd gotten over his initial rage at Katie's doctors, trying to put himself in their shoes. Every effort ended in puzzled frustration. *I don't really know much about Grueneberg and Burton, except they came highly recommended by Katie's other doctors. But what makes them tick? What if they're wrong? Will they admit it?*

"He's gone back to sleep." Katie's words momentarily derailed his train of thought.

Where was I? Oh, yes, what makes them tick? "How much do you know about Grueneberg and Burton?" he asked. "I mean, I know all about their credentials and professional achievements, but who are they?"

Katie snickered. "Typical man, trying to hack his way through an emotional thicket using only the left half of his brain. Will knowing more about them make either of us feel better?"

"It might make me less suspicious."

"I don't understand *why* you're suspicious. You think they're playing a game with us?"

"I never said that."

"You didn't have to. You were suspicious of Vangelis too, as I recall. Maybe the problem is Andy Lyle's built-in distrust of people." She took his hand and gave it a gentle squeeze.

"Well, it would make me feel better if I knew more about them."

"We haven't had the opportunity for much small talk, but I know Grueneberg's father was Jewish, his mother Catholic. They survived the Holocaust and World War II, came to this country with nothing, and became quite successful in the business of importing luxury goods."

He smiled at her. "That helps a little. What about Burton?"

"His father was a general. He had a brother killed in Vietnam. He told me his mother died when he was in college, and I think it was from cancer. He's divorced, and some things he's said suggest he's worried about his relationships with his kids."

"What that says is they're typical doctors, high achievers. Sometimes high achievers aren't so hot on their people skills."

She nodded and was about to say something when her face scrunched into a grimace. She gave a soft, "Ohhhh."

"What's wrong?"

"Nothing. It just hurts a little."

He didn't wait for instructions. He rose and went at once to the master bedroom, returning with a pillbox and a glass of water. She swallowed two tablets, drank the water, and leaned back. She closed her eyes and took a series of shallow breaths.

"Babe, are you all right?" Andy's alarm bells were ringing at maximum volume. "Can I get you something else?"

She shook her head. Tears rolled down her cheeks. She cried silently for a few minutes while Andy rubbed her neck and shoulders. "Thank you, darling. I'm sorry to be a bother."

"Where does it hurt?"

"My back, mostly, and a little in my belly."

"Sit up. Just lean a little forward."

She complied, and he began massaging her back with his powerful fingers. He kept this up for a short time then moved his hands to her abdomen. When she started drawing deep breaths, he exhaled a sigh of relief.

Katie opened her eyes. She leaned forward and kissed him. "It's all better now."

Andy's mouth wrinkled. "I'll massage you until my hands are raw if it makes you feel any better. I'll do it for as long as I have to if it helps you deal with the pain."

"You won't have to. It can't last much longer." She looked at him and saw that his lips were quivering. "My poor sweetheart, don't cry. It isn't as bad as you think."

"You don't need to put up a front for me. If you can take it, so can I."

Her eyes radiated peace at him. "It's not great, but it's as good as it can be. Eric and Clark did what they could. Now, we've got Luke and Diana to look after us."

He picked her up and carried her to bed.

———

IT TOOK ANDY a long time to fall asleep. When he began snoring, Katie got up, disarmed the alarm system, and went outside. An October breeze brought on an involuntary shiver, causing her to draw her bathrobe closer around her frame.

Six weeks. No, less than six weeks. I know my doctors well enough to know when they're putting up a front. The fears she fought down in the warmth of an autumn sun came out to play at night. *I've lived with this nightmare for four years, but I've kept it in the back of my mind. Now it's right in front of me. And it's not just the fear. I hurt too much to sleep.*

She had a bottle of high-powered painkillers with her. Slipping back into the kitchen as quietly as possible, she drew a glass of water, and shook out two of the pills, whose soft pink patina suggested a benign nature at odds with their potency. *Diana Karras said NEVER to take more than two of these every four hours.* The nurse's warning had been blunt: The prescription medication subdued the ache in her back and gut. Even a slight overdose, however, could lead to accelerated shutdown of her liver and kidneys.

Katie turned off the floodlights and stretched out on a chaise longue upwind from the grill where Andy prepared his signature dish: baby back ribs. Memories of the mingled aromas of charcoal smoke and barbecue sauce, and the sound of Andy whistling "Orange and Blue" while he was grilling, taunted her in the darkness. She began to cry, tears that formed a prayer rising into the night, toward the uncaring constellations. *God, can You hear me? Are You listening? Are You even there?* No answer came. The barking of a neighbor's dog broke the silence, a sound almost joyous, as though it had stumbled on a hitherto undiscovered rabbit warren.

Is it better to be human? That dog's going to die too, but it's not worried, not in the least.

Prior to starting chemotherapy, Katie had taught science to high school students. She wondered about everything she'd ever learned. *Is it really better to know just how little time I have left? It's only going to get worse.* She slipped her left hand into a bathrobe pocket and fondled the bottle of painkillers, rubbing it with the soft touch she used in the darkness to let Andy know she wanted him.

Where did it come from? Of all my close relatives, only Opa died from cancer. She looked up again. *Is this Your doing? Dude, You out there, whatever Your name is, is this Your kind of trick? You told Your own son He had to die, at least that's what I've always believed. Why should it bother You to bump off a few humans for an evening's amusement?*

Once again, there was no answer. Katie recalled something she'd read in college, the writings of a doctor who talked about what he called "the genetic tape." His idea was that our lifespan, the diseases that could kill us, even the possible hour of death, were all fixed during pregnancy, perhaps even as far back as the moment of fertilization. She wrestled with the idea that, on a night in the heart of 1973, a routine act of love between her parents had started a clock that was now ticking down through its final hours to the moment it would stop forever.

If that's so, can I hate Mom and Dad for what they did? The savage implications of something she'd read fifteen years earlier stopped these morbid speculations cold.

When she started back to bed, she realized she'd locked the back door after her first trip inside. Her keys hung on the keyboard by the garage door. *I don't want to wake Andy.* With a sigh that sounded something like the final breaths of a dying soul, she settled back onto the chaise longue and fell asleep.

46

ANDY, KATIE, LUKE, and Diana drove home from the Georgia-Florida game in fine spirits. The Lyles had sold their season tickets to the Gator games when they got Katie's terminal diagnosis. When Luke heard Katie express her admiration for Tim Tebow, he obtained four seats on the forty-yard-line from a source he called "my friends at the top."

"What's going to happen to the Gators next season?" Katie asked.

Luke showed no surprise, as if every person with a month to live talked casually about football games she would never see. "I'd say they'll do better than Tebow will. Every defensive back in the NFL will be gunning for him next season."

Andy laughed. "How can I tell Timmy he was conceived after watching the Gators stomp the shit out of South Carolina five years ago?"

Katie's smile faltered when she heard her son's name. Luke, at the wheel, saw her expression in the rearview mirror. He asked, "Have you talked with him yet?" The silence from the back seat gave him the answer. "Would you like me to sit down with him?" His voice was even softer than usual.

The Lyles looked at each other. Andy said, "I guess we can let you try."

———

TWO DAYS LATER, Diana took Andy and Katie to North Coast Medical Supply to get Katie an infusion pump that would dispense pain medication at the touch of a button. Luke stayed with Timmy.

A slow, sullen autumn rain thwarted Luke's plan to take Timmy into the backyard. After a few minutes of coaxing, the boy sat next to Luke on the sofa.

"Timmy, do you know why your mother is sad?"

"She cries a lot at night. She thinks I don't hear."

"She's sad because she's going to leave you soon. She's going to take a long, long trip."

"Is she going to heaven?"

The boy's directness stunned Luke. He sat back. When he looked into Timmy's eyes, he saw curiosity but nothing that looked like fear or sorrow. "Do you know where heaven is?"

"I know Mommy's Opa is there. He went there last year."

"It doesn't matter what you call it. Mommy will always be close to you but in a different way soon."

"Why? Does she have to go away because she did something wrong?"

"What makes you say that?"

"Herbie's daddy's in prison. Herbie says he can't come home."

"Who's Herbie?"

"A friend from Aunt Lisa's school."

"Do you know why Herbie's daddy can't come home?"

"Mommy said he killed somebody. Did Mommy kill somebody? Is that why she has to go away?"

Luke didn't answer at first. When he brushed back the hair from Timmy's forehead, he noticed the boy struggling with tears. "No, Timmy, Mommy didn't kill anyone. Mommy is very sick."

"You're a doctor. Can't you make her better?"

"Yes, I can. But Mommy has to come with me, and that means she's got to leave you and Daddy. Nobody did anything bad. Sometimes bad things happen, and it's nobody's fault. Do you believe me?"

"No."

The doctor put a hand on the boy's shoulder. "That's all right. I understand. Someday you'll understand too."

"When is she coming back?"

Luke had to turn away for a few seconds. *I should've seen that coming.* "She won't come back. But someday she'll call you, and you'll go to see her, and then you'll never be apart ever again."

"Can I go with her?"

Best to confront this now. "Mommy hurts a lot, Timmy. She doesn't want you to hurt like she does. If you were to go with her, you'd have to leave Daddy and your friends."

"Do you live in heaven?"

"I live here, Timmy. I go to lots of places, but I'll never be far away from you. I'll be here when you need me."

The youngster gazed up at Luke with a look that seemed to the doctor a mingling of sadness and wonderment. The rain had stopped, and the sun's rays were breaking through. "Timmy, would you like to go for a walk?"

"Where to?"

"Just a few blocks away. We can talk over an ice cream sundae."

———

"HOLD MY HAND, Dr. Luke. Mommy always makes me hold her hand when we go walking."

Luke enveloped Timmy's pudgy hand in his own. "Mommy does that because she loves you and wants the best for you. You know that, don't you?"

"Yep. She never says mean things to me or Daddy. Dr. Luke, why does Daddy not like Gran Marilyn?"

Another minefield or perhaps another skeleton in the family closet. "Timmy, people sometimes have trouble telling other people they love them. I had a brother like that."

"You didn't like him?"

"I didn't understand him. Because our daddy had to bring us up after my mommy died, I was afraid he loved my brother more than me."

"I wish I had a brother. I'd never be mean to him."

"You're very wise. Sometimes I'd give anything just to have my brother back with me."

"If I love Mommy enough, can I keep her?"

Don't let him see the look on your face. "Love is the greatest power there is, Timmy. It isn't always enough, but that doesn't mean we should ever stop loving."

———

ANDY, KATIE, AND Diana found Luke's note explaining his and Timmy's whereabouts. Katie looked at Diana and asked, "Is this good news or bad news?"

"When Luke talks to children, he always winds up with an ice cream sundae or a burger. It's a good sign. They'll be back soon."

Katie picked up the orange and blue tote she'd bought to hold her infusion pump. "I think I need an ice cream sundae myself."

Andy said, "I'll get the car."

Her eyes flashed scorn. "Big strong man's got to drive everywhere he goes, right? I'll see you at the Double Dipper. Right now, I feel like walking."

———

TIMMY'S EYES LIT up when his parents walked into the ice cream parlor, but he didn't get up and run to her as he usually did when she came home. With a puzzled look on her face, she sat down beside him. He looked at the tote. "Is that where you keep your medicine, Mommy?"

"Why, Timothy James Lyle, whatever gave you that idea?"

The boy looked at Luke and turned back to her. "Dr. Luke told me the medicine's what makes you not hurt so much."

Katie shot a questioning look at the doctor. He nodded in silent response. She took her son's hand. "The pain is why Mommy cries sometimes. I don't want you and Daddy to worry about me. Do you remember when you got sick last winter, how that icky medicine you had to take made you feel better?"

"Yes, Mommy."

"It's the same thing. Even grownups have to take their medicine."

Luke winked at Timmy. "Doctors do too."

The boy gave Luke a puzzled look. "Do doctors get sick too?"

Luke's eyes glowed with a warmth that reached out to the boy. "Yes, we get sick sometimes. Everybody does. We're all human, Timmy. Do you know what that means?"

Timmy shook his head.

"When you were born, the body your parents gave you will last for a long time but not forever. We all have pain."

"Mommy says pain is something is bad."

"She's right, most of the time. Some pain is good. As you grow up, you'll have times when it becomes something different, and that may hurt, but it's not bad. But what Mommy is living with is what we call 'suffering.' It's the bad kind of pain. That's why there are doctors. We all want to stop suffering."

Timmy looked at him with inquisitive sorrow, the kind of look that made Luke wish he hadn't chosen to study medicine. "Why can't you help Mommy?"

"Mommy hurts because doctors don't have a way to stop every kind of sickness. Doctors don't like to admit it. We think we can do anything, but we can't. That's what I meant by doctors taking our own medicine."

Katie put a hand on the back of Timmy's head. "Dr. Luke and Nurse Diana make Mommy hurt less. That's how I know they love me."

Luke bowed his head. "But doctors can hate too. Sometimes that's good, and sometimes it isn't."

"Hate is bad. That's what they taught me in Sunday school."

"Yes, that's right, when you hate somebody. A bad man killed my mommy when I was your age, and I hated him for a long time. I only stopped when I learned it didn't hurt him, it only hurt me. But it's good to hate things like suffering from sickness. I'll never stop hating the things that are making your mommy sick."

Katie embraced her son. "And Mommy will never stop loving you, no matter how much it hurts me."

47

ANDY'S PARENTS CAME over when they returned from a trip, entering via the garage door on which was posted a sign: "QUIET PLEASE. THERE'S A SLEEPING CHILD IN THIS HOUSE."

Andy ushered them to the deck, stopping by the fridge to get his father a beer and his stepmother a bourbon and Diet Pepsi.

"Where's Katie?" Tom asked. He exuded the take-charge aura of a man built for success, a prime specimen of American manhood who still moved with the grace of the All-SEC cornerback he'd been in his college days. "Is something wrong between you?"

"I can answer that," Katie said, slipping silently through the door from the kitchen. "There's nothing wrong with us, Big Tom. It's all about me."

"What do you mean?"

"It's the cancer. I'm dying. My oncologist gives me maybe a month or five weeks."

"When did you find this out?" Ginny's voice cut through the background noises – children at play, lawnmowers and Weed-Whackers at work, dogs romping through a nearby wood – like the slice of a dull razor.

"Last week. I'm under the care of a hospice now."

Tom reached out and took Katie's hand. "You should've called us as soon as you knew." He gave her a querulous look. "Is this the same oncologist who told you things were hunky-dory back in June?"

"Yes. But the cancer's showed up in places that chemo can't reach without running the risk of killing me."

Throughout Tom's career, he'd cultivated the skill of quick decision-making. "Here's what we'll do. You need to see another doctor. Tell you what, I've got a classmate who's a former head of the Tennessee Doctors' Guild. Let me give him a call and see what he recommends."

"You ought to sue the living daylights out of that oncologist," was Ginny's contribution to the discussion. "Where did he get his degree from, a Cracker Jack box?"

"What good would that do, Mama Ginny? If he's right, if he's anywhere close to being right, I'll be gone before we even get to court."

"Somebody has to pay for this."

Katie shot a glance at her husband then said, "I've already paid. I've been paying for four long years."

Ginny stood up, her eyes blazing, a Brünnhilde returned from Valhalla. "Do you know how much it's cost my husband's company, all the money we've paid to some damned quack?"

"Eric Grueneberg is no quack. He's got a degree from Johns Hopkins, and he's been treating cancer patients for over twenty years."

Andy started to edge his way into the conversation. Tom beat him to the punch. "What Ginny's saying is, 'Why give up now?' As long as there's life, there's hope. This guy, Grueneberg, is ready to run up the white flag."

"It's not running up the white flag to say I'm tired. I remember what your father went through in his last few months. Andy and I don't want that."

Ginny plowed ahead, undeterred. "You've got to fight to stay alive. If that doctor's not doing his job, he ought to get sued right out of business."

Katie bounded out of her chair. "I don't think this conversation is going anywhere."

"Mommy, I can't sleep." At the sound of a childish voice, all four adults looked at Timmy, who'd just emerged from the kitchen. "Why are you and Gran Ginny shouting?"

Tom picked up his grandson. "We're sorry, Tim-Tim. We were just talking grownup. Will you go back to sleep if I take you upstairs?"

"I'll try, Big Tom." The two of them went into the house.

Andy and Katie glared at Ginny. After a tense pause, Katie said, "I think we all need to take a chill pill. It's bad enough for us to argue about this, but we don't need to drag a four-year-old boy into our disagreements. I'm okay with that. Are you?"

Ginny pursed her lips. "All right. Let's talk about something pleasant."

The conversation shifted to small talk about church events and sports.

———

LESS THAN A week after the confrontation at Andy and Katie's house, the phone rang in Tom Lyle's office. "Tom Lyle here. What can I do for you?"

"Is something wrong?"

Tom recognized the voice in an instant. *Marilyn*. He struggled for a reply.

"Tom, are you there?"

"Yeah, I'm here, Marilyn. To what do I owe this pleasure?"

"Sarcasm was never one of your gifts. I called because I heard some bad news."

"What do you mean bad news?"

"How is Katie doing?"

"Who said anything about her?"

"Audrey McKenzie called me and told me someone had placed Katie Lyle on the prayer list for the senior women's Bible study group."

Tom saw no way to be diplomatic. "Yes, Katie's in pretty bad condition. Why do you ask?"

"Are her doctors any good?"

"Well, we don't know 'em personally, but they've gotten good ratings from the online sources I checked out."

"Well, Audrey told me that a friend of hers went to some Dr. Grueneberg for cancer treatment and couldn't stand him. She said he came across like a big-city doctor, always seemed to be putting her down. She said Dr. Grueneberg was Katie's doctor."

"I don't know him personally. I don't see how criticizing him does any good now."

"Jack and I want to come down and talk to Andy and Katie. Jack thinks he can find grounds for a malpractice lawsuit."

Tom bit his tongue to keep from saying something personal and nasty. As he debated what, if anything, to say, she spoke up. "All right, I know you don't like him, but this is important enough to put aside personal likes and dislikes. We're coming, unless you tell us we're not welcome."

Tom gave a defeated sigh. "All right. I'll try to smooth things out with Andy."

———

TOM WAS WAITING in Andy and Katie's living room when the doorbell rang. He opened the door to see Marilyn and Jack, dressed as if they were going to a performance of the symphony. Memories of past set-tos occasioned by his ex-wife's disdain of his down-to-earth dress and manner. *Put a cork in it, Tom. At least I got Ginny out of the house. But I don't have any idea how Andy will react.*

"I should tell you that Andy doesn't want to talk to you," he said. "I've persuaded him to be civil, at least. Please watch your step."

Jack looked as though he were searching for a snappy retort, but Marilyn's face showed a trace of the mockery for which she'd always displayed a gift. "Well, I hope my son remembers some of what I taught him about good manners."

"Good afternoon, Mother. Good afternoon, Jack." Andy's voice was level, a forced monotone.

At least she didn't try to kiss him. That would've been too much. Tom said, "Let's talk here. Katie is fetching Timmy from a kiddie soccer game."

"Very well." Jack pulled an expandable file from his briefcase. "You may want to look at this information. It seems your Dr. Grueneberg was reprimanded by a county medical association in Texas a few years ago. That's why he's in practice here."

Andy took the folder and began perusing the papers while Tom went to the kitchen to fix drinks. After a few minutes, just at the moment Tom returned, Andy said, "It looks to me as though the reprimand was for trying too hard, using a backdoor channel to get an experimental treatment for one of his patients. In any case, we don't know anything about his critics. They might be some off-the-wall group that call themselves 'Metroplex Medical Society.'"

"Grueneberg's shown a willingness to bend the rules, if not break them."

Marilyn took a sip from the glass of Pinot Grigio Tom brought her. "This guy sounds like one of those doctors who used to grind up peach pits and mix them up for a miracle cure. He plays fast and loose with his patients' lives."

Jack nodded. "He's got pretty poor survival rates for his patients."

Tom handed Jack an Old Fashioned. "That's only one indicator. One thing Katie has brought to my attention is that Grueneberg takes on some patients other doctors won't touch. He's like a St. Bernard, going out in all kinds of weather, so to speak."

As Andy continued his review of the file, the sound of a car door slamming made Tom perk his ears up. "Marilyn, would you please come with me?"

A puzzled look on her face, she rose and followed him into the kitchen. At that moment, the door to the mud room opened, and Katie and Timmy walked in. Katie's eyebrows jumped.

Katie said. "Go give Gran Marilyn a kiss."

Timmy complied, although to Tom the kiss looked perfunctory rather than heartfelt.

The sound of Andy's raised voice sent them back to the living room. "Jack, I don't see a damned thing here except a bunch of lawyer's bullshit. Is this the only reason you came down here?"

Tom saw the two men on their feet. The atmosphere reminded Tom of his Army hitch at Cam Ranh Bay, when he'd seen barroom brawls break out. "Gentlemen, you'd both better shut up. There's a small child in the kitchen, and he doesn't need to hear this." He stepped in between them.

Jack and Andy fell silent. Marilyn, Katie, and Timmy came in from the kitchen and sat down. After a strained half-hour of conversation, the visitors rose, saying they needed to catch a flight back to Atlanta. As they left, Andy shook his mother's hand, pointedly spurning Jack's effort to be polite.

When they had gone, Timmy turned to his mother. "Mommy, why do you hate each other?"

"It's not hate, Timmy, it's bad feelings. Someday, when you're older, Daddy will explain it to you."

"Why can't you tell me now?"

Tom, Andy, and Katie looked at each other. No one had an answer.

———

AFTER TOM RETURNED home, Andy and Katie put Timmy down for a nap and went out to the deck. "Can I get you something to drink, babe?" Andy asked.

"Just a ginger ale."

He brought her a can of Canada Dry and kept a beer for himself. When he set the beverage in front of her, she said, "I need you to make me a promise. I warn you, it won't be an easy one."

Andy took a deep breath. "Is it something to do with Mom and Jack?"

She nodded. "You've got to find a way so you can be in their presence without giving Timmy any more reason to get upset than he's going to be."

This matter-of-fact way of reminding him that he would soon have to settle quarrels without her presence made Andy look down at the deck. When he looked up, he said, "I know I've got to. Maybe Mom can't help herself. She can't resist the opportunity to put a needle up Dad's butt whenever she gets the chance, for no good reason other than that he's a South Georgia country boy. I know Dad wasn't the easiest guy to live with when all of us were kids, but that was because he was breaking his back trying to give us the kind of home Mom said she wanted. Whatever he gave her was never enough."

She squeezed his hand. "Life puts stripes on everybody's back. That's what Opa once said. He told me about his stepfather and how he never could forgive him for failing to replace his real father. What made it worse was that his stepfather never tried."

Andy put a hand up to his forehead. "You know what's ironic about the whole Mom-Dad business?"

"No. You'd better tell me."

"Mom loved Big Daddy, although he was a lot cruder than Dad was. When he got sick, she kept sending flowers to his hospital room.

At first, Dad would throw them out, until he realized he was hurting his own father in an effort not to give Mom credit for anything."

"So, he had to change his ways."

For the first time since Marilyn and Jack's arrival, Andy smiled. "It was a compromise. He left the flowers but tore off the cards so Big Daddy wouldn't know who sent them."

"May I tell you a secret?"

"Sure, babe. Is it important?"

"Haven't you noticed how your Dad goes out of his way not to start a fight with either Marilyn or Jack?"

"He's a bigger man than I am."

She kissed her fingers and touched his cheek. "Well, this is a chance for all of us to do some growing up."

48

ERIC GRUENEBERG KEPT his personal life out of his patients' sight. He rationalized this stance with the thought that cancer patients needed to concentrate on their own struggles, not listen to a doctor's "war stories." Other than his close family, Helen was the only person who could scale the self-protective wall around him. In the cool of a fall evening, Eric sat on his deck. He sipped a gin and tonic and watched a mother duck and her ducklings swimming in the manmade lake that bordered his property.

He heard the opening bars to Mozart's *Eine kleine Nachtmusik*, the ringtone for a personal call on his cell phone, but he decided not to answer. *Let it roll to voicemail.* When he went inside for a refill, Marina said, "That call on your cell phone is from Helen Ferguson. It's not like her to call you at home."

"Yes, that's true." He picked up the phone and hit "Call Back." When she answered, he asked, "What's up, Helen?"

In a voice less businesslike than usual, she replied, "No emergency here. I'm just worried about you. You seemed unusually preoccupied yesterday. I just wanted to call and see how you're doing."

He hesitated. The brooding that had enveloped him over the last few days was a recurrence of the episodic mild depression that had bedeviled him for years. "It's a long story," he said. "I don't want to tether you to a phone."

"Maybe I should come over, unless you think that's presumptuous."

"Where are you now?"

"I just finished a round of golf with my usual foursome. I can be there in ten minutes."

"Why don't you call Bob and the two of you come over for dinner? It's been a while since we all got together."

He heard laughter on her end of the line. "So sorry, boss. You and Marina will have to take just me or nothing. Bob's been held over in Washington for another week."

"Well, that's the life of an indispensable man," Eric said. "Just come on and join us. I'll defrost another steak."

The impromptu dinner went well. They talked about children's colleges and careers, about sports, about how the proposed legislation called "Obamacare" might affect their medical practice. After cleaning up the dinner dishes, they took cups of espresso out to the deck. In the evening stillness, the cooing of doves in nearby trees played a soothing counterpoint to the croaking of frogs, the chirping of crickets.

Helen got to the point. "Eric, I know you sometimes have these spells, but it seems pretty bad this week. What's wrong?"

"It's not one thing, it's a combination. It's just one of those juxtapositions life sometimes throws at us."

"So, what's the combination that's got you in the dumps?"

"Yesterday was my father's birthday. He would've been eighty-nine. I spent a lot of time thinking about him, about how he faced danger."

"He had a remarkable life. Didn't your sister publish a book about your parents?"

He nodded. "*Vati* never ran from a fight. The things he did to stay alive during the war, a fugitive Jew trying to avoid the death camps, were blood-chilling."

Marina interjected, "Yes, my dear, but we've talked a lot about that in the past. What else is bothering you?"

"It's a patient of mine, a young woman named Kathleen Lyle. Helen knows about her, but I haven't said anything to you. She's got terminal melanoma, but she just seems resigned to accepting the worst."

"Well, 'acceptance' is a stage," Marina said. "That's where hospices come into the picture."

"Yes, I know, but . . ."

"But what?"

"She seems almost joyful about this. I know that's a bad word to use, but it's as though she *needs* to die."

"Why is that a problem? We all must die sometime."

"Of course, but when someone goes looking for death, bad things have a way of happening."

She asked, "How does this relate to your father?"

Eric turned to Helen. "I've never told you how my father died."

"No, you forget that you told me he was gunned down in East Berlin."

"That's not all." He paused. "He was dying when he went overseas." Another pause. "They did an autopsy before they shipped his body home. His colon was eaten up with cancer. He wouldn't have lived three months if he'd come back safely."

In the darkness, he couldn't see Helen's face blanch, but he did see her eyes widen.

"Do you think he went looking for death?" she asked.

"I'll never know. *Vati* was fifty-five, and he could've claimed that he'd lived enough for three people. He struggled to the end. I guess I just don't understand why Katie seems ready to give up."

Marina said, "We all fight the same fight, just in different ways."

Helen added, "Sometimes the best we can do is to choose how we live, not to worry so much about dying."

Eric looked into the darkness. When he turned his gaze back to the women, he started to speak, stopped, started again, then fell silent.

———

HELEN CALLED LUKE from her car when she left the Gruenberg house. She remembered that Luke had said something that alluded to his own wish for final release from his spiritual burdens. His phrasing had been almost identical to her response to Marina. *That's why I said what I did to her tonight.*

"Hello, Helen, this is Luke. What's on your mind tonight?"

"I know it's late, but may I come see you?"

"Now?"

If I wait until in the morning, I'll chicken out. "Unless it would seriously put you out."

She heard what sounded like Luke stifling a laugh. "You know, we've got to stop meeting like this. Once was wonderful, twice may be pushing our luck."

"I promise to be a good girl."

During the drive to Fernandina Beach, she kept wrestling with two contradictory thoughts: *Luke wants to let go. I don't want to let him go.*

He was clad in a bathrobe when he greeted her at the door. "Coffee? Or something stronger?"

"Do you have decaf?"

"Give me five minutes."

When he returned from the kitchen, she said, "I had a very interesting visit tonight with the Gruenebergs."

"What did you learn from them?"

"Something about us."

"Such as-?"

"I think I understand why it seems like you can read people's minds. Did you know Eric's father was dying when he went to Europe to get Eric's sister out of trouble in 1976?"

"No, I didn't know that. The first time I met Eric, he just mentioned that his father was deceased but had come through World War II by the skin of his teeth. I didn't know anything about the circumstances of his death."

"Luke, are you dying?"

"I hope so."

"Don't make jokes with me. You know how I feel. I've lost one man I loved. I just can't deal with the idea I may lose another one."

"It's no joke, Helen. Do you have any idea how damned tired you get when you've lived as long as I have and have seen as many innocent people die as I have?"

"For God's sake, you're not planning, suicide, are you?"

Luke bowed his head. "There's something I've never told about my business. All these years, when you collaborated with Diana and me on cases, I waited for the right minute. Now, I've waited too long."

"Why do you say that? Frankly, you're scaring the hell out of me."

He chuckled. "There never was any hell in you. There was in me."

"In you, not in Nate?"

He took a deep breath. "I knew what kind of person he was. I guess it's because I helped make him that kind of person."

With a puzzled look, she asked, "Why do you say that?"

"I think it was because I let him know, in several not-so-subtle ways, I was more of a hotshot than he was. I married a girl from a rich family, while he partnered with a girl from the Baltimore working class."

"I'd say you more than made up for that by how you've treated Diana. She really should've been your daughter."

He rubbed his left palm across his forehead as if he were trying to wipe away some beads of psychological sweat. "When Diana and

I got to the Wicomico County morgue that day back in eighty-one and realized what had been going on between Nate and Connie, Diana poured out a whole boatload of anger on me. Long story short, she told me if I'd been more attentive to Connie's needs, she wouldn't have 'stolen' her father from her. As best I can remember, those were her exact words. That drove a wedge between us. She told me she didn't want to see me again. I didn't sit with the family at Nate's funeral. She didn't come to Connie's graveside service. You were the bridge that helped bring us back together. You and Sonny Widener."

He saw Helen's face shift from horror to astonishment to inquisitiveness all in the space of a few seconds. A long pause followed while he waited for her to say something. When she remained silent, he continued. "After you miscarried Nate's child, it must've affected Diana in some mysterious but positive way. When she lost Hector and the kids in that murder-suicide, and I plucked up my courage enough to go to the visitation, she let me stay for a long time."

"I remember. I was there."

He nodded. "It was Sonny who showed us how to bury all our anger and hatred."

"We hadn't started working together at that point. What did he do?"

"We spent a lot of nights at his veteran's shelter as his Parkinson's got more advanced, trying to help him keep things afloat. He showed us how meditation and prayer gave us the power to reach out to those gone from us."

"Meaning . . .?"

"We learned how to help the dying pass through the life-death barrier in peace. As we continued to work on our own forgiveness, I began to understand the vision I'd experienced at Mama's funeral. That's when I left GWU Hospital and persuaded Diana to join me in founding Eleni Hospice."

"So that's how it got started. Why do you think you're near the end of your 'borrowed time?'"

"The first thing was that Diana told me she'd finally managed to forgive Hector for what he did. The second thing is that now I'm certain Timmy Lyle is my successor."

She took his hand and squeezed it. "Perhaps so, but he's got a long way to go."

He leaned over and kissed her. "You're the one who'll take my place. You and Diana will guide him."

"I hope you're wrong. I don't think I'm strong enough."

Luke threw back his head and laughed. "Not strong enough? Hell, Muhammad Ali said *he* was 'The Greatest,' but he never met you. If he had, he'd have laid down his crown."

He saw that she appeared to be on the edge of tears. He rose. "Think about what I told you."

Helen nodded. He leaned over and gave her a parting kiss. There was something on his face, a look he sometimes gave the family members of the dying but a look she had never seen there before, one that mixed love and pity.

49

ANDY WRESTLED WITH angry, morbid thoughts on his drive to work. *You're losing control, aren't you, fella? That's what you're afraid of. As much as it hurts to see Katie slip away, isn't what you're worried about that Andy Lyle might not be the big shot, the go-to guy for answers?* Andy's success in working his way up through the ranks of the family business had instilled in him an exceptional confidence about rising to business challenges.

Emotionally at sea, he oscillated between anger and helplessness, between sorrow and the desire to slink into an emotional cave and stay there. *I believe nothing can come from nothing. Clark and Eric tell me this all started with a stem cell that was supposed to become skin tissue to replace cells that normally die off. They say it didn't 'differentiate' correctly and turned into the father of a gang of murderers. By the time Dr. Morton caught it, it had already gotten into her liver.*

His left-brain persona told him it was absurd to think that one rogue cell spelled doom for his wife. The right half of his brain was a closed room into which he shoved all the thoughts he couldn't handle. *Katie is thirty-five. She won't make it to thirty-six. When Timmy graduates from high school, she'll be just a faint memory to him. And when she's gone, I won't be able to reach for her at night, to take comfort in the warmth of her love.*

His unresolved anger at the doctors rose to the surface at odd times. Sometimes it boiled over into weird, inexplicable dreams. Whenever the anger started to boil, it took control of his thoughts. Preoccupied, he changed lanes without signaling or checking his rearview mirror. The frantic braying of a horn, the screech of brakes suddenly applied, the jolt of a sideswiping brought him back to reality: A Ford F-150 had been in his blind spot. The damage to both vehicles was, fortunately, repairable. A sheriff's deputy arrived within a few minutes. Both drivers exchanged the required information. The deputy took statements and issued Andy a citation for failing to yield right of way. He went on his way, chastened by the realization of how close to the edge he was.

Tom and Tom Jr. were at the site of a waterfront development under construction just off I-295. Andy went to his office to read the e-mails that had arrived overnight. When this chore was done, his mind went wandering again, back to his concerns about the doctors. He decided to do an online search and entered "Lukas Vangelis" in the search box. The first hit that came up was for a profile on a professional social media site. The profile revealed that the man was an immigrant, born in Izmir, Turkey to parents who subsequently fled an anti-Greek pogrom and settled in Boston. He was a graduate of Northeastern University and the University of Virginia Medical School. He had been an emergency room physician at George Washington University Hospital for thirty years. He had an impressive list of professional publications, all of which appeared to be in emergency medicine. The man was an expert in trauma response. *So, he's not an expert on cancer.*

There's nothing there that tells me who the guy really is. Frustrated, Andy shut the door to his office and began an in-depth quest for more information.

"HELLO, ANDY. CAN you talk for a few minutes?"

"How important is it, Mother? I'm busy right now. I'm trying to find out as much information as I can on this Dr. Vangelis."

"Are you too busy for me to say I'm sorry about our last visit? Neither Jack nor I was at our best that day. Jack's concerned about closing his practice. He was willing to represent Katie at no charge. It just didn't come out that way."

A likely story. "Okay, I understand. I hope *you* understand that it's damned hard for me to be at my best for my wife when it seems like Jack's eyeballs light up with dollar bills whenever he sees someone else suffering."

"May I say something in his defense? You don't give him credit for what he's done that you don't know about. Do you have idea how much legal work he's done for Habitat in Cobb County without taking a penny in compensation?"

Andy said nothing for several seconds, then responded with, "All right, I'll reconsider. It may just take some time, given what I'm dealing with right now."

"I know that. I love you. Tell Katie and Timmy I love them."

Andy knew he should've responded directly to Marilyn's good wishes, but the only thing he could say in parting was, "I'll be sure to tell them that."

50

THE PHONE RANG in Luke's cottage just before bedtime.

"Hello."

"Luke, are you awake enough for me to talk to you?"

"Helen, you can talk to me any time. You know that. Why do you ask?"

There was a pause. "I, uh, it's hard for me to say, given what we've been through. I'll just tell you that I've thought seriously about asking Bob for a divorce."

"Helen, why are you talking nonsense like this?"

"Because it's only since you took Katie Lyle as a client that I've come to recognize something about myself. I'm still in love with you, and I'm ready to throw over a marriage to a man who has never done one thing to hurt me. As long as we're this close, there's always the danger that we'll do something foolish."

"There's always that danger."

"No. I've got to make a choice. Either my job or my marriage."

"What are you talking about?"

"I'm handing in my resignation on Monday. If I don't have to deal with you professionally, maybe I can keep from thinking about you when I'm at work."

He heard a slight slurring of her words as she made this last disclosure. *What the hell? If we lose Helen, we lose a connection that could destroy our ability to help Katie and her family.* On an impulse, he asked, "Have you talked with Bob about this?"

"Can't. He's in Washington until next Wednesday."

"Don't go anywhere. I'm coming over to your house."

There was a click on the other end of the line. *Oh hell, in for a penny, in for a pound.* He dressed quickly and headed out the door.

———

AS HE PULLED back into his driveway, his mind whirled through a replay of the hours he'd spent dissuading Helen from pursuing her plan. He watched the sunrise and then went inside, uncertainty roiling his soul.

It came as no surprise that he couldn't sleep more than three hours. There had been no disturbances since he went to bed.

Because it was Sunday, the hospice was closed for all except emergency calls. When he got up, he checked his cell phone, found no voicemails or text messages, and fixed a breakfast of Greek yogurt, fresh blueberries, and coffee. *How many years did I eat a diet of wolfed-down junk meals? If I was what I ate, it's no wonder my life was a mess.*

When he felt sufficiently re-invigorated, he showered, dressed, and went for a walk on the beach. A chilly breeze gave a refreshing counterpoint to the sun's warmth as he crossed the highway and the dunes.

Connie always loved the water. Should we have built a house somewhere on Chesapeake Bay? Would she have taken up with Nate if we had? No, Luke, stop rationalizing. She took up with your brother because he gave her the attention you couldn't find time for.

He cleared his mind of these disturbing thoughts and replayed the previous night's encounter. It had culminated when Helen, apparently at the end of her emotional rope, said, "Make love to me. I'll never know if you don't."

"I can't. You are my true love, and I'd throw myself between you and anyone who tried to hurt you. But I'd rather hurt you myself than live a lie any longer."

Helen's mental toughness, always an admirable feature of her personality in Luke's eyes, deserted her. In a voice clogged by tears, she said, "Why? In God's name, why have you lied to me?"

He reached out and squeezed her hand. "I couldn't tell you the truth. Diana and I have a special mission."

"What? Is it so special you can't take me with you? You can't even be honest with me? Do you think I deserve this torture?"

He fought down the tears that filled his own eyes. "You didn't do anything wrong. If I could make you happy now, I'd cut off an arm to do it. But we don't have a future. We're almost at the end of the road."

"What are you telling me?"

"Just this." As carefully as he could, he recounted the encounters with Sonny that had led to their "commissioning," as he put it. He gave her an abbreviated history of the intervening years. As his long recitation spun out, he could see a kaleidoscope of emotions pass across her face – puzzlement, skepticism, impatience, anger. To his great relief, though, the despair he'd detected earlier was gone. When he spoke of Timmy Lyle's pivotal role, he concluded by saying, "I've got to find some way to explain things to him. That's my last hurdle."

For the first time since his arrival, he saw a smile cross her beloved features. In a half-whisper, she said, "I understand. Let me help you."

He nodded and stood up. His right hand reached out to her. She took it and they walked hand in hand to the bedroom.

51

CLARK BURTON SAT bolt upright in bed, his pillow drenched in sweat. He leaned against the headboard and took several deep breaths. In the five years since his divorce, he'd filled his bed with a succession of nurses and lab technicians, but none of those relationships had endured. *How did my life get so screwed up?* He didn't mind sleeping alone, except when the dreams came calling. Then he wished for someone, anyone, to talk to.

The oddity was that he seldom dreamed, but when he did, the dreams came in groups, an ever-shifting kaleidoscope of images. One of the scenes tonight was a variation that started back in his teenage years, 1967 to be exact. He, his parents, and his two sisters stood in a single rank at Andrews Air Force Base. When the flag-draped casket that held his brother's remains was carried off the transport, his father snapped to attention and saluted. His mother and sisters dissolved into weeping. Wanting to be like his father, he'd saluted, not noticing the tears staining his father's cheeks.

He'd had waged a *jihad* against cancer for thirty years. It was a war to which he had dedicated himself since he was twenty, standing by his mother's bedside as ovarian cancer choked the life out of her.

The dream scene shifted to a hospital room. In tonight's dream, though, the wasted figure on the bed in front of him wasn't Maggie Burton Hoeltscher; It was Katie Lyle. His mother stood at the head of the bed, gently stroking the young woman's cheek. His father, in dress blues, appeared to be kneeling in prayer on the other side of the bed.

Maggie turned to him. "Son, you're a doctor. Can't you do anything to help her?"

"I've tried, Mom. I've used every drug I can lay my hands on that might help her. Nothing works."

The scornful look on her face was a bayonet thrust to the gut. "Men! You're as useless as your father. All that firepower in Vietnam, and it couldn't keep Robbie alive."

Major General George Burton rose from where he knelt. "Maggie, we're not doctors. Let Clark get advice from people who know about cancer. Like you." He pointed just to Clark's left.

Clark half-turned, only to behold a young woman whom he'd treated for breast cancer five, maybe ten years ago. *Why can't I remember her name?*

"Fight for her, Dr. Burton," the woman said. "Her son needs her. Don't let her go."

"Like hell," a middle-aged man to his right interrupted. "I fought multiple myeloma. I weighed two fifty when it was diagnosed. I was down to a hundred forty when I died. Can't you see all she wants to do is die?"

Suddenly the hospital room was crowded with angry patients, clamoring to give him advice. As the cacophony erupted, Katie gave no sign that she heard anything being said.

A disembodied voice broke into his dream. "There's a lot more that Lukas can tell you." *Who the hell is talking?* The voice was one he'd heard years ago, but he couldn't assign a name, or a face, to it. It was, in fact, the long-dead Dr. Athanasios Vangelis, giving a word of guidance to a former student.

He awakened at that instant. The bedside clock showed it was a few minutes before five. Clark groaned and got up. *Maybe a caffeine fix is what I need.*

He never failed to follow up with the men and women he treated, and Katie Lyle aroused all his protective instincts. He'd referred many patients to hospice care, although few had been as young as her. He regarded each such referral as a provisional confession of failure. As he drank his first cup of coffee, he booted up his tablet and accessed an online medical journal. In the table of contents, he honed in on an article by a well-known cancer research center. The FDA had approved for general use a Swiss-developed cytotoxin that showed great promise in putting even Stage IV melanoma into remission. His thoughts immediately went to Katie.

––––––

THAT AFTERNOON, HE called his colleague in Jacksonville. When Eric came on the line, he asked, "Have you heard anything from Katie Lyle? There's a new therapy that might be worth a try." A quick exchange between the two doctors revealed that Eric hadn't yet looked at the latest literature. He told Clark he would read the online article and, if he concurred with Clark's evaluation, call Katie in for a discussion.

Eric called back the next day. "Clark, it's getting screwy. Before I tried to call Katie, I decided to follow up on her hospice care. My folks called every hospice in this area. Not a one of them recognized the name 'Katie Lyle' and they all swore no one had notified them that she was being referred. None of them had a referral letter."

"Problem with communication on either your end or theirs?"

"I wish it were that simple. Our records show that Helen called four separate hospices in succession, yet none of them shows a contact from us."

"Do you think it's deliberate, maybe, that she doesn't want to communicate with us? I presume your people tried e-mail as well."

"Right. We kept 'read' receipts for every e-mail, but there again, on their end, no record."

"So what can we do?"

"Let me check this out personally."

Eric had his office reschedule all his afternoon appointments. He left the office early, complaining of a sinus headache. Instead of driving to his home in Ponte Vedra Beach, he headed north on I-95 and took the exit for Fernandina Beach. His GPS guided him to the address for the Lyles. When he was a block away, he saw a vehicle with the words "St. Raphael Hospice" on the door. He pulled over under a live oak, cut the engine, and did a name search of hospices on his tablet. The only website that came up was for a Washington-based firm. It didn't show a local address.

Damn, I'm hot. It's November. What gives? He went to brush back his thick gray hair and found it was sweat-soaked. He got out of his car and stood in the shade, letting the autumn breezes tranquilize him. As he relaxed, he saw a woman, in her mid-thirties by appearance, come out of the house and get into the van. She cranked it up and headed in his direction.

Acting on instinct, Eric jumped back into his car and turned his face away from the street as the van passed him. When it turned a corner four blocks away, he took out his phone and dialed Clark's emergency number.

"Clark here. Eric, is something going on?"

"I think we have a major problem. Have you ever heard of a 'St. Raphael Hospice' in this area?"

"No, but I'm not an expert. Can your office try to locate them?"

"Perhaps, but I've already searched online, and there's no such organization within two hundred miles of Jacksonville."

"What should we do? Call the cops?"

"We may have to. Let me do one more thing before we try that."

———

DIANA PULLED OVER and called Luke when she had put about a mile between her and the Lyle residence. "We've got trouble. Did you know that one of Katie's doctors was supposed to come calling this afternoon?"

"No. What makes you say that?"

"I saw someone who answered to the description Helen gave me for Dr. Grueneberg sitting in a car a block from the Lyle house." She read off the tag number.

There was a pause of almost a minute. She waited, knowing that Luke was running a check on the license plate. He told her, "That's Eric Grueneberg, all right. What is *he* doing there? That's not supposed to happen."

"I have no idea. But I'm pretty sure he got a good look at the van."

"Well, you're right. That is a problem. Let's get together, and we'll talk about what to do next."

———

ERIC RANG THE doorbell, noting that a bronze plaque was mounted by the front door. It read, "House of Lyle, Founded June 9, 2001." *Am I an undertaker for the death of a dream?*

Katie's eyes widened at the sight of Eric standing on her front stoop. "Dr. Grueneberg, this is an unexpected pleasure. What brings you here?"

"My wife called and said she needs me at home. I thought I'd just look in on you on the way."

"Please come in. May I get you something to drink?"

"Ice water with a slice of lemon or lime would be just what this doctor ordered."

When she returned with the cold beverage, he asked, "Has your hospice been good about meeting your needs?"

"They've been absolutely the best. It's funny, I'd never heard of St. Raphael Hospice until now, but I guess since you recommended them, they had to be good."

Eric hoped his face didn't show his astonishment. He said, "Hmmm. Would you please bring me your notes about that recommendation?"

"Is something wrong?"

"No, but I *thought* I recommended North Coast Hospice since they have an office only a few blocks from here."

Katie went to a bedroom, returning with a manila folder. When Eric opened it, a referral letter listed several hospices, with "St. Raphael Hospice" as the first name on the list. His eyes narrowed; the signature on the letter was unmistakably his. *What is this? Am I going mad? Or did someone else forge my signature?* He gave her a pensive look. "So I guess they've been responsive to your needs."

"Yes. How did you know Dr. Vangelis? Did you go to school together?"

Vangelis. Why is that name familiar? Got to check it out. Make up something. Play for time. You've got to find out what's going on. "Actually, I think we met at a conference where I sat in on a session about end-of-life care."

They chatted for a few minutes until Timmy came in from the backyard. He dashed through the kitchen but came to a stop, his face showing surprise at the presence of a stranger. Katie smiled and said, "Timmy, this is Dr. Grueneberg. He's one of Mommy's doctors."

Eric started to get up. Timmy's eyes widened. Without saying a word, he turned and ran to his bedroom. *This has gone completely off the rails. Has Vangelis said things to make the boy afraid of doctors?*

Katie gave him a shocked look. "I'm sorry. Timmy's a sensitive boy, and he gets upset easily."

"No need to apologize. I was scared of strange people when I was his age. I think Timmy associates me with bad things." Eric's train of thought had been so disrupted by the boy's reaction that the idea of talking to Katie about the new elixir from Switzerland had slipped his mind.

"I'll make sure it doesn't happen again."

The look on Katie's face when Timmy fled was all the reason Eric needed to continuing bird-dogging the mystery of St. Raphael Hospice. Saying that Katie needed to spend time with her son, he told her good-bye and withdrew.

———

HE RETURNED TO his office that night and shut himself in. He obtained Katie's chart from the file and perused it for what seemed like the thousandth time. Try as he might to read between the lines, he found nothing to explain a series of events that seemed seriously out of kilter.

Am I going mad? He remembered how, in the weeks after his father's death, he'd spent hours with his mother, looking at the few pictures and letters she'd been able to bring on the family's flight from ruined Germany. He closed his eyes, sinking into deep reflection.

"I never told you, my son, how close I came to going mad." Liesl Grueneberg handed him a photograph. It showed a family group, mother and father, two sons, one daughter.

"When was this picture made, *Mutti?*"

"It was August 1940, as I recall. After Franz Josef came home from the invasion of France, Papa wanted a portrait made. They were so proud of him. It was the last time we were all together."

"Please, *Mutti*, don't go over that again. It'll only make the hurt come back."

"Do you really think looking at pictures can hurt me? When I saw how my parents died, burned to death in their own house. If that and losing my brothers in the war didn't drive me mad, nothing can. Your father kept me from going out of my mind."

"*Vati*'s strength kept us all going."

"You've got to be the strong one now, my son. Your sister and I depend on you. I'm come such a long way. I don't think I can go on much longer."

This conversation was a moment captured forever in the amber of memory, something he returned to again and again in the years after Liesl died.

He opened his eyes, turned to the bookshelf behind his desk and took down the picture, now beautifully framed. As he scanned the beloved dead faces of his mother's family, he gasped. In a flash, he understood why Katie's plight had broken through the veneer of his professional reserve: The resemblance between her and the youthful Liesl was uncanny.

52

DIANA AND LUKE decided to meet in the picnic area of Ft. Clinch State Park. When she arrived, she saw him sitting at a table reading a book titled *How We Die*.

"What's going on? Don't we know enough about that already?" *Luke is always so serious. He needs to loosen up.*

"No. I need to have another talk with Timmy, so I can try to explain what's happening to Katie."

"Is he asking too many hard questions?"

"Not yet, but I expect them to start anytime now. He doesn't understand death."

"That's no surprise. Very few people do," she said.

"We're among the fortunate ones. We should do a better job of explaining."

"Have you figured out how we can handle Grueneberg and his snooping?"

"Let's take a walk." They strolled down a nature trail, newly-fallen leaves crunching under their feet. "That's the sound of autumn. If we have to explain death, it's the best time of year."

My thoughts exactly. Diana looked around, watching leaves drift here and there, borne along by a breeze that had the bite of approaching winter. They walked on in silence, stopping where the St. Marys River spilled into the ocean, a pathway through the eternal decay of tidal marshes. "Maybe this would be the place to bring Timmy. Show him that death's all around us, but it's nothing to fear."

"That's a good idea, but I'm afraid Katie and Andy won't allow it unless I can get her doctors off my back."

Diana picked up a broken cattail, turning it over and over, admiring the brown velvety texture of the tiny flowers embedded in the head. "They call this a bulrush in some parts of the world, don't they?"

Luke stopped and slapped his forehead. "Of course! That may be how I can deal with Dr. Grueneberg."

She drew back, a gesture not of fear but of utter puzzlement. "What brought this on?"

"It was just one of those wild out-of-the-blue thoughts. You mentioned 'bulrush,' and I thought of Moses, set afloat on a basket made of bulrushes."

"Why mention this now? This is today, not thirty-five hundred years ago."

"Jews never forget. Grueneberg is half-Jewish. I've got something that will jog his memory."

Diana had seen such occasional flashes of something oddball, something that seemed to come out of nowhere. *He's a superior being. He just gets these wild thoughts, but somehow it always works out for the best. I've got to trust him.* "What's your great plan? Gonna let me in on it?"

———

LUKE HAD PONDERED one plan after another, but he still wasn't certain that any might be successful. He described his latest brainstorm while they strolled around the park. By the time they reached the parking lot, he'd decided.

"Let me call Katie and ask her for a favor." He walked about fifty feet and took out his cell phone. When the call ended, he said, "I can deal with Timmy first, then target the nosy Dr. G."

"I know you feel close to Timmy, but Grueneberg seems to be the larger problem."

"Perhaps so, but Timmy is more important in the long run. I've finally figured out why."

———

TWO DAYS LATER, Luke drove Timmy to Ft. Clinch. After a tour of the old bastion, they sat down for a picnic lunch. Timmy downed two peanut butter and jelly sandwiches, a banana, and a bottle of apple juice. He asked Luke, "How did you know what I like?"

"Your mother gave me some hints."

"Can we do this again sometime?"

"Of course."

"When Mommy gets back from her trip, me and her can come here."

Control yourself. Doctors aren't supposed to show their emotions. "Timmy, Mommy can't come back. She's got to go a long, long way. But I'll be glad to bring you back here."

"Where's she going?"

"Farther than you can imagine, but closer too." Hearing the honk of migrating geese, he pointed to a gaggle of southbound birds. "Those birds have more than one home. Right now, they're going to one of their homes, but they'll come back in time. Mommy will have a new home, but she'll always be close to you and Daddy."

"Aunt Lisa told me Mommy's going to be an angel. Are you an angel?"

"No, son, I'm just a man like Daddy. I'm older than he is. Someday you'll be a man just like me."

"Is Daddy going away with Mommy?"

Luke shook his head. "Mommy's got to make this trip by herself."

"Are you going with her?"

"I promised you once I'd always be close to you, and I'll keep that promise."

"Cross your heart and hope to die?"

If only it were that simple. "Cross my heart and hope to die."

"Dr. Luke, I told Daddy you and me talked about Gran Marilyn."

"Did he say anything to you about her?"

"No. I heard him talking to Mommy later. He said you ought to mind your own business."

"Well, Timmy, Daddy's got a point. But I can't help Mommy unless I can help you and Daddy too. I hope Daddy doesn't feel about Gran Marilyn the way I felt about my brother."

———

KATIE, ACTING ON Luke's suggestion, called Eric as soon as Luke dropped Timmy off. Eric, in turn, called Clark. "Something interesting just happened. Katie called to schedule an appointment. She asked if I could get you to come as well." He gave his colleague the date.

"I'll make a point of being there," Clark said. "This time, we *have* to talk about additional chemo."

———

TIMMY HAD GOTTEN worn out by the trip to Ft. Clinch and the talk with Luke. After an early supper and bath, Katie and Andy put him to bed, where he fell asleep within a few minutes.

In the middle of the night, he found himself back at Ft. Clinch. This time, not with Luke, but with Opa. Even at four, Timmy understood this was a dream. Unlike his "night frights" from a couple of years earlier, he could sense a blanket of comfort wrapped around him.

He and Opa walked hand in hand down one of the nature trails. Opa was wearing a floppy-brimmed hat, an old favorite which he told Timmy was a "boonie rat" hat he'd worn in Vietnam.

There had never been any discussion of "Vietnam" in Timmy's presence. Before Timmy could ask him any questions, Opa said, "Boyo, you need to trust Dr. Luke. You want to know why?"

"Why, Opa?"

"It's because a long time ago, in a place called Bastogne, Dr. Luke saved my life."

"What did he do, Opa?"

"I was in a hospital bed one night when the Germans started bombing us. It hurt me too much to move, so I couldn't get away. Dr. Luke threw himself on top of me just before a bomb hit the hospital."

"Was Mommy my age then?"

"She hadn't been born yet. Your grandma hadn't been born yet either, and so Dr. Luke made it possible for you to be here. So, trust him, and he'll take care of you."

"Me and Mommy?"

"You and Mommy, but it's different with Mommy. Remember I'm near you and so is Oma and so is little Katie. Mommy will still watch over you, even if she's not here with you."

Opa reached out and pinched Timmy's cheek. Then, he disappeared.

Timmy slept soundly the rest of the night.

53

A THUNDERSTRUCK LOOK spread across Eric's and Clark's faces when Katie and Andy arrived, accompanied by Timmy and a man in a medical coat. "*Shalom u-verakah*, Dr. Grueneberg," the man said. "Peace and blessing to your house. It's been a long time."

Eric and Clark looked at each other, disbelief on their faces. "What are you doing here?" Clark asked. "You're dead. I read your obituary in the *Baltimore Sun*."

Luke laughed. "You're thinking of my cousin Athanasios."

"That blows my mind. You're a dead ringer, if you'll pardon the pun. How did you know he used to greet Eric with those very words?"

"We were very close. I understand your confusion. At Athanasios's request, I delivered a couple of lectures on trauma response to a class the two of you took at Johns Hopkins."

Eric's features slipped back into his usual expression of professional calm. "That explains your appearance. Your cousin and I talked a lot after *Vati*, uh, I mean my father, died. Athanasios used that greeting when we sat down together."

Andy asked, "Would you mind explaining what all this is about?"

Luke said, "I've been told that my esteemed colleagues have some doubts as to my authenticity. I decided to take this bull by the horns."

"Okay, but why'd you ask us to bring Timmy?"

Luke looked at the little boy. "Timmy, why don't you tell these gentlemen about our talks?"

Timmy didn't hesitate. "We talked about Mommy and what's going to happen to her. Dr. Luke told me Mommy has to go away so she can get better." He turned to his mother, on whose lap he sat. "Dr. Luke said I'd see you again someday."

Katie pulled her son to her breast. "Yes, darling, a very long time from now."

Eric stood up and walked out of the room. Katie handed Timmy to her husband and followed him. When she saw him in the hall, she stopped in her tracks. Eric was leaning against the wall, his shoulders shaking, his left hand over his face. She went to him, placing an arm around his shoulders. To her surprise, he didn't pull away. He stood there, muttering, "*Vati, Vati.*"

"What's the matter?"

"I never got to tell my father goodbye. He went to Europe on a business trip in '76 and came home in a box."

"Oh God, I'm sorry. It was you trying to help me that led to this."

The doctor took her hand and looked straight at her. "I'm only sorry because I've been a fool. All these years I've misled my patients."

"Excuse me? You've never misled me."

"Not directly, no. But I've always told my patients my job as a doctor was to be their protector against sickness and death."

"But that's right, isn't it?"

He shook his head. "That's only part of it. I've played the god of medicine, letting my patients think that curing them was just a matter of coming up with the right potion. When I ran out of medical magic, I'd become very detached, very clinical, observing how they died. I guess I hoped that, from enough observation, I could put all the pieces of the puzzle together. But I should've told them that sometimes the only thing I could do was to give them a chance to say goodbye."

"You and Dr. Burton gave me that chance. God bless you for giving it. Dr. Vangelis told me that the difference between 'curing' and 'healing' was that I could be cured without gaining any understanding about myself. But gaining that understanding is part of me being healed."

It took a mighty effort for Eric to refrain from saying anything. He looked at her, and the words that had formed in his throat remained stuck there.

———

WHEN LUKE RETURNED to the hospice, he gave Diana an account of the meeting with Eric and Clark. His mention that he'd invoked her father's name drew a question: "Why did you mention him?"

"It was a deception to buy us a little more time. As I told them, I met them a couple of times when they were students. Nate told me that Burton and Grueneberg were two of the finest students he ever had. He suggested I keep an eye on them, so I did. They'd be shocked to know how much background information I have on them. But it's not time to let them in on the real secret."

"Did you explain why they'd never heard of St. Raphael Hospice?"

"I couldn't tell them who our spy was. I showed them the website and explained to them that we're just moving into Florida. Showing them the letter from the Center for Medicare and Medicaid Services also helped. It's good when the director of the Center is a former colleague."

She cast an amused glance at the November sky, then turned to him. "So the threat of having them dig too deeply into our services has gone away. That's good. It means a lot of tough questions we don't have to answer. What do we do now?"

"Help Katie finish her goodbye."

54

ANDY LYLE WAS still unready for final acceptance. Frustrated, he called Eric the day after the office visit. The receptionist promised him a prompt callback.

When the two made contact, the doctor said, "Thanks for jogging my memory. There's something Clark and I forgot to mention in the hullabaloo yesterday."

As Eric gave a layman's explanation of the new drug's possibilities, Andy felt his temper do a slow boil. "Do you think Vangelis knows about this?"

There was a long pause on the other end of the line. "Probably not. Oncology isn't his specialty, and he's more interested in keeping Katie comfortable."

"I've *got* to let her know about this. She may change her mind if she knows she doesn't have to give up and resign herself to dying."

"Andy, just a friendly word of warning. Katie is in a delicate psychological state right now. As much as I don't want to let her go, should you convince her to try this? Do we dare rekindle her hopes? It might be a false dawn, so to speak. There's still a lot we don't know about this drug."

"I know my wife better than anybody else. I'll play the ace of spades."

"What's that?"

"Timmy. She won't do it for herself, but she'll do it for him."

"I'll see what I can arrange."

Eric called back before Andy left the office. "There's a window of opportunity. One of my colleagues at Shands has already started using the drug with a couple of patients. It's too early to tell for certain, but he thinks it has real possibilities. Can we meet at Shands on Saturday?"

"Let's go together. We'll pick you up."

––––––––

"WHY SHOULD I? What good would it do?"

Andy was too shocked to reply at first. He glared at his wife. "Because I've always believed you'd rather live than die. Has that quack Vangelis poisoned your mind against trying something that could give you a fighting chance?"

"No, he's been up front about everything. It's easier for you to say 'fighting chance.' You're not the one who has to do the fighting."

Andy forced himself to lower his voice so as not to wake Timmy. "How will it help Timmy if you give up?"

Her lips tightened. "I'm the one who took the pain of bringing him into this world. I know our son at least as well as you do. I can make him understand."

"Will you at least talk to Eric and Clark?"

"I'll think about it. I'm too tired to argue, and I need some time to myself. Good night." She got up from her recliner and went to bed.

With a groan, Andy took off his shoes, picked up a handmade throw showing lighthouses of the eastern seaboard, wrapped it around himself, and lay down on the couch.

––––––––

THE NEXT MORNING, after Andy took Timmy to Lisa's preschool, he returned home instead of going directly to work. When he walked in, he saw Katie sitting at the breakfast nook table, a steaming mug of hot tea in front of her. When she turned to face him, it was obvious she'd been crying.

"What's the matter, darling?" he asked.

"I'm sorry I was so harsh with you last night. I wasn't in the best mood to discuss Eric's suggestion. I hardly slept at all after that."

'That makes two of us." He gave her a kiss and sat down facing her. "How do you feel this morning?"

"Depressed. You know being tired does that to me."

"I meant about Eric."

"Do you really think there's any hope?"

He bowed his head for a long moment. When he looked up, he saw her smiling. "I want to believe," he said.

"I guess maybe I do too. Why don't you call Eric and tell him we'll go ahead with the visit to Gainesville?"

"Sure thing, babe. What's the worst that could happen?"

———

THE FOLLOWING SATURDAY, they drove to Gainesville. Leaving Timmy with the Warrens, Eric and the Lyles departed on what was, to outward appearances, just a friendly weekend outing.

Clark met them at Shands Teaching Hospital along with Dr. Allen, the onocologist who'd started using the Swiss drug. After a long talk, they met Allen's patients. One was a man suffering from liver-metastatic melanoma. He said the new therapy caused severe nausea, but the pain had dwindled to where it was controlled by non-addictive painkillers.

The other patient, a middle-aged woman afflicted with Stage IV melanoma, had a private discussion with Katie. This gave Katie a glimmer of hope. Dr. Allen told her she could begin treatment in three days. She departed with five pages of instructions.

They'd driven to Gainesville under partly cloudy skies. By the time they left the hospital, granite-gray clouds had rolled in from the Gulf. The rain started just before they reached U.S. 301. They hadn't gone ten miles before the bottom dropped out. Andy cut his speed to forty, then to thirty as the windshield fought a losing battle against a rare fall monsoon.

"Andy, I'd seriously recommend pulling over until the worst of this is done," Eric said.

Katie, sitting in the back seat, shook her head. "I want to get back to Timmy. Just take it slow."

Andy's attention focused on a minivan just behind them, tailgating with its high beam headlights on. "What is that crazy SOB doing?"

A semi blew by them, throwing a torrent of water against the windshield. There was a blinding flash and the boom of thunder.

The minivan had already swung into the left lane. Andy cut his speed, intending to let the driver get clear of them or pull into the space between him and the semi just ahead. Katie shrieked as the minivan cut them off. Andy slammed on the brakes, but it was too late. Above the rumble of the thunderstorm, there was the sound of tearing metal and breaking glass. The two passenger vehicles skidded to a stop on the shoulder.

Heedless of the downpour, Andy bounded out of his Yukon. He saw that a lightning bolt had split a live oak just off the right of way. The top half of the tree had crashed onto the rig between cab and trailer, sending the eighteen-wheeler into the median strip, where it rolled onto its side.

Andy and Eric huddled under the dubious shelter of a golf umbrella as they walked toward the overturned semi. A tall man was helping the driver, miraculously only slightly injured, out of the cab. When he turned, Andy and Eric halted. Luke Vangelis was guiding the shaken driver to where Diana Karras stood holding an umbrella.

Luke looked at Andy. "Would you please call 911?"

A highway patrolman arrived in short order. After taking statements from the witnesses to the accident, he returned to his cruiser just as the thunderstorm ended.

Andy looked at Luke and said, "I called you a crazy SOB. I'm sorry. If you hadn't cut us off, I'd have skidded right into the back of that semi. What the hell were you doing out here on such a godforsaken day?"

Luke gave him a wry smile. "Trying to catch you. It was mostly good luck that I saw the lightning flash in time to react. I had to get you to stop."

"How did you know we went to Gainesville?"

"A little bird told me."

"Huh?"

"A little bird named Bonnie. I tried to call you at home. When I got no answer, I started checking with your contacts. I got your mother-in-law, and she told me where you'd gone."

"When did you catch up to us?"

"Credit Diana for that. I was trying to navigate through the storm. She spotted your vehicle headed back to Jacksonville. I made a U-turn and just managed to catch up with you."

"If you'd caught us before we got to the hospital, what would you have done?"

"Nothing. I would've let you do whatever you believed was right."

The crow's feet around Eric's eyes crinkled in a pattern that betrayed uncertainty. He looked at both of them. "Well, we damned near had a disaster in the process."

Luke nodded. "A near-disaster may be the only way to keep something worse from happening."

A feminine voice behind them said, "I think I know what you mean." They turned around to see that Katie, draped in a poncho, had joined them.

"What are you talking about?" Andy asked.

"This search for a cure almost destroyed us. If Luke and Diana hadn't caught up to us, we might both be dead now. Timmy could've lost both his parents at once." Her lip quivered for an instant, and then she smiled. "Letting death destroy who we are is much worse." She smiled at Luke and kissed Andy on the cheek. Turning to Eric, she said, "Please tell Clark I've changed my mind. I know you think it's the best thing, but I want to spend the rest of my time loving those who love me, not fighting for a deliverance that may never come. Do you understand?"

Eric said, "If you're sure this is what you want, we won't interfere."

"I'm sure." She touched her husband's cheek. "Do you understand?"

Andy pulled her close. "Yes, darling, I understand."

55

THE CANCER PROGRESSED rapidly after the trip to Gainesville. Within a few hours of their return home in a rented vehicle, the pain had worsened to the point that Luke convinced Andy to move Katie to the inpatient hospice at Amelia Island Community Hospital. Family and friends agreed on a constant vigil, despite her protestations that she didn't want to disrupt others' lives. Andy always brought Timmy by on his way to preschool. Art, Bonnie, Tom, and Ginny each took a daily four-hour stint. Family friends covered the remaining hours of each day.

Luke came in early every morning to check on her and assure there was an adequate supply of pain medication. Diana put in an appearance every evening. On the Saturday evening after Thanksgiving, everything changed.

Despite John Donne's advice to the contrary, death's pride shows in the indignities it inflicts on the most blameless of us. The cancer that ravaged Katie's body had, in the end, shown itself in the deterioration of her outward beauty. Where her blonde tresses had once been the crown of her face, now only a close-cropped yellow mat remained. Most of the time, she lay silent, with an oxygen mask providing a steady flow of air to her lungs. When her eyes opened, the lovely hazel irises focused on an infinite distance, searching for something not visible to her companions.

Diana found Katie alone, due to a mix-up in communication within the families. She made a swift appraisal of the situation: major blockage of the intestinal tract, with severe fluid buildup. Hating to leave Katie alone, even for a minute, she hastened down the hall and told the nursing supervisor, "Mrs. Lyle is dying. Please call her family at once."

When the supervisor went to Katie's room, Diana called Luke on his cell phone.

After listening to her description of Katie's appearance, he said, "I'll be right down."

The head nurse returned and began calling family members. Diana went back to sit with Katie, whose face was obscured by the oxygen mask. Her eyes had closed. *Comatose. God, I wish I'd been here earlier. I could've let her family know.* Against all the canons that prescribed keeping a distance between patient and healer, Diana took the dying woman's hand and began crooning a lullaby, words from long-vanished ages in a strange tongue. She continued singing until Luke arrived. Both of them waited in silence for the family to arrive.

When Andy arrived, Luke gave him a brief update. The Warrens showed up a few minutes later, accompanied by a priest wearing a purple stole. Luke slipped out quietly.

———

KATIE AWOKE IN a strange place, a clearing in the heart of a dark wood. She couldn't tell if it was night or day. The shadows that surrounded her couldn't keep out an eerie light, coming from neither sun nor moon, as if a million stars had gathered around her, the light from each faint, yet collectively powerful.

It's a dream. Something about it was different; however, there was no pain. When she'd dreamt in recent weeks, the pain was always there, ready to yank her back to the world.

"Katie." She turned to face the voice and saw Luke. She'd known it was him, although the voice sounded as though it came from everything around her. *This has to be a dream. What is he doing here?*

"Hello, Luke. Where am I?"

"In the same place as I am, as you can see."

"Am I dead?"

"You can be. Or not, at least for a little while. It's still your choice."

"Don't play word games with me, Dr. Vangelis. What does that mean?"

"Just this. Take a look." He pointed to a spot behind her.

She turned again and gasped. Standing in a darkened room, she could make out her own figure lying on a hospital bed. Andy and Bonnie sat at the head of the bed, each holding one of her hands. Lisa sat at the foot of the bed, sniffling into a handkerchief. Diana entered the room. She checked Katie's pulse and respiration, then went back out. Katie involuntarily said, "Oh!"

"Do you want to go back? You can if you'd like to."

"What if I do?"

"The pain will come back. That's how you'll know you're alive."

"How long do I have to decide?"

"No hurry. Things are different now."

She pondered for what seemed like only an instant. Light began to creep through the blinds. The door opened and Art entered, Timmy riding on his back. "Yes, yes, let me go back."

Katie opened her eyes. Her mother sat up and brushed back a loose hair from her forehead. "Hello, Katie-poo," she said.

"Hello, Mama."

Art brought Timmy to her. When she tried to sit up, the pain came flooding back. Seeing the tears trickling down her cheeks, Andy and Bonnie each put an arm behind her and raised her up.

"Goodbye, my sweet boy," Katie said. "Mommy will always love you."

The little boy leaned forward and gave her a kiss. Following his great-grandfather's advice, he tried to be brave and failed. When he started crying, his grandfather took him out of the room.

Bonnie kissed her. The pain was a wave, dragging Katie under. She whispered, "I love you, Mama."

Bonnie forced a few words through trembling lips. "My beautiful little baby. Oh God, I'd go through the pain of bearing you a thousand times over if I could keep you with us."

With a supreme effort, Katie reached up with an emaciated hand and brushed away the tears from her mother's cheeks. Then she kissed her fingers and placed them on Bonnie's lips.

She turned to Andy, his beloved features backlit by the sunlight now filling the room. "My heart," she whispered. She looked straight into his eyes, pouring a lifetime's love into a look that stretched out into eternity.

He kissed her. As he struggled for words, her gaze became fixed, her pupils dilated. Her mouth opened, and her hand fell limply onto the bed.

Diana quietly entered the room as Bonnie's wailing broke the morning stillness. She drew the weeping mother away from the bed, folding her in an embrace.

56

LUKE, CLARK, AND Eric stood in the line of mourners that stretched from the open casket up the aisle of the funeral home chapel, overflowing into the lobby.

Luke looked at Clark and asked, "I know what Eric's been dealing with these last few weeks, but how about you?"

Clark swallowed twice. "I need to let those I can't save find peace in whatever way they can, even if it wounds my pride."

"Well, that's good advice. Anybody in particular?"

"I know it sounds screwy, but I'd start with my brother Robbie. When he was killed in Vietnam, it drove a wedge between my parents. Dad tried to tough it out, regular Army style. Mom never recovered. It may seem goofy, but I think her cancer may have grown out of anger and guilt."

Luke smiled, the smile of a teacher who's just heard a student voice an original thought of unexpected profundity. "Eric, do you think Clark's onto something?"

Eric looked at the line of mourners, which now stretched out the front door. "I'm too confused to think right now." His appearance underscored these words. He wore his father's yarmulke, while at the same time clutching his mother's rosary beads. "How did you get to

Katie before any of the other hospices? And why can't we find any records of contacts from our offices to theirs?"

"It helps to have friends in high places, but it's even more helpful to have someone on the inside."

"Who is 'someone?'"

"Helen Ferguson. She made sure all the contacts went to us."

"Should I fire her over this?" Grueneberg's face bore an expression out of keeping with the somber atmosphere of the mortuary.

"You need to hear the full story before you do anything rash. Athanasios treated Helen's first husband for ALS. He insisted on putting the poor guy through some experimental, highly unpleasant treatments. They didn't help, and he died a needlessly protracted death, always hoping for a miracle."

Eric drew himself up, like a peacock in the presence of one with more gorgeous feathers. "She shouldn't be practicing medicine without a license, even if she meant it for the best, referring Katie to you."

"Helen's not exactly unqualified. She has a doctorate in psychology. Her specialty is thanatology."

"She never told me that."

"No matter. She knew what Katie needed. It's that ability some people have to look past the veils we put on and understand someone else's needs."

"So she ran all the communication through you. The other hospices never heard about her case."

"That's right."

They reached the bier and bowed before Katie's body. Passing down the line of relatives, they offered consoling words, doing their best to alleviate a pain that lay beyond their power to cure.

———

AFTER THE VISITATION, Luke suggested that they go for a drink. They drove to an oceanfront restaurant and settled in at a booth away from most of the other patrons.

Clark spoke first. "I still don't understand how you can look just like your cousin did in '77 and '78."

"I misled you. Athanasios was my twin brother, not my cousin. Diana is his daughter."

Clark's gaze narrowed. "Well, that explains one mystery, but there's another. All the biographical info I could find on you says you were born in 1921. If you're eighty-eight now, you're the youngest-looking octogenarian I've ever seen."

Luke nodded, his eyes almost mirthful. "You're right on the age. I found the Fountain of Youth."

Clark broke in. "Well, Ponce de Leon, are you going to show us where it is?"

"It's inside me. It's inside you as well, if you recognized it. Loving and forgiving is what keeps us looking young. We still age, but it doesn't show."

"Quit playing games."

"A little family history first. My mother was killed by a drunkard in a hit-and-run accident in 1925. You can imagine how a four-year-old reacted to that. Our parish priest did a lot of talking to Athanasios, my father, and me. He kept reminding us of the need to forgive. Papa and Athanasios never believed him. I can't explain why, but his words set something off in me."

Clark raised one eyebrow. "You mean to tell me the words of a priest are the secret to not growing old?"

"No. I always remembered what he told me, but I didn't do it for a long time. I didn't know how. I was a surgical orderly in the Army during World War II. After medical school, I was at an Army hospital in Seoul during the Korean War. I saw some pretty grim sights. That's where I met your father."

Clark's mouth dropped open. After a moment he recovered, "How were you able to change? And what does that have to do with you not aging?"

"I finally learned about healing. All right, you ask where these powers come from. For most of my life, I had no clue that I'd inherited them from my mother. It's only in recent years that I've gotten an understanding of some things. Let me put this in context."

"What do you mean by 'context?' And these powers you're talking about?"

"A little personal dirt first. Athanasios and my wife had an affair behind my back for several years. Neither Diana nor I ever knew what was going on. The truth came out when they were both killed in a head-on collision coming back from a tryst in Ocean City. Diana and I wrestled with anger for months after that."

Clark whistled. "When did this happen?"

"It was back in '81. We went through a lot of counseling, but it wasn't until we met a holy man that we learned what we needed to know."

Eric looked at him, one eyebrow raised. "You really believe in holy men?"

"I need to tell you about Sonny. He was sort of a John the Baptist. He and Diana's husband Hector served together in Vietnam. Hector killed his two children, then committed suicide in a very bad flashback. Not long after that, Sonny became a patient of the doctor Diana worked for. He was diagnosed with Parkinson's disease, possibly resulting from Agent Orange exposure."

"So what made him 'holy,' to use your words?"

"When Sonny found out Diana was Hector's wife, they started having some long conversations. She confessed to having hatred because of what Hector had done. Sonny talked about his own life, all the tough times he'd gone through, before and after Vietnam. He'd worked for years with homeless veterans, but it was only after he'd gotten the Parkinson's diagnosis that he started working on forgiveness."

Eric interrupted, "And just how did you and Diana come into this story?"

"We started providing medical care for the veterans at his shelter. One night, when we were taking a break, we sensed something odd going on. We both got a vision of Athanasios and Connie, my wife, with us. That's when we started working on forgiveness."

"Did these powers just come to you all of a sudden?"

"It's a long story, if you'll bear with me."

"Okay, go ahead."

"I told you about my mother's death. At her funeral, a deacon sang a dirge called 'Eternal Memory,' while our family went up for a last look at her. While we were standing there, I saw a shining image before the coffin, as if Mama was transparent, with the sunlight streaming through her hair. I didn't realize it then, but many years later, at Sonny's, I heard her again, saying, 'The gift is yours, my son. Preserve it for those who will follow you.'"

"You saw your mother after her death?" The incredulity on Eric's face told Luke he had to take more risks.

"Mama was the first healer in our family. I only learned the full truth a few years ago, not long before I met Clark's father and Katie's grandfather in Washington. Mama gave me a vision of what had happened long before that. When the Greek army invaded Smyrna, or Izmir as it is today, there was looting and killing. Mama went to the aid of some Turks, even if the only thing she could do was to comfort them while they were dying. She loved, even when it put her in danger."

Clark spoke up. "Suppose I accept your notion of talking with ghosts. Why don't more people have these powers you speak of?"

"Not ghosts, spirits. Most people do have the power, but perhaps they never have the chance to recognize that fact. We humans inhabit the visible world, yet we're much closer to the invisible world than we know. There's a fine line that most of us only cross when we die. And it's not a matter of ghosts or goblins. It's about the preservation of who we truly are, even in death."

Clark wiped sweat off his brow. Luke paused for a few seconds, expecting him to say something. When he remained silent, Luke resumed. "Those things that are invisible can still be very real. Have you ever walked close to high-voltage switchgear? That buzzing you hear is a warning not to get too close. Maybe only those who can use these powers for good get the chance to. I don't know why Diana and I were chosen to use the powers. I'm certain that, in some way, Katie has passed them on to her son. Do Diana and I deserve credit for helping? I guess we'll never know."

"This certainly goes against anything I've ever experienced."

Luke took a sip of ouzo and gave him a beatific smile. "'There are more things in heaven and earth,' as the Bard wrote."

———

FIVE MINUTES BEFORE the funeral home closed its doors for the night, a rental car pulled up in the parking lot. Marilyn and Jack Pilcher entered the chapel only to find that Andy had already left, leaving Art, Bonnie, Tom, and Ginny to greet late-arriving visitors.

"How are you doing, Tom?" Jack asked.

"I'm all right. As you might guess, Andy's taking it hard. He left because he wanted to give Lisa a chance to come pay her respects, and she couldn't do that while watching Timmy."

"I was hoping Andy would still be here," Marilyn said. "We'd have arrived earlier if our flight hadn't gotten delayed."

"The funeral mass is at ten tomorrow morning with burial immediately afterwards. You'll have time to talk with Andy then."

The Pilchers approached the casket and stood there for over a minute. Marilyn broke into sobs, and Jack put his arm around her. Tom came up to them and did the same.

57

LUKE DROVE HOME after the talk with Eric and Clark, intending to get a good night's sleep before the funeral. As he approached the seaside cottage, something inside needled him, a voice saying, "Stay awake. You don't need to sleep just yet."

He decided to brew a pot of coffee. While it percolated, he took out his favorite Cross pen and began writing on the notebook he'd started when he first met Timmy. He drank cup after cup, filling two dozen pages with a neat cursive so different from his normal doctor's scrawl that an expert would've sworn it couldn't possibly be the work of the same hand.

He finished drinking coffee and writing at the same time. As the grandfather clock in the hall chimed four-thirty, he took the notebook to his study. He set it on a shelf next to a set of volumes bound in dark green leather, inserting the folded letter to Timmy he'd written earlier that night. He removed the jeweled watch from his wrist and set it on the notebook. His last act before returning to the living room was to write "Diana" on the cover.

He settled back into his chair. Despite the amount of caffeine circulating in his veins, he dropped off to sleep without delay. He dreamed, the dream that had set him on the course that brought him to this hour. Eleni Vangelis, clad in the dark gown which she'd worn in her coffin, hovered over him.

"Lukas, my child. You have sought my peace all your life. Now you have it."

This is something new. She's never said that before.

"I don't understand, Mama. What do you mean?"

"You've found the one who is to follow. Already he knows what path he must walk in life."

"How can that be? He's only four."

Eleni's eyes were deep wells, from which compassion surged in an unending stream. "He will learn. You have directed him well. Others will guide him."

As awareness slowly awakened, he said, "Diana and Helen?"

"Yes, my son. Rest in my love."

Through the deep blue peace of sleep, he muttered, "I'm so tired, Mama."

"Come with me. It's time to return home." She reached out and touched him.

He stood up and walked with her, out the front door and across the road, through the sand dunes, to the edge of the ocean, where a late fall sunrise heralded the start of a new day. Eleni kissed him and walked to meet the incoming tide. She turned her back to the sun, spread her arms as if reaching to embrace the landscape, and vanished. Luke walked east, into the great waters that, decades earlier, had washed the shores of his birthplace. He went forward, fear vanquished, enveloped by a peace that was, curiously, cold.

58

WHEN KATIE OPENED her eyes, she was back in the woods with Luke standing next to her.

"The pain's gone forever, Katie. It'll never come back."

"Who are you in reality?"

"As I told you, Lukas Vangelis, M.D. My business is healing."

"Am I healed?"

"Yes. I told you we were on the same road. What have you learned from our journey?"

"How precious life is and how love makes all the difference. I understand how I can always be close to those I love, wherever I am."

Luke began to hum a hymn. It was a familiar melody: "For all the saints, who from their labors rest . . ."

"Is this where I'm supposed to rest?" she asked.

"You'll find things are very different now. Work and rest, they're mortal words. They don't apply any longer. Sickness, tiredness, even frustration and anxiety, that's all over and done with."

"So I'm dead. Is this heaven?"

"This is eternity. It's not heaven yet, but it can be. How about coming with me?" He took her hand and led her through the trees a short distance to where a parking lot was filling up with cars.

"What's going on?"

"The funeral procession is about to start. Your family's inside the funeral home saying their last goodbye before we go to the church."

"Can I see them?"

Luke nodded. With only a thought, without apparent exertion, they crossed the parking lot and went inside.

Katie gave an involuntary gasp when they entered the chapel. Her parents, Andy's parents, her two sisters, and Andy's sisters and brother had gathered around the casket. The women wiped their eyes while the men's faces showed individual struggles to maintain their composure. An attendant came to escort them outside to the waiting limousines. Art gently placed a hand on her forehead. Bonnie and Andy, the last to leave, kissed her on the lips. As Katie and Luke stood there, the funeral director folded the casket lining, moving with fastidious slowness, forming a protective cocoon around the body before he closed and locked the lid. She looked at what had been her mortal garment and said, "They did a good job. I didn't leave them much to work with."

"Nonsense. You've always been beautiful, and you're even more beautiful now."

"Where's Timmy?"

"You'll see him soon."

"So this *is* heaven."

"Remember what I told you. You can make it heaven. If you want it to be, you'll have lots of help. Shall we go?"

"Where to?"

"There's one thing left to do."

Again without any effort, they moved, this time to a grassy slope where a funeral home canopy rose, sheltering a group of gravestones. An Indian summer sun cast a mellow light on the trees. Just to her right stood a headstone with "CHRISTINA MUELLER THOMPSON 1921-1996" and "BRIAN ALBERT THOMPSON 1917-2008" chiseled into it. A few feet away, the open grave with its metal vault waited. "Here close to Oma and Opa," she said. "How long do we have to wait?"

"I told you things are different now."

As they waited, Diana came down a gravel path that bordered the plot and joined them. When she saw Luke, she asked, "Did you intend to leave this at home?" She held out Luke's wristwatch.

He shook his head. "It doesn't belong to me anymore."

"Your car was in the driveway, so I went inside to check on you." Her face bore a puzzled expression. "Did you call a cab? Why didn't you wait for me to pick you up?"

"I decided to go for an early morning swim. You should get a call from the Sheriff's Department pretty soon." At that instant, Diana's cell phone buzzed and she checked to see who the call was from. Awareness dawned on her face and Luke saw that she was battling for self-control. "Our paths diverge now. You must stay, and I must go."

Diana replied, "For how long?"

"You'll be the one who guides Timmy to his inheritance, to the blossoming of his special powers. You'll find everything you need to know on the shelf in my study."

Diana held out the wristwatch Luke had left in his study. "And you forgot this."

"Deliberately," he said. "I reset it when Katie died. Now it must go into other hands."

Katie, observing this exchange, asked Diana, "May I see that?" She looked at it for a long moment. "Wait a minute. The calendar just says 'Day 1.'"

"Very observant. It's my talisman, the last gift I can give Timmy. He will have it when he has learned how to use his powers."

"It's strange. It looks like the hands don't move."

"You're very observant. You died just over six days ago, in human time. That's a mere instant as *we* reckon time." He held up the watch, showing her that the second hand was at six seconds after midnight, then passed it to Diana.

"We -?" Before she heard the words, she heard a familiar tune, a man whistling "Hi Lili Hi Lo."

"Yes, Katie-poo. It's how we do things here." Brian, Christina, Andreas, Eleni, Nate, Nikki, Hector, Andrew, Athena, and Connie came to where they stood, watching as the funeral procession arrived. Diana bowed to her parents and embraced her children.

Brian walked past Katie to the headstone. As the pallbearers took Katie's casket out of the hearse, Clark, Eric, and Helen emerged from a throng of mourners. Clark came toward them and stopped at the marker. Removing the two-flag lapel pin Eric had seen on his lab coat, he laid it on top of the stone. Then he stepped back, came to attention, and saluted. Eric stood next to him, eyes closed. Helen's face was a mask, but her eyes were visibly red.

Eleni nodded at Luke and took his hand. Diana watched, eyes dark with sorrow, as her family turned and walked away, disappearing into the trees that lay just beyond the cemetery. She embraced Katie, then left Katie, Brian and Christina to stand beside Helen.

Only an instant later, a ray of sunlight shot from behind one of the scattered clouds that had moved in. The sunbeam lit up the casket's lid, warming the metal and giving a glow to the spray of flowers that adorned it.

Katie's family took their seats under the canopy, surrounded by a flock of mourners. Marilyn and Jack Pilcher came and stood directly to Andy's left. Timmy reached up and held his grandmother's hand.

A priest opened a prayer book and began the committal service. Diana whispered something to Helen during the committal, and Katie saw Helen bury her face in her hands. Knowing the message that passed from one woman to the other made Katie close her eyes for just an instant, trying to shut out the pain she saw.

After the final prayers were said, a funeral home attendant opened a small bird cage. A dove, seeing the path of freedom, took wing and headed for a home hardwired into its brain.

As the crowd of mourners dispersed, Andy lifted Timmy up and let him place a small hand on the casket lid. Taking out a handkerchief, Andy wiped his eyes. He pulled a carnation from the floral spray and gave it to his son. He patted Timmy's head and said, "Mommy will live on in you."

Timmy looked up, and a smile lit his face. "Mommy's here," he said, and held out the carnation toward where Katie stood.

Katie blew a kiss and gave them a goodbye wave. Brian and Christina took her hand and led her away, toward a landscape that grew darker with each step. Yet in the darkness, she felt no fear. As they moved forward, a million points of light surrounded them.

THE END

ABOUT THE AUTHOR

STEVE GORDY TOOK up creative writing as an avocation in 2003, when he joined the South Carolina Writers Workshop (now the South Carolina Writers Association). Since then, he's had a number of pieces published in anthologies by SCWW and the Savannah Writers Club. His submission of the first chapter of *Faith, Hope, and Dr. Vangelis* was selected as runner-up for Novel First Chapter in SCWW's Carrie Allen McCray literary awards for 2014. He has served as a chapter and state leader in the association.

In 2012, he organized a group of writers in the Aiken-Augusta area under the name "The Aiken Scribblers." In 2013, this group published an anthology of stories and poems about the horse statues in Aiken, South Carolina under the title *Nights of Horseplay*. It's available at www. amazon.com/Nights-Horseplay-fantasies-Carolinas-thoroughbred/ dp/0615831060.

In 2017, he published a collection of his own stories, many previously published, titled *Tangled Woods* and *Dark Waters*. It's available both in paperback (www.amazon.com/Tangled-Woods-Dark-Waters-twisting) and as a Kindle e-book (www.amazon.com/Tangled-Woods-Dark-Waters-winding-ebook).

Steve is an educator and is retired from the Savannah River Site and Piedmont Technical College. He holds degrees from the University of Florida and Yale University. He and his wife, Ruth, have lived in Aiken since 1988.

His next writing project, *Meredith's Song*, is about the life, loves, and legacy of Meredith Legg Stapleton (1987-2014), whose remarkable life has inspired hundreds with her motto, "You have to do your best every day and never give up."